AFTER ALL I'VE DONE

AFTER ALL I'VE DONE

A Novel

MINA HARDY

CROOKED
LANE

NEW YORK

Copyright © 2020 by Megan Hart

Published in the United States by Crooked Lane Books, an imprint of The Quick Brown Fox & Company LLC.

Crooked Lane Books and its logo are trademarks of The Quick Brown Fox & Company LLC.

Library of Congress Catalog-in-Publication data available upon request.

ISBN (hardcover): 978-1-64385-470-0
ISBN (ebook): 978-1-64385-471-7

Cover design by Nicole Lecht

Printed in the United States.

www.crookedlanebooks.com

Crooked Lane Books
34 West 27th St., 10th Floor
New York, NY 10001
First Edition: November 2020

10 9 8 7 6 5 4 3 2 1

To Lori, my best friend, who is in no way an
inspiration for anything that happens in this book.
Thanks for the decades of friendship and support!
Here's to many more!
For Robert, my best husband, who also is in no way an
inspiration for the circumstances in this story.

CHAPTER ONE

Diana

Imagine yourself in a dark room.

The difference between closing your eyes and keeping them open is the flicker of lashes on your own cheeks, and that's all. You keep your eyes open, trying to see, because you haven't yet given up the hope that somewhere, somehow, you'll catch a glimmer of light. That you are not a prisoner here in this endless night.

Wait long enough, try hard enough, and you'll see hints of light, maybe around a door frame. Maybe it's the end of a hall or a tunnel. It could be the pressure of your own eyes, straining so hard that the blood vessels burst. Then the light is gone, and you're back to staring at nothing but darkness.

That's my mind.

Laundry
Groceries
Transfer money
Cancel dentist
New phone
Pay RC

The yellow legal pad I just found in my nightstand features a list, written in my own handwriting. It's my own list, the items crossed off or circled to remind myself of the minutiae of my life, but I don't remember writing it. I don't remember completing any of those tasks.

New phone. My phone was lost in the accident, but I wrote this list before that happened. Who—or what—is *RC*, and why did I need a reminder to pay? Did I ever visit the dentist, or do I need to reschedule?

"Babe, I can't find my red tie," Jonathan says from behind me. "The one with the polka dots?"

Quickly, I shut the nightstand drawer and turn to face him. My husband used to laugh at me when I walked into a room and looked around, perplexed, before walking out without whatever it was I'd gone in there to find. We joked it was old age, although at forty-five, I'm nowhere close to old. We used to joke a lot. We don't anymore.

The days of walking out of a room without remembering why I went into it have now become a *real* joke, laughable. That's normal forgetfulness. What I have is deeper, more pervasive. Darker.

"Have you seen it?" he asks when I don't reply at once with the location of his missing tie.

"I haven't. It's not in the drawer?" Already I'm crossing to the walk-in closet so I can help him search. "Where did you take it off?"

"Uh . . ."

"Never mind. I'll look around for it." I force fake cheer in my voice so that neither of us has to address his awkward silence.

"Thanks, babe. You're the best," my husband says. "I gotta run. Oh . . . yeah, in case you forgot, I have that board meeting tonight. Don't wait up."

That word *forgot* hangs between us, more uncomfortable even than a few minutes ago when he couldn't own up to where he'd probably left his tie. Jonathan has always thought he was a better liar than he really is. There's no board meeting, but he doesn't realize that I've already figured out what he's really doing all the nights he's "working late."

I accept his kiss and wave him off to work the way I've done for the last ten years of our marriage. Like nothing's wrong. Like we are fine, or at least as though I am.

I am not fine.

About five weeks ago, on the last day of September, on a dark and stormy night, my car hit a deer. I lost control and ended up in a ditch—or so I was told. I can't, perhaps thankfully, remember the car accident. The car, my baby, a cherry red Camaro that was flashy and ridiculous and utterly, completely mine, was totaled and hauled off to the junkyard before I woke up. Me? I opened my eyes in the hospital to find multiple incisions in my abdomen from an emergency surgery to rip out my gloriously infected gallbladder, both my arms immobilized in slings from two broken collarbones, and a lot of pain. I still hurt like hell when I get up in the morning, mostly throughout the day and always, always when I try to go to sleep. There's still a vague, persistent ache in the space below my ribs that hits me when I'm not expecting it. My digestion's a wreck. I don't miss my gallbladder at all, but the two broken collarbones have really messed me up.

When your collarbones break, you lose the use of your arms.

Without the use of your arms, you basically become an invalid.

It's much better now, but for the past month it's been rough. I've barely been able to feed myself. Forget about personal hygiene. The last time I needed someone to wipe my butt for me, I was four years old. This sucks.

I was lucky, though. I could have gone head-on with the eighteen-wheeler coming at me, the one that stopped to make sure I was all right after I ran into the ditch. I learned later that the driver called the ambulance for me. He stayed with me until it arrived. For all that, I don't know his name. Can't thank him. And of course, I don't remember him at all.

I don't remember anything after Memorial Day weekend five months ago. Driving to the beach with my best friend, Val, the windows of my sexy car rolled down and the summer's pop hits cycling through the radio stations that changed from town to town. It's called anesthesia-induced amnesia, and there's no cure.

I might, one day, spontaneously recall what happened between the end of May and the first week in October, but it's more likely that I'll never get that time back. Instead, I have pain and lists I can't remember writing and a husband who lies to me every day. I have a brand-new reality, and nothing in it makes sense. The accident didn't kill me, but I'm not sure how I'm going to survive it.

3

CHAPTER TWO

Valerie

Jonathan tastes like chocolate when I kiss him. His mouth is warm. Hot, even. I breathe him in and pull him close, and I hold him next to me until he rolls away and tosses off the covers so he can leave the bed.

Don't, I want to say. *Don't go.*

Of course I don't say that, no matter how much I want to. It would sound desperate and grasping, and even if that's how I feel about him and this situation, it's not how I want him to think of me. I watch as he gets out of bed and walks naked to the bathroom. I listen as he takes a long hard piss, the water in the toilet splashing. He doesn't close the door. I guess we've been together long enough to feel comfortable with an open bathroom door, long enough that we don't have to pretend that we don't have bodily functions. With someone else, this would be irritating. I'd want to keep the "magic," whatever that means. With him, it's intimate. I want to make it permanent.

When he comes back to the bedroom, he looks me over. I haven't pulled up the covers. I want him to see me naked. I want him to crawl back into bed with me, to cover me with his body, to put his mouth on mine. To kiss me there, and in lower places. I want to make him cry out my name the way he does every single time.

There've been other men. So many of them. But none of them ever made me feel as beautiful as they told me they thought I was.

I don't want him to go back to *her*.

"I'll call you later," he says. "After she goes to bed."

4

She goes to bed early now because of the pills. Jonathan and I will get a few hours of phone time, giggling in the dark like teenagers up past curfew. If I'm lucky, that is. Lately the phone calls have been cut short by yawns and complaints of having to get up early for work. It's not like it was in the beginning, but then I guess nothing ever really is.

I love you, I think but don't say. I never say it, but he has to know it's true. Does he love me? His eyes say he does. The way he kisses me says so too. But Jonathan never says it with words.

He pauses to kiss me, bending over the bed. I don't grab him by the neck to pull him down, even though I imagine myself doing that. I guess I do have a little pride after all. It doesn't last. I leap out of the bed and catch him at the bedroom door. I'm still naked. He's fully clothed. Sometimes being naked is a weakness. Sometimes it's a weapon.

His hands roam over my bare skin. His breathing quickens. His kiss is fierce, but fast.

"I wish you could stay," I tell him.

I don't want to cry. I know he doesn't want me to. The tears I can no longer hold back make him uncomfortable. I never used to be that sort of woman. The kind to cling or chase or beg.

Funny how things can change.

He grips me gently by the upper arms to put some distance between us. He looks into my eyes. He's got lines at the corners of his, new since we started this . . . whatever it is. More lines bracket the corners of his mouth. It used to be that we laughed together all the time. We haven't laughed about much of anything lately, and there are times, like now, that I worry we never will again.

"Soon." He says it like a promise, an answer to a question I didn't ask. Not aloud, anyway. Not this time. "Soon."

Then he's gone, and I'm here alone in a room that still smells of him, and even though I never used to be the sort of woman to cry herself to sleep, that's what I end up doing.

CHAPTER THREE

Diana

"Hallooooo!" My mother-in-law's familiar trill rings through the hallway. She's let herself in through the garage, the way she usually does, and I hear the click-clack of her heels heading away from me, toward the kitchen.

Not for the first time, I consider changing the code for the garage door's keypad lock. It would at least give me a warning that I'm about to be . . . well, *invaded* seems like a harsh description, especially since I'm not sure what I would have done without her in those first weeks after the accident.

Jonathan has never been the sort to fuss and coo, so he didn't take vacation time to stay home with me. Harriett was the one who helped me use the toilet and take a shower. I couldn't even brush my own teeth. The first time I tried to wash my hair, I threw up from the pain. I'm able to do most of it by myself now, but the embarrassment of it all, the shame of being so vulnerable, is a memory I definitely wish I could forget. I'll never be able to, though, because Harriett will always be around to remind me.

Invaded might be harsh, but it's how it feels. Ten years ago, when I moved into this house with Jonathan, Harriett moved out of it and into the in-law quarters above the detached garage. She'd promised then that even though she'd be just steps across the yard, she would respect our privacy. She's kept her word, mostly, until the accident. She's been over here every day since I came home from the hospital, sometimes at all hours. Eventually, tired of being woken up at dawn every time Harriett let herself in to start the coffee, I turned off the phone notifications from my camera security system. I appreciate the coffee. I hate being woken up. Still, I wish she'd at least text before she came over—but how can I ask her to do that when, without her help these past six weeks, I'd have been lost?

After all, she's the only one I really have left.

"Diana?"

"I'm in the den." I'm out of breath as I slowly, carefully, move through the set of daily mobility exercises I'm supposed to do.

My left arm hurts the tiniest bit less because the clavicle on that side is only broken in one place, not three. I lift it slowly to chest height. The agony in my collarbone, sternum, and shoulder slices and dices me, stabs like an ice pick, way down deep. It's a hum like a tuning fork, vibrating nonstop. At the faint feeling of the bones grinding together, my body runs hot and cold. My stomach twists, and I make a weird, strangled sort of combination groan of relief, frustration, and agony. The pain doesn't stop right away, but it fades. Every day, a little more, it fades.

"Diana? Are you upstairs?"

I find enough air to answer more loudly this time. "In the den!"

I slip my arm back into the sling. I'm not supposed to be out of the slings for too long. It can take six to eight weeks or longer, even up to twelve, they've told me, for the bones to heal well enough to allow for full use of my arms. I can expect it to be some more weeks after that before it won't hurt at all. I might always have residual pain there, but I didn't hear that from the doctors. I found *that* out on the internet.

The only good thing about all of this is the meds. It turns out that anesthesia-induced amnesia is considered enough of a psychiatric burden that there's reasonable justification for me to have weekly therapy sessions with my psychiatrist, Dr. Levitt. I also get to take the good stuff. A pastel rainbow of opioids, anti-depressants, and anti-anxiety tablets, capsules, and pills. Put them on my tongue, I go flying.

"I just had your prescriptions refilled—oh, Diana. What are you doing?" In the doorway between the den and the hallway, Harriett sighs and shakes her head.

I taste sweat on my upper lip, and I hope my mascara hasn't run. It was hard enough to get it on once already today. I'm going out with my friend Trina in a bit, and I'd rather not look like a toddler with a fistful of markers helped me do my makeup. It'll be the first time I've gone anywhere except a doctor's appointment since I've been home from the hospital.

"Just doing my exercises."

"Your face is practically gray, and you're sweating like a pig. Here. Take your medicine."

She opens the bottle and tips some pills into her palm. Pale green-blue oblong pills. I have a few different prescriptions, so without reading the label, I'm not sure exactly what they are. I think they're the pain pills. They upset my stomach, which requires more pills to offset the random nausea. Dr. Levitt says these random bouts of sickness could also be my body's reaction to the stress of my mind missing so much time. Either way, I've lost close to fifteen pounds since the last time I can remember weighing myself, and I was never in need of a diet.

"I'm okay." I shake my head when she thrusts her hand in my direction. There's no way I'm going to let Harriett see how much I'm hurting. I want her to think I'm healing, even if I'm not convinced of it myself. The sooner she thinks I don't need her help, the better. "I'm trying not to take so many."

"There's no sense being in pain. You've had some serious injuries. Your doctors wouldn't renew your prescriptions if they didn't think you needed the pills." Harriett proffers the pills again.

"I'm okay, Harriett. Really."

Truthfully, the dull ache in my collarbones has ramped up from doing those exercises, and I *do* want those pills. I want a glass of wine with Trina even more, though, and I'm not about to mix pain meds and alcohol. My last dose was last night before I went to bed. Since then, I've thought about taking more meds about every fifteen minutes or so, but the promise of a perfectly chilled glass of chardonnay, maybe even two, has held me off. I can't remember the last time I relaxed with a glass of wine and a good friend. Literally cannot recall.

Her frown knits her brows together. "You're going to end up hurting yourself even more. I wish you'd just let me *help* you."

Why do you have to be so stubborn, so ungrateful? is the thought that comes to my mind. Harriett doesn't say that, of course. That's *my* mother's voice talking, the voice I have not quite learned to ignore, even after all these years.

"You do too much for me," I tell her.

Harriett flutters and blushes as though I've paid her a compliment, which was not my intent. "Oh, hush. I'm happy to do it. You know I am."

Oh yes. I know how Harriett is. I knew it before I married her son a decade ago. Back then, I thought she was exactly the sort of mother I'd always wanted. Now . . . not so much.

Guilt overwhelms me. I used to love Harriett more than my own mother. Somewhere along the way, everything I used to think was so great has become irritating. Smothering.

My husband has always taken this motherly love for granted, but I never have. Because of that, I'm the one who makes sure "he" remembers to order her flowers for Mother's Day, to make dinner reservations on her birthday, to pick up exactly the sort of flannel nightgown she adores for Christmas. My husband does not appreciate having a mother who cares, so I do it for him. Harriet is probably the only reason I'm still here. If I'm going to be honest, she's the only reason I'm here at all.

I wish I could remember why I hate her so much now.

"What time is Jonathan going to be home? I'm going to start dinner." Harriett tosses this over her shoulder as she heads down the hallway toward the kitchen.

I follow. "I don't know. He's working late tonight."

She whirls to face me, her eyes wide. Harriett literally wears pearls, and she literally clutches them. "Again? That's the third time this week."

"Again," I agree mildly.

Harriett keeps closer track of my husband's schedule than I do. I stopped paying attention to it a long time ago. I mean, up until about six months ago, I had my own career. My own late working nights to worry about. What I know, though, that she obviously does not, is that her son is not at the office all those nights he says he's working late. He's sleeping with another woman, that old cliché. Worse than that, it's my best friend.

"He works too hard," Harriett says with a frown as she putters with something in the cupboard. Pill bottles rattle. She closes the door and turns. "I'm going to message him. I really wanted him to be home for dinner. It feels like ages since we've all been around the same table, like a real family. I'm making pot roast. It *used* to be his favorite."

Jonathan has been a vegetarian for as long as I've known him. He's even been leaning toward becoming totally vegan. If pot roast used to be his favorite, it's far from it now. I *do* love pot roast, though, especially the way my mother-in-law makes it. All that rich gravy served over mashed potatoes that are swimming in butter. Mushrooms and carrots. A side of peas, cooked just enough so they're still crisp. I'm a terrible cook. I learned, out of desperation and necessity, the bare minimum required to feed myself so I didn't starve, but it's never been one of my accomplishments. I can't compete with the divine expertise of Harriett's pot roast.

"Well," she says, "I suppose I can count my blessings that at least I have you."

Harriett beams and moves toward me to offer one of what I think of as "Harriett hugs," an all-encompassing, thoroughly comforting embrace, but stops just short when I make a warning noise. "Oh dear. I keep forgetting not to squeeze you. How's the pain?"

It's worse than it was twenty minutes ago, but I don't want to tell her that. "It's bearable."

"Are you sure you don't want to take any pills? I really think you should." Her eagle-eye gaze snags on the book I left on the kitchen table, and she's distracted. "Where did this come from?"

"It's a library book."

I got the overdue notice in my email yesterday. I couldn't remember that I'd checked out that book, but I finally found it on an end table with a bookmark three-quarters of the way through it. I couldn't bring myself to renew it, not even to find out how it ends. It's the stupid little things that sting the worst.

"I'll return it for you," Harriett says.

"You don't have to. I'll take care of it."

"Don't be silly, Diana. You don't want to get a fine."

"I already owe a fine," I tell her tightly. "I'm going to take the book back tonight. My friend Trina's coming to get me in a few minutes."

Harriett looks confused. "Where are you going?"

"I have an appointment with Dr. Levitt. Trina is picking me up, and we're going to grab a drink afterward. It's trivia night."

"Trina? Driving you? But you didn't mention an appointment."

This gives me pause because I most certainly did. "I told you last week."

"You didn't," Harriett insists. "After all, I've been the one taking you to all your appointments. You see that doctor on Wednesdays. It's not Wednesday. I definitely didn't know you had an appointment with Dr. Levitt today. I would have written it down if you'd mentioned it."

"She's going on vacation, so she asked if we could switch to earlier in the week." I give a guilty look at the large whiteboard on the kitchen wall. Harriett has been so diligent about keeping it updated for me with all of my various doctor appointments and medicine schedules. I hardly ever look at it, and I certainly haven't ever written anything on it. Writing hurts too much, and anyway, I keep my own lists. "I'm sorry. I thought I said something to you."

"I'm sure you *thought* you did, but just . . . well." Harriet presses her lips together.

Unlike her son, Harriett won't actually say the word. *Forgot* has become a curse word. I'm not sure how to respond to Harriett about that. My amnesia is localized between two points in time. The first, several months before the night of my gallbladder surgery, and the second, when I woke in the hospital after it. Yes, my recollections of that first week after the accident and my surgeries are fuzzy, but they're not completely blank. To my knowledge, I haven't been any more forgetful about my daily life than I was before.

"Are you all right? Not having any new . . . trouble?"

"You mean mentally?" I ask and watch her mouth twist. I know she doesn't approve of me seeing a psychiatrist, but Harriett would never say so out loud. She'll drop comments about it, of course. Ask pointed questions. But just say what she means? Never. "I'm fine. It's just a little rearrangement of the schedule, that's all. No big deal. I promise."

"Not . . . remembering?"

"No," I answer curtly. "I'm not remembering anything."

I wish I could check my phone to see if Trina messaged me that she's running late, but it's in my purse. I'd have to have Harriett dig it out for me, maybe even enter the passcode to unlock it, since the exercises really have me aching. She has, and she would, but I'm trying hard not to ask her to do that sort of thing for me anymore.

"I wish you'd told me, that's all. I can still take you. I need to go to the drugstore and pick up your prescription refills. And run some . . . errands." Harriett is already looking around for her coat.

I know errands means cigarettes, although she won't admit it. You won't ever catch her smoking. She does it in secret, like you can't smell it on her clothes and breath. I don't judge her for it. We all do things we don't want anyone else to know about.

I glance toward the kitchen cabinet. Through the glass doors I can see the lineup of pill bottles. I have always hated the glass-front cabinets. They put everything on display, so everything has to be neat and tidy all the time. It stresses me out.

"I thought you said you already got—?"

"Oh yes, well. Of course. I'm just all flustered now." Her hands flap as she frowns. "I'm just all discombobulated, Diana. Let me grab my coat and keys."

I've never said a word to Jonathan or Harriet herself about possible memory issues on her part. Feels too close to home, I guess. Anyway, we don't talk much about anything anymore, Jonathan and I. At least not anything important, and in this moment I wonder, did we ever?

Gently, I say, "I've already made plans with my friend."

"But I was just about to put the roast in the oven—" Harriett falls silent when I shake my head.

"Don't worry about it. I appreciate it, but you really don't have to make anything."

She presses her lips together. I've hurt her feelings. "I was only trying to help."

"I know. Thank you. I do appreciate it." I'm not lying. I'd have starved without her cooking these past weeks.

"I'll just text Jonathan to make sure he's going to be late."

"Be my guest. I've still got plans." I snap the response, not meaning to sound so nasty, but I don't want to be the one to tell my husband's mother that he's messing around, and every time he misses dinner, the likelihood grows that I'll have to. If I have to tell her, I will have to tell him that I know, and after that . . . I'm not ready to think about what happens after that.

I can see this throws her. When I first met Harriett Richmond about twelve years ago, she was the volunteer contact for Sunny Days Adoption Services, the children's charity my company supported. I'd been tasked with updating their office's ancient security system, so I spent a lot of time working with her. Jonathan's father had died long before I met her, but I'd always known that Harriett's life had been built around taking care of her husband and son. I understand that it would never have occurred to her that she could go out with a girlfriend and leave her husband at home to fend for himself, but this woman has known me for a long time. At no point in my marriage have I ever given any indication that wifehood was the reason for my existence.

"He works so hard. He was late yesterday too. Last week, I don't think he made it home before seven any day except Friday. And then he's always going out to the gym so late at night too."

"He works as hard as he has to," I say cryptically, but fortunately his mother doesn't take it as anything but praise.

Harriett sighs and purses her lips. "Have you thought about when *you'll* go back to work?"

"I haven't."

I don't have to go back to work, not for a while at least. I took the early retirement package and payout I was offered when my company underwent restructuring, and that happened, conveniently, only a couple weeks before the time when my mind goes dark. Jonathan had encouraged me to take the summer off and spend as much time as I could at the beach house. Back then, I'd thought it was generous. I know the truth, now, about why he wanted me gone as much as possible.

"No wonder he has to work late so often, paying all the bills." She mutters this, not quite soft enough so I don't hear it.

Anxiety and anger knot my stomach, but I draw in a breath to keep my voice steady when I answer her. Yelling at Harriett is like chastising a kitten. Even if it's being naughty, you hate yourself for doing it. "I love your pot roast.

You know what would be great? If you left it for me in the fridge. Can you try to remember to slice it up first?"

"Well. My goodness. I suppose I certainly *could*. Even if you won't be home to eat it at dinner time, and I *was* making it especially for you." Harriett can't hide the trembling of her chin.

I've still managed to hurt her feelings. Great. Now I feel guilty again. I guess that will give me one more thing to talk to Dr. Levitt about. If I'd known wrecking my car was going to be what drove me into therapy finally, I might have started reckless driving sooner.

I know I can be a bit standoffish, but I am not a monster. I can't hug her with both my arms still in slings, but I try to sort of press myself against her so she can hug me. Gently.

"I'll let you know next time if I plan to go out, so you don't expect to make dinner," I promise.

"Of course you want to spend time with your friends. I understand. Don't you worry a second about it." Harriett pats my back. "I'll just finish up the pot roast and leave it for you. But you text me when you get home, all right? Or else I'll worry."

"I will. I promise."

My phone buzzes from my purse. I assume it's Trina, telling me she's in the driveway. I get up from the small kitchen table and use the tips of my fingers to snag the strap of my purse. At only an inch over five feet tall, everything about Harriett is petite, tiny, delicate. Standing beside her, I'm gargantuan, even after the weight I've lost. I'm bumbling, clumsy. There's no way I can get a coat on, and November in Pennsylvania can be more than chilly. They're calling for snow before Thanksgiving this year.

"Can you help me with my shawl?"

I wince at the minor weight of my bag, a tiny clutch with a thin strap, just big enough to hold my phone and wallet. I can't carry my usual tote-sized bag. Still, I always feel like I'm forgetting something—well, I am. Almost half a year of my life.

Harriett helps sling my shawl over my shoulders, taking an extra minute to tuck it closed at my throat. I have become the child she seems to wish I would be. Maybe we both wish it. Such a simple gesture, but I feel it deep inside. The caring. The concern. It's good to feel loved, and if sometimes, just sometimes, Harriett's love also feels a tiny bit like I'm being strangled . . . well, nothing good comes without a catch.

She goes with me to the front door and waves goodbye as Trina helps me with the passenger door. Harriett lingers, watching from the doorway as Trina buckles me in with a laugh. I shift to help her, both of us giggling at the absurdity of how difficult it is to situate me.

"Thanks for this," I say. "I really needed to get out."

"Hey, what are friends for?"

Trina's words are meant to cheer me, but I have to turn my face to the window to make sure she doesn't see the tears I'm certain glitter in my eyes. That's how I see that Harriett watches us until the curve in the driveway takes us out of sight.

Trina catches me up on the small-town gossip as we drive. She even runs the library book inside for me, along with the money for the fine. She drops me at Dr. Levitt's office, promising she'll be back in an hour.

The office is outfitted with a low leather couch. Such a cliché. I've never lain on it, even though the pillow and fuzzy throw blanket look comfortable enough; it's just too hard for me to get up and down into a prone position. At home I have to use a huge wedge pillow to sleep, and getting in and out of bed requires an entire rigamarole.

Instead, the doctor and I usually sit in the overstuffed chairs facing each other. She always offers hot tea served in a delicate teacup, but that would mean taking an arm out of the sling to drink it, and today I'm saving up all my aching and paining for those glasses of wine with Trina.

When I tell her this, Dr. Levitt chuckles. "Can't say I blame you. A glass of wine with a friend is usually worth more than a session with me."

"I haven't been out in forever. I always thought I was a homebody until I couldn't leave on my own. I was really glad she called me."

I don't mention that Trina and I had become much closer over the years that Val lived away. When Val moved back to good old Lebanon, Pennsylvania, to take care of her dad and then stayed because she lost her job in New York City, I'm ashamed to admit that Trina and I stopped getting together as often.

We talk a bit about my forced convalescence. Dr. Levitt says to focus on my progress instead of the setbacks. I can text now, carefully, if I don't overdo it. I can read books on my tablet since I only have to tap the screen instead of turning a page. I can feed myself if I'm careful to eat things that don't require a lot of cutting and I take it slow. That's a lot better than the first week or so, when I mostly ate soup or drank milkshakes through a straw. Every day, I'm closer to being out of the slings and back to my independence. We talk a lot about how important that is to me. Being able to take care of myself.

We haven't really started talking about why relying on others is such a hardship for me. To do that, we're going to have to delve deeper, and since I've only had three appointments so far, Dr. Levitt's barely had time to scrape the surface of what seems to be a disturbingly deep well of psychological issues. I mean, we all have them. You don't get through life without baggage. I'm sure it's all going to come up, but so far we've been focusing on the present.

Eventually, Dr. Levitt steers the conversation to my memory loss. There's not much she can do to help me regain my lost memories. Anesthesia-induced amnesia is a medical condition, not the same as a trauma-induced memory loss, even though the circumstances surrounding the loss were traumatic. She's here more to help me with my emotional reactions to finding a sizable blank space in my brain, to teach me how to cope, and to monitor the meds I'm on as part and parcel of all of this.

And to talk about the dreams.

"I didn't have the nightmare last night," I tell her. "That's three nights in a row without it. Maybe they're going to stop."

"Maybe." Dr. Levitt inclines her head toward me as she takes down a note or two on the pale lavender legal pad in her lap. I want to ask her where she got it. It looks just right for making a lot of lovely lists—once writing with a pen is no longer the equivalent of tearing myself to pieces.

My chuckle lifts on a sigh. "You don't think so."

"I think your nightmares are part of your emotional reaction to the stress and trauma of what happened. Even if your mind can't actively remember the night of the accident and the surgery, your body does. It can scarcely forget, after all. You're still in pain every day."

16

"But I'm also getting better every day. Do you think when I stop hurting, I'll stop having the dream?"

"I don't know," Dr. Levitt says. "It would be out of line for me to even guess at that. But I do think, Diana, that dreaming about burying someone in your back yard is a reflection of your frustration with your physical condition and your inability to remember such a significant portion of time. Now, I don't put too much stock in dreams as a whole. But in your case, it seems fairly obvious to me."

Oh, it's obvious, all right. Dreaming about having killed someone? I know exactly why I dream that. Just not why I'm dreaming about it *now*.

"I just feel like, if I only try harder . . ." My fists both clench, and I wince, making sure to relax my hands. "My memories are in there. If I can just get to them, I'll be able to remember."

"Your condition was caused by the anesthesia you were given for the surgery, not any head trauma." Dr. Levitt says. "You *may* regain them someday, but it might help you to stop thinking of your memories as being *buried*. The harder you try to dig for them, the farther away they're going to feel. Instead, perhaps try to think of them as being covered by water. Give them time to float up of their own accord."

"Great—then I'll start dreaming about drowning."

She laughs. "We'll deal with that when we get there. Okay? Anything else you want to talk about?"

There's always something, even if I haven't managed to bring myself to talk about it yet. But we started this therapy to help me figure out how to deal with my memory loss, not to negotiate the scorched wasteland of my childhood and adolescence or the current shambles of my marriage. Most of the time, Dr. Levitt reminds me that everything that happened in my life brought me to this point, and so whatever is going on with me now will always be tied to what happened to me then, much like anything that happens to me moving forward is likely to be affected by my amnesia and how I'm reacting to it. Memory loss is traumatic. It leaves scars.

"It's hard. Feeling so dependent on Jonathan. I mean, he's always made more money than I do."

She wrote something on her pad. "You weren't completely dependent on him before—you had a career and your own income. You even kept your own name, Sparrow, when you married. But now you feel as though you need him more than you want to. It's been rough on you, having to rely on someone else to do what you feel you should do for yourself. It would be hard on anyone."

"He's the one who really encouraged me to leave GenTech during the restructuring. It was supposed to be supportive. You know, giving me the chance to 'retire' early, so to speak. A chance to find out if I wanted to do something different. He'd take care of all the money, you see, so I didn't have to worry . . ." I stop myself from straining to see what she's writing.

"And you don't feel it was?"

I'm silent for a moment or so, struggling to put my thoughts into place. "I guess I'm just feeling stuck. That's all. And yet it's lucky I'm not working right now, because of all of this. The injuries would be bad enough, but I'm pretty sure amnesia would really mess me up at work."

"You should be out of those slings as early as a couple weeks from now. Perhaps even sooner. And things will change for you before you even know it."

I can't tell her that's what I'm afraid of.

"How about life at home?" Dr. Levitt asks.

Before I can answer, the bell dings to tell us the time's up. The hour always seems to pass so quickly, but today, I'm glad. There's so much to talk about with her, but so much I'm not ready to say.

CHAPTER FOUR

Valerie

The Blue Dove Inn used to be a dive bar, but new ownership bought it about four years ago. They cleaned it up, put on a big addition, and added a deck out back where they showcase local live music in the summers. Their specialty cocktails menu is longer than the appetizer list, and the craft beer selection even larger. It's one of the nicer places to eat around here and also the closest place for me to order takeout.

Tonight is trivia night, so it's crowded. I've had to wait longer than usual. Usually I prefer to cook for Jonathan because he's mentioned more than once that *she* never does, but tonight I got out of work too late to get to the grocery store for the fresh veggies I was planning to stir-fry. I'm in the corner, scrolling through a news blog on my phone while I wait for my name to be called, so when I hear it, I look up at once with the expectation that it's the hostess with my food.

"Val! Hi!"

It's Diana. She still has both arms in slings, so she can't hug me, but she moves close enough, like she means to. I can smell the wine on her breath, and she weaves a little bit. Gross. It's only eight o'clock on a Tuesday night, and she's drunk. *Like mother, like daughter,* I think, and can't hide the twist of my mouth or the way I draw back. How could she think I would hug her? How could she think I would even acknowledge her? After all I've done for her and how she completely went back on everything she promised? She's lucky we're in public, or else I'd have no problem telling her exactly what I think of her.

Trina Kauffman is with her, which explains part of it.

"Hey, Val. Haven't seen you out in forever," Trina says.

"Been busy," I say.

The three of us have known each other since high school, but Trina has always been more Diana's friend than mine. She and I don't hang out or keep in touch beyond saying "hi" if we bump into each other. She probably doesn't know what's going on between the two of us, although I wouldn't put it past Diana to have told her. Gain sympathy points. Make herself a martyr. But the fact that my former best friend went out of her way to say hello tells me she's saving face in front of Trina.

Trina laughs. "You must have a new guy taking up all of your time."

Maybe Diana did tell her.

An awkward silence falls over the three of us. Diana's still smiling at me. I know her well enough to see that it's a little strained, but only a little. There's something else in her expression too. A kind of longing. I look away from her.

"I'll go grab the car and bring it around," Trina offers to Diana with a nod toward me and a friendly smile.

Sure, because Diana is *so* disabled she can't possibly walk herself down the steep concrete stairs and across the parking lot. What a crock of shit. I hear my name again and turn, without saying anything else, to get my food from the hostess. It smells delicious, but my stomach is churning. I hope Diana will be gone when I turn back, but she's still outside the front door, waiting for Trina.

"Hey," she says in a quieter voice. She looks at the bag in my hands. Clearly there's enough food for two. Her lips press together a little, but she meets my gaze without hesitation. "I've been meaning to call you."

"Why?" I clutch the white paper bag closer to me. Its warmth ought to be a comfort.

Diana's brow furrows. "I . . . because . . ."

"Just. Don't. I'm supposed to be in Punta Cana right now." My words are clipped, but I'm pitching my voice low so nobody can overhear us. New housing developments and a few new stores in the strip mall haven't made this town any bigger than it's ever been. People have had enough to say about me over the years, and I'm not about to give them anything else.

A blue Subaru rolls up, Trina at the wheel. Diana shoots a glance at her as Trina gets out and goes around to the passenger side to open the door for her. Diana looks back at me.

"I don't understand," she says.

I lean close enough to hiss into her ear, "Yes, you do. Don't you dare act like you don't. Don't you fucking dare."

"It's about Jonathan."

I blink rapidly to keep myself from staggering at her sheer fucking audacity. Then I focus on her. "Of course it's about Jonathan."

"I know about the two of you," Diana says quietly, not making a scene.

I stop myself from feeling grateful that she's not shouting. How can she stand in front of me, looking like butter wouldn't melt in her mouth?

"Of course you do," I manage to bite out. "You're the one who asked me to fuck him in the first place."

CHAPTER FIVE

Diana

I stagger, clumsy-footed. *I asked her to do what?*

"Stop pretending you can't remember," Val says. "Just own your shit, Diana. For fuck's sake, how could you do this to me?"

"Me . . . do . . . but you're the one . . ."

"Diana?"

I turn at the sound of Trina's voice, and Val pushes past me to take the steps down to the lower parking lot. Trina helps me get in the car, but we don't laugh and joke this time as she buckles me in. I can tell she wants to ask me what's going on, but she waits until we pull into the driveway before saying anything.

"You okay?" she asks.

"Yeah. I just . . . we had an argument." Is that what it was? Honestly, I don't know what the hell we had, just now or, obviously, before.

Trina grimaces. "Sorry. I know you two are tight. I hope you get it worked out. But hey, if you want to talk about it, you have my number. If you need a ride, or whatever. Just call me."

It's too embarrassing to cry about this, so I force a watery smile. "Thanks. It's been a rough bunch of weeks."

By the time I get inside my house, I no longer feel like crying. I manage to get my phone out of my purse with a minimal struggle. Cradling it carefully, I open a message window and type out a text to Val. We've had arguments in the past. Sisters always do, and she's always been as much a sister to me as a friend.

What's going on? We need to talk.

But the message keeps showing "Delivered," and she doesn't reply.

CHAPTER SIX

Valerie

SEPTEMBER, TWO YEARS AGO

"That is a shit-fire, fuck-me, hallelujah lot of money," I said when Diana waved the check in front of my face.

She'd come to Brooklyn for a rare weekend visit. It had been six months since the last time we'd seen each other. I missed her, but my life there was different. I got away from that prison of a small town. She chose to stay behind.

"What are you going to do with it?" I poured us both glasses of wine from the bottle she'd brought. Briar White, her fancy brand with the white rose on the bottle.

We'd both grown up with next to nothing, but Diana had moved up in the world. Nice house in Pennsylvania. Another at the beach in Delaware. She worked, but didn't really have to. Her husband kept her in style, and it had become more and more obvious over the years that she'd become accustomed to it. We saw each other so infrequently now that it really stood out—but could I blame her? She'd chosen her prison, but it came with thousand-thread-count sheets.

"Spending her money feels dirty," she said. "Like it could be enough to make up for everything she pulled. Like it could ever change what she did. I'll never forgive her."

She tucked the check into her pocket and sat beside me on the couch I'd rescued from the neighbor's trash, her feet tucked beneath her. She looked too fancy. Some of her dark hair fell in tendrils around her face, the rest of it pinned up high. I wanted to reach around and yank it free. Mess her up a little. Get her down on my level. We used to be so alike when we were young, but we'd both changed.

"You don't have to forgive your mom," I said, "but don't let that stop you from spending the money she left you."

"And it is all mine. I don't have to share a single cent of it. He doesn't even know about it. See? It's made out to Diana Sparrow. He couldn't cash it even if he tried."

"You didn't tell him?"

"He met my mother *once*," she said flatly. "Two months ago, when she came back around and said she wanted to make her amends. Whatever she felt she owed me with this check, Jonathan has nothing to do with it."

She talked sometimes about how fast her husband went through money. Less often, she let it slip that he was a lot less cool about her doing the same. I'd mention that he was financially controlling. She'd point out that she lacked for nothing.

I'd never even met Jonathan before he and Diana got married. I'd heard her talk about him the few times she'd managed to visit me in Brooklyn. I went to the clinic with her when she decided not to have his baby. Nothing she'd ever said about him had made me think I needed to make the effort of knowing him, until suddenly they were engaged. I'd never tried to talk her out of it, the way I should have.

"Fuck Jonathan," I said and raised my glass.

"No, thank you," Diana replied. "You can be my guest, though."

"He's not my type."

We clinked our glasses and sipped. No matter how long we spent apart, it was always easy to fall back into the patterns of our friendship. We talked about our celebrity crushes and how terrible her husband was and why I'd broken up with my last boyfriend, who'd really been a one-night stand that had lingered past the expiration date.

Another bottle of wine later, Diana pulled the check out of her pocket again with a triumphant flourish. "I know what I'm going to do with it."

"Pay for a hit man to off your asshole husband?" I thought she'd chastise me—after all, it's one thing to complain about the dude you've bound yourself to in unholy matrimony, but it's another when someone else does it.

Instead, encouraged by sweet white wine and girl time, we both burst into peals of laughter. She shook her head. Drained her glass. Put it on the coffee table.

"Nope," Diana said. "I'm going to buy myself a car."

* * *

That was a little over a year ago. The money she'd inherited from her mother would have paid a year's rent on my Brooklyn apartment, but Diana didn't need to worry about anything as banal as her living expenses. True to her word, she'd used it to buy her precious red Camaro. She'd been as careless with that car as she'd been with our friendship, and now both were wrecked.

Thinking of that weekend and how she'd spoken about Jonathan, I run hot and then cold with chills of fury. If she'd left him back then, we wouldn't be where we are now. When my phone pings with a text from her, I've had enough.

Swipe.

Block.

Delete.

I owed her for a long time because of what she did for me, but I don't owe her anything anymore.

CHAPTER SEVEN

Diana

Cold rain hammers at my skull as I drop to my knees in the mud and dig, dig, dig. I pull clots of earth with my bare hands. There's a hole at the base of the tree, and I am the one who made it.

I made this hole, the size of a child. The child I never had. The one I did not want.

I taste blood. My mouth hurts. My fingers hurt and are also bleeding; there's blood and mud and rain, cold as ice. All around me. I'm digging. Deeper. My fingers work the earth, and worms wriggle between them. My hands part the earth, separate it, make an emptiness.

I'm putting something in the hole by the tree.

I'm covering it up.

I've buried something.

I've buried some*one*.

* * *

I wake from the dream with the sour taste of bile in my mouth and the uncomfortable heaviness of heartburn settled at the base of my throat. It's only ten at night, but I feel like I've been sleeping for days. My collarbones ache, probably because I was writhing around in bed. The triangle pillow I've been using to prop me up and help ease the backache that happens from being unable to shift positions or to sleep on my side is shoved too far over, close to the bed's edge.

Dr. Levitt has assured me over and over again that if I'd hit a person, not a deer, there's no way I could have buried them in the back yard. Even if the first responders on the scene hadn't noticed a dead person, my injuries would have made it impossible. I know that my guilt and fear stem from something totally unrelated from the accident, and yet the dream lingers.

Jonathan's side of the bed is still made pristinely. I can see the emptiness in the glow from the window. I left the outside lights on for him, but he's not home yet.

I steel myself for the pain as I push myself upright, feet onto the floor, and swallow over and over until the horrible taste fades. I need a drink. I swear I turned down the thermostat before I went to bed, but the room is sweltering. I'm sticky. I use the phone app to dial back the temperature to something more reasonable.

I want a lukewarm shower to rinse away the sweat of the nightmare. At this point, I think I would sell my soul to the devil for a long, luxurious shower and the ability to wash my own hair. I want to shave my armpits, which I am embarrassed to be able to smell. The slings are disgusting too, even though Harriett has tried to wash them for me. Grotty gray, and I hope I'm only imagining the faintly sour odor clinging to them.

The doctors have all told me there's no set science about when collarbones heal "enough." My next checkup isn't until next week, but I am suddenly so desperate to be clean, to be healed, that I take off first the left sling and then the right. The right collarbone break was worse and hurts more, but I slowly raise and lower both arms and bite back the groans. This time I'm able to push off the bed and stand.

I need to do this. To get back on my feet. To take care of myself.

In the shower, I run the water and step in with a deep sigh. Moving like an arthritic tortoise, I manage to soap and rinse. Again, turning so I don't twist, I wet my hair and fill my palm with shampoo from the pump bottle, but I can't raise my arms high enough reach the top of my head. The pain rises until it chokes me, and I'm terrified to push through it, scared I will re-break myself. I can't do this.

A memory rises.

* * *

"Let me." The ice cubes in the plastic bag rattled as I folded the dishtowel around them to protect Val's skin from the coldness.

Her eye was already swollen. I helped her wipe away the blood from her nose, but her split lip still leaked crimson. She was lucky she hadn't lost a tooth. *Lucky*, I thought, *like luck had anything to do with this bullshit.*

"Ouch." Val winced as I put the bag of ice on her face. "Shit. That hurts."

"You're going to have a shiner."

She rolled her good eye at me. "Think it'll make me look *tuff*?"

She said it like Ponyboy in *The Outsiders*, the movie we'd obsessed over for years. Nothing about our lives was like the Curtis brothers'. No Darrel, no Sodapop, no Johnny. Maybe most importantly—for me, anyway—no Dallas Winston. Still, something in that book and movie called to us enough that we could quote it, line for line, because of how often we'd consumed both.

"Yeah. You look *tuff*." I sat next to her on the bed and listened for any sounds from outside her room. Her father's rampage had worn off before she called me. I got there as soon as I could, but wished I could have been there in time to stop him from hitting her. I wasn't sure what I'd have done, but I liked to think it would have been impressive.

I took care of her this way. Ice for her eye. Chicken noodle soup heated on the stove in a battered pot. She didn't cry about any of it. I mean, neither of us ever did. Tears don't do any good. You deal with what your parents hand you and wait until you're old enough to get out. At sixteen, we only had a few more years to go.

I took care of Val, my sister-friend, until it was late and both of us were yawning. The ice had long since melted, and I emptied the bag into the sink of the bathroom down the hall. I pushed the dresser in front of the door and crawled into bed next to her. I was careful not to shift her too much. I saw the bruises blooming on her back and shoulders.

"It's the last time," she said with her eyes closed. "I swear to God, he's never going to hit me again. I'll . . . I'll kill him if he does."

We didn't talk about what we did together in her mother's hospital room, or how what we did contributed to where we were now. I touched her split lip. She'd have a scar.

"I'll always take care of you if you need help, Val. You know I'll do anything for you."

Val opened her eyes. She held up her hand so we could link our pinkies. "Same. Anything."

*   *   *

Val should be here to help me wash my hair. To help me get into my comfy pajamas. To laugh with me at old sitcoms. She would have been, not so long ago, but everything between us has changed. After all I've done for her. After all she's done for me. This is where we end?

"You're the one who asked me to fuck him in the first place."

Wine, Brooklyn, the check from my mother. Yes, I remembered the conversation. The toss-away comment I'd made over a year ago had come back to haunt me.

I've known about the affair since a few days after I got home from the hospital. My phone had been lost in the accident, so my husband got me another one. He even set it up for me—by logging in to his own Cloud account.

My husband, as it turns out, is a very stupid man.

I saw their texts. All of them. *Ping, ping, ping,* one after the other, until I managed to get to the settings and turn off the account. Using my arms hurt. Finding out Val was sleeping with my husband was worse. I don't remember knowing before I read those texts . . . yet somehow, I was not totally surprised.

It explained why I hadn't been able to get in touch with her about the accident, why she hadn't visited or even checked in. I didn't tell Jonathan I'd found out. Just home from surgery with busted-up bones, missing memories, exhausted and sick, how could I have been expected to deal with this too? Short answer, I could not.

I.

Could.

Not.

I still can't. Seeing her at the Blue Dove last night, I'd been unable to stop myself from reaching out. If *I* could pretend I didn't know, then *she* could pretend it wasn't true. Right?

I've seen Val lie. I know she can do it straight-faced, not so much as a blink to give her away. She was not lying to me at the Blue Dove, and if she was telling the truth, that means this is far more complicated than I already thought it was. I remember that I no longer love him, but I have no recollection of ever planning to actually leave him. Is this how our marriage ends, just like that? How can it?

Weeping, I stand beneath the water until it goes cold.

I manage to get a towel around my waist. I take my comb into the bedroom to sit on the edge of the bed while I drag it through my wet and unwashed hair, but again, I can't lift my arms high enough. I'm dry mouthed from the pain and shaking from the effort.

All I want is to have clean hair and a good night's sleep. It's almost eleven at night, but my husband is still not home. Harriett's lights are on. I know she suffers from insomnia. I know she almost always waits up for his car to make sure he got home all right. She never says anything about it, and I'm sure he doesn't know, but I do.

Harriett is always coming over the to the main house unannounced, but this is the first time I've ever done it to her.

"Diana," she says when she opens the door. Her platinum hair is done up in her curlers, covered with a triangle of fabric. Without makeup, her face is soft and pale and not young, but younger looking. "Come in. What's wrong?"

"I wanted . . . I wanted to wash my hair . . ." My voice shakes with sobs. I want so much more than that, but I don't know how to ask her without telling her everything about Val and Jonathan. The carnage and ruin that has become my life. Once it's said, I won't be able to take it back. The end of my marriage will be real, and I will have to face it.

I'm just not ready.

Marrying Jonathan had been settling. I've known that for a long time. Harriett had spoken so glowingly of her son, a good man, a fine catch, and I'd been at a low point after the loss of my father, so I'd let her set us up on a date. One date had turned into two. I had found him, if not intriguing, at least unobjectionable.

And then we were married, and I'm not sure how or why, except that I loved his mother and I'd been alone for a good long time, and he asked. In the end, that's what it comes down to. Jonathan asked, and I thought that if he was the kind of man I'd never be able to rely on, well . . . then he could never let me down.

I've cried in front of Harriett before, but it's been a long time. No matter how frustrated I've been since the accident, this is the first time my emotions have up and run away with me. I may have forgotten a good four months of my life, but I haven't forgotten how many times I've leaned on her in the past.

"Oh dear. Come in. Come in." She stands aside to usher me in. I yelp when she puts an arm around my shoulders. "I'm sorry!"

"Can you please help me?"

Harriett nods. "Of course. Yes. Come into the bathroom, and I'll get you all set up."

Her apartment has an open floor plan, lots of space, and the bathroom is set up specifically to accommodate someone with limited mobility, including a sink at the right height for hair washing. The place was clearly built for some-one who needs assistance . . . or will. For someone who means to live there until the end of her life.

I close my eyes and lean back in the chair to let the back of my neck rest on the sink edge. It's a little uncomfortable, but I'm willing to put up with it. Har-riett tucks a rolled towel beneath me without a word. She runs the water warm and sluices it through my hair. Her fingers work in the shampoo. She uses a pitcher to help rinse. Then condition. Finally, she combs through it, apologiz-ing every time she hits a snag. There are a lot. My scalp is stinging by the time she's finished, but it feels so much better.

"It's close to midnight," Harriett says. "You should get some sleep."

"Thank you, Harriett. So much."

"You know I'm always here for you, Diana." She walks me to the door. The outside lights are off next door. Jonathan's finally home, but neither of us men-tion the late hour or where he might have been this whole time. She has to know he wasn't at work.

"Goodnight, Diana. I'll be over in the morning."

You don't have to rises to my lips, but I pinch off the words before they can escape. She doesn't have to—that's exactly it. But she will anyway.

In my kitchen an empty plate sits on the counter, smeared with gravy and mashed potatoes, a few strings of pot roast from the sandwich I'd had when I got home, tipsy from my night out with Trina. I thought I had put it in the dishwasher. Leaving it out is something that Jonathan would do, not me. I'm too tired to make the gymnastic effort required to clean it up now.

The sound of the television from the den tells me Jonathan hasn't even made it upstairs, which would explain how it's possible he has no idea I wasn't home when he got there. I creep down the short hallway to the den and peek in at him. He's in his recliner, remote in hand but head tipped back and mouth open. He's snoring. After my mother left, my dad used to sleep in the living room on the couch with the television running constantly, but that had never been my husband's habit . . . at least, not before he started needing a reason to hide what time he came home.

I should wake him up, encourage him to come to bed so he doesn't have a sore back in the morning, but I don't. Truth is, I don't want him in the bed with me. Not even if he takes a shower, which it doesn't look as though he's done, which means he's come back into this house with my former best friend's touch still all over him. I want to wake him up then. I want to shout in his face. Accuse him. Let him know that I know the truth. Tell him to get out, go back to his mistress. I want to laugh in his surprised face when I tell him I know *all* about her.

But I don't, do I?

I don't know when or why it started. I don't know my part in it. All I have is that yawning void in my memory, and my cowardice and inability to face any of it.

I do not confront my husband. Instead, I shake a few pain pills from the bottles in the kitchen cupboard. Harriett has helpfully left them all opened so I don't have to fight with the childproof lid. I hope they will quiet the ache of my knitting bones and let me get back to sleep. I go back upstairs to bed and get under the covers. I situate myself against the pillow and, motionless, feel the pain in my bones ease enough that I should be able to sleep. There might be more nightmares if I do, but I close my eyes anyway. The dreams are better than staying up for hours thinking about all the ways someone who loves you can betray you . . . or how you can betray the one you love.

33

CHAPTER EIGHT

Valerie

LAST DECEMBER

Diana and Jonathan have had a holiday party every year for as long as they've been married. I'd made it to all of them, even when I still lived in Brooklyn. I never thought I'd come back to the town I grew up in, much less move back here, but my dad was dying. I was all he had. I didn't want to be, but that's how it worked out.

That night, I left him behind with the hospice worker. I could still smell the lingering stink of his sickness on me, beneath the soap and deodorant and perfume, but my sparkly red dress and matching heels made me feel better. I'd put my hair up. I wore a pair of my mother's diamond earrings, the ones my father told me I'd never get to have because I was a "gold-plated little whore."

"Don't think I don't know," he said. "I know what you did, you and that girlfriend of yours."

Joke's on you, Dad. I took these earrings right from my mother's jewelry box before I left home the first time. I'd had them for years. They sparkled for me as much as they ever did for her.

As always, when I pulled into my best friend's driveway, I took a moment to look at her house and think how far we'd both come. Or at least how far I'd gone before coming back. I was living in the childhood home I'd run away from as soon as I turned eighteen, and Diana lived in a nineties-built mini-mansion her husband had been gifted by his mother. As soon as my dad died,

I'd be out of this piece of shit little town again. Diana . . . well, she was stuck here for good.

Through the windows of the in-law apartment above the detached garage to the left of the main driveway, I saw Jonathan's mother in her kitchen. Harriett Richmond made the cookie platter every year, and since I was a little early, I took a minute to stop at her door to see if she needed help. She must have ducked outside while I was locking my car, though, because before I could knock, we startled each other as she came around from the back of the building.

I caught sight of a scowl before her expression smoothed into confusion. "The catering should be delivered next door."

"I'm Val," I reminded her. "Diana's friend." We'd met a handful of times, for example, every year at this party. I tried not to be offended she didn't remember. Or that she thought I was "the help."

"Oh yes. Did she send you over to fetch me?" Another flash of a frown slid across the expertly applied crimson of her lips.

"No. I just saw you through the window, and I thought maybe you'd need some help with the cookies."

Harriett blinked. "The cookies?"

"You make the cookies every year for the party . . . don't you?"

"Oh. Yes. Well, yes, I do. From scratch. I was just getting them ready. But I don't need any help, honey. You go on ahead to the party." The older woman smiled, showing me a bit of lipstick on her teeth. She smelled of smoke. Cigarettes, not wood stove or campfire.

It had been a warm winter so far, but as I made my way across the driveway toward the main house, a few snowflakes skittered down from the dark skies and salted my bare arms. I hadn't bothered with a coat.

Diana opened the door and looked past me for a moment, perhaps catching sight of her neighbor/mother-in-law. She greeted me with a grin and a long hug. I could smell the wine on her breath, pungent, fruity. I wanted some immediately.

Diana breathed into my ear. "He's making me *craaaaaazy.*"

"Wine?" I patted her on the back.

We'd always told each other we weren't going to get married. That we'd live together in a male-free commune. Wine afternoons and no sleepovers with boys allowed. Just us girls, making sure to have each other's backs. I hadn't seen her since that day last September when she'd told me about buying her car, but nothing much seemed to have changed.

"This way." Diana took me by the hand through her two-story foyer—in her house it was a *foy-ay*, not a *foy-er*.

The family room was decorated for the party with plenty of candles and string lights, but no tree this year. Diana always put one up for her husband's sake, even though she'd given up Christmas for herself years ago. I wondered if she'd ever told him why.

She saw me looking to the corner where it was usually placed. "He didn't do it this year, so I didn't either. I warned him if he didn't take care of it, we wouldn't have one. I guess he doesn't care, at least not enough."

"Nobody else will either," I assured her. "Not so long as there's plenty of food and booze."

"Harriett will."

"Well, I guess she could have come over and put up a tree, then, right?" My quip was meant to be light, but a shadow flitted across Diana's face.

Not even a frown could turn my beautiful friend ugly. She would always be "the pretty one," and I would always be jealous.

I let her lead me to the bar set up in the kitchen. A full spread of liquor and wine. She poured me a glass of white. Then one for herself. Not from the bottles she had chilling in festively colored buckets, but the special white she saved only for herself. And for me.

"Pinkies up," we said at the same time, and clinked our glasses together.

The party got into full swing. There was plenty of food, including the platter of cookies sprinkled with colored sugar that Jonathan's mother brought. I hadn't eaten all day, but now a single plate of barbecued meatballs and cheese with crackers was too much to finish. I tried to pace my drinking, but the wine, even when I switched to what had been put out for the regular guests, was crisp and chilled and trickled into every crack and crevice. Filling me up until I feared I might overflow.

Every time someone from high school tried to get me to talk about the good old days, I wanted to throw up all over them. They'd never left home because they loved it here so much they chose to stay, or they had left but were home for the holidays because they loved it here so much they missed it when they were gone. I was the only one who didn't want to come "home." The only person who seemed to hate this shitheel town, and here I was. Trapped again.

But I put on the face of someone who loved it there. I bragged about my job, the old job, the one I'd lost two weeks ago because of all the time I'd had to take off since my dad got sick. I talked about my amazing life in the city, not mentioning that I'd lost my apartment there, that I was in debt I couldn't repay, that I'd broken up with my last boyfriend because he wanted someone who was "wife material." I laughed and held up my ringless hand when they asked if I was married, did I have kids. Maybe a cat or a dog or a parakeet?

"No, no," I said. "Too smart for that."

Some of them envied me, and some of them pitied me. I told myself I didn't give a damn what any of them thought, but I must have, because every conversation was another slice, a digging cut, until my insides were a handful of fluttering ribbons. I was drunk. I should've gone home. I'd given up smoking a few years ago, but I wanted a cigarette.

Christmas is a hard time of year for a lot of people, and this year it seemed I was one of them. The lights, the festive music, the sparkly red dress, the wine and food and people laughing at the party—all of it left me feeling down and dark. This wasn't sadness. This was despair.

I want, I thought as I pushed my way out the French doors in the kitchen and onto the deck, as I stumbled toward the garbage pails set at the back of the in-law apartment. *I want, I want, I want.*

I want . . . to die.

It was not the first time I'd had the idea that ending my life would be better than living it, but it had been a few years, at least, since I'd last entertained that idea. As soon as the thought rose to my mind, though, it felt right. I got calm. Outside, under the steadily falling snowflakes, I tipped my face to the dark sky and let the chilly flakes coat my face for a moment before I brushed them away.

I had a choice. I always had a choice. I did not have to stay here, in this life.

I didn't have to have a life at all.

When the call from the hospice worker buzzed my phone, I let it go to voicemail. I waited for a minute or so, giving her time to leave a message. I read the transcription of it without listening. I already knew what she was going to say.

"Sorry." A male voice interrupted me, and I turned the phone downward so the light wouldn't show him my face. "I didn't see you out here. You okay? Val?"

I turned, already weary, but it wasn't Tom or Jim or Steve from high school; it was Diana's husband. Jonathan. His black and silver hair glinted in the shaft of light filtering from his mother's kitchen.

"Needed some air," I said. "Great party, though."

Jonathan leaned against the back of the apartment and pulled a lighter and a pack of cigarettes from his pocket. "Sure."

"Can I have one?"

Without a word, he shook the box to give me access to one of the cigarettes. Then he offered the lighter. The first drag was heaven. The second buzzed my head. I took my time before drawing again.

"Don't tell my mother I'm out here smoking," he said in a low voice, but with a chuckle.

"What about your wife?"

"My wife," Jonathan said, "doesn't give a shit if I get lung cancer and leave her a widow."

It was the sort of thing I should tell him wasn't true, except I'd heard Diana bitch about him enough to know that maybe it was true. I stayed quiet and smoked my cigarette. I stabbed it out against the side of the garbage can, then lifted the lid to toss the butt inside. The can was full to the brim with trash, and the most notable thing on top was a set of those plastic containers from the grocery store that hold baked goods. Sugar cookies, according to the label I glimpsed. I let out a laugh. So that's what she'd been doing. That old bat made such a show of her "homemade" treats, and all she did was pick them up in bulk from the market.

"What?" Jonathan asked.

"Never mind."

"I guess I should get back inside," he said without moving.

I watched him. "I should get home. My dad's sick. I should see how he's doing."

Both of us stayed still.

"Is it just me," Jonathan asked after a moment, "or are most of my wife's friends . . . assholes?"

I shook my head. "It's not just most of them."

"You're her friend."

"Yeah," I agreed, "and I'm also an asshole."

"No, you're not," Jonathan denied with a laugh. "At least, not like they are."

"You don't even know me!" My protest was a little too loud and could attract attention if anyone else had decided to come outside. I looked around automatically, but we were still alone.

"I should know you though, shouldn't I? The infamous Val? I feel like I should know you." He moved a little closer to me.

He was drunk. Drunker than me, and I was having a hard time focusing with both eyes open.

Jonathan stepped into a patch of shadow, closer still, his voice a low but amused mutter. "She talks about you all the time. Sometimes I wonder if I should be jealous that she loves you more than she loves me."

"She doesn't love you at all." The words tripped out of my mouth. Too late to take them back. Too drunk-honest to wish I could.

"I know."

I was not expecting him to kiss me, but he did. I melted into the embrace as easily as if we'd been flirting with each other for years. Our mouths opened. Tongues dipped and twisted. Sloppy, no skill in it, but when his hand slid beneath my hair to cup the back of my neck, tipping me harder against him, I gave that kiss everything I had. In that moment, all I could think was that it might be the last kiss I'd ever get.

"My father died," I told him, without mentioning that it had happened only a few minutes ago.

"I'm sorry," Jonathan said.

I wasn't. I hadn't gotten a last word with my father, but I didn't have anything to say to him, even if I'd had the chance.

"About that? Or about the kiss?"

"Both, I guess."

"Don't be. Shit happens." I shrugged like none of it mattered, even though it did. Diana didn't love him. That didn't mean she wanted someone else to have him.

We were both silent. I thought about asking him for another cigarette but didn't. I didn't want to smoke away the taste of him.

"I don't think it's okay to cheat on your spouse," Jonathan said finally.

I shrugged again. Said nothing. I wasn't the married one, and I sure as hell was never going to tell her.

"I'd better get inside," he said.

I followed him back to the house, where it was warm and bright and full of the off-key yodeling of party guests doing karaoke in the living room. I watched him find Diana with the focused intent of a predator looking for its next meal. I watched him kiss her, and I watched her let him.

Eight months later, I was in love with him, and she was supposed to be letting him go.

CHAPTER NINE

Diana

Pain. A knife, stabbing into my side, wrenching upward. Ripping me apart. I can't breathe. Move. I'm dying, I am being murdered, someone is killing me.

I am not dead.

Run, run, running on wet earth, the ground beneath me soft with mud so that my feet slip out from underneath me. I dig in the ground. I make a hole. I fill the hole.

My hands are covered in blood.

I taste it in my mouth, a thickness, sour, choking me. Sick.

I know what I've done.

* * *

I never used to sleep late or go to bed early, but since the accident, I do both. In bed by nine PM, up by ten AM, and that's only if I set my alarm to wake me up.

"It feels like I'm never going to get enough sleep," I tell Dr. Levitt now. "I think the pills are making me too tired."

"We can certainly take a look at them and adjust if you want, but keep in mind it truly does take time for your body to get used to medications, particularly in the aftermath of trauma like yours. Sleep is a great healer. Here." She sets the delicate teacup filled with steaming, sweet tea on the small table next to my chair. "Let that sit for a few minutes, or you'll burn your tongue."

It's such a motherly thing to say, and for a moment, a surprising and embarrassing moment, I'm speechless from the tears clogging my throat. I blink them away and sniff, but I can't wipe my face. A single tear slips out of my right eye and down my cheek. Dr. Levitt hands me a tissue, tucking it into my hand inside the sling.

"Sorry. I'm feeling down today," I tell her.

"If I had a dollar for every time someone said that to me, I'd be able to take a Caribbean cruise."

We both laugh at that because that was exactly where she'd been two weeks ago.

"My doctor's appointment last week was a disappointment," I tell her and wince as I carefully ease my arm from the sling and blot the tears. "I thought I'd be out of these by now."

"Soon," she promises and settles into the chair across from me. "Collarbones are—"

"I know. Hard to predict. They keep telling me that." I lean back in the chair and let my arm rest outside the sling, testing the vibrating pain for a few seconds before giving up and putting it back inside the cloth harness. By the time I'm done, the tears are gone. Pain's good for shoving away sorrow, but I learned that a long time ago.

"And the dreams?"

I hesitate before answering. "I had one last night. It woke me up."

I don't mention that I'd screamed loud enough to hurt my throat, or that my terror hadn't woken my husband because, once again, he hadn't been there. It had been midnight this time. He was staying out later and later. I guess he's counting on the pills keeping me knocked out.

"Everything the same?"

They're always the same, with minor differing details. There's blood on my hands. I've killed someone and buried them under a tree in my back yard.

"Yes. But this time I also had the feeling someone had been trying to hurt me, or they *had* hurt me. Not just that I'd done something to someone else, but very clearly, that I was in danger."

"Interesting." Dr. Levitt scribbles a note. "When you woke up, were you still scared?"

"Sometimes I wake up and my heart is pounding, I can't breathe—maybe I've even screamed a little. Or it feels like I have. But lately the dreams have been feeling so real that when I wake up, I . . ."

She waits.

I haven't touched my tea yet, not because I'm afraid it'll be too hot, but because reaching for it is going to hurt. Drinking it would give me a reason to be silent for a few more seconds, though. I reach for the cup but then sit back in my chair. I know Dr. Levitt won't say a word until she thinks it's necessary, so she can give me as much time as I need to speak.

I have a confession. It might have something to do with these recurring dreams, or it might not. But it's not mine solely to make, and even though Val has betrayed me, I can't bring myself to do the same to her. Not with someone I've only known a few weeks.

I blow on the tea before sipping. "Pinkies . . . out."

The phrase Val and I always said catches in my throat, and Dr. Levitt gives me a curious look. I haven't told her about the affair. I haven't told her about a lot of things. Withholding information from your shrink isn't the best way to get through your shit, I know. But I'm so, so tired, and there's so, so much of it, and only an hour a week is never enough time.

"My friend Val and I used to say that," I explain.

Dr. Levitt writes something on the lovely lavender pad I've been coveting. I sip more tea, then put the cup down, careful not to spill, moving slowly to keep the pain at bay. It's worse today than it has been, and I blame the dream. I woke up thrashing around.

"The last few times, after I've woken up, I've had a hard time remembering that they're not real. That they are dreams, not memories." I cough as I tuck my arm back into the sling. The relief isn't instant, but it's better. I look her in the eye when I continue, "I have to remind myself that I have not ever buried someone under a tree in my back yard."

"Let's hope you haven't done anything you're dreaming about," Dr. Levitt says—without a laugh this time.

I don't laugh either.

"I want to stop taking the meds. I don't like being reliant on them. I can deal with how much it hurts," I say. "I'm just going a little nuts with how long it's taking for me to get better."

"When you were young, how much responsibility did you have for taking care of yourself?"

So, there it is. The question I've always known would come my way as soon as I started seeing Dr. Levitt. Expecting it doesn't make it easier to answer.

"A lot," I say.

She nods and scribbles another note, like she was expecting this. I'm sure she was. Her silence is meant to prompt me into speech, but I'm having trouble finding the words. I've been waiting to dive into this subject since the first time I came into her office, and still I don't know what to say. The only person who really knows all about it is Val. If Dr. Levitt wants to know about my childhood, though, she doesn't probe. Instead, she changes the subject.

"We've spoken briefly about you going back to work. Have you given that any more thought?"

I shake my head. "No. I took the payout with the idea that I'd do some freelancing. Maybe look for something new. I mean, money's not a problem. Jonathan does very well."

"You're in a fortunate position."

I acknowledge that with a nod. "I know."

"And yet . . ." She gives me an expectant look.

"And yet?"

"So much of your independence seems to be tied to your ability to provide for yourself. I realize you have a comfortable financial position, but it seems to me that even though you'd decided—and remember deciding—to take some time off, you're feeling ill at ease with nothing much to do."

"'Remember deciding'—that's the key," I say. "And, yes. I'm bored out of my mind."

Dr. Levitt chuckles softly and makes a note. "I get that. So. Have you thought about doing something?"

"Like another job?"

"Or something else," Dr. Levitt offers. "Something creative."

I blink at her. "Creative?"

"Perhaps taking a class of some kind? Perhaps a writing class. Journaling can be very helpful, and you've shared with me about your to-do lists, so you already enjoy the process of keeping track of your thoughts via a written medium."

The idea is . . . appealing. "I never considered making lists to be particularly creative."

"I'm going to go out on a limb here and guess that you never thought of *yourself* as particularly creative," Dr. Levitt says.

I am quiet for a moment. "My mother painted."

It's the first time I've really referenced my mother. A real two-for-one today. I expect Dr. Levitt to write something down about this, but she only stares at me with a neutral, pleasant expression.

"There you go," she says.

I look at her and shake my head again. "I never did. I mean, she never . . . encouraged it."

"You've spoken sparingly of your mother. What was your relationship like with her?"

"She's dead now. It doesn't matter," I tell her flatly.

"How did she die?"

"She had a long history of depression and addiction, and eventually it caught up with her," I say.

Dr. Levitt nods as though she understands. I don't, so I'm not sure how she could. "What did she paint?"

"Landscapes. Oils. She was a surrealist." I laugh now. "She was surreal, all right."

"Maybe you inherited some of her skill?"

That's impossible, but I can't get into why without opening a gigantic, squirming can of worms. "No. Thank God, I didn't inherit anything from that . . . from her."

If Dr. Levitt wonders at why I bit my tongue at the last second, she doesn't show it, but I explain anyway.

"My mother cursed like a sailor. I swore I wouldn't let myself be like her. Vulgar."

"I see. You don't want to be anything like her at all." Her pen scratch-scratches. I scowl. "No."

"You're not alone. Many people struggle to distance themselves from parents with whom they have a dysfunctional relationship. But my advice would be not to let something your mother was good at prevent you from seeing if you might also be good at it."

"I've never been much of a writer," I tell her. "It seems too much like telling a bunch of lies, over and over again."

She laughs, and I do too, although I'm the only one who really knows why what I said is funny. "When I'm healed, do you think I should continue seeing you, Dr. Levitt?"

She looks up at me, her sleek, pale eyebrows raised. She taps her pen lightly on the pad before answering. "If you think you'd like to, of course."

"But do you think I need to?" I insist.

"I think," Dr. Levitt says, "you would benefit from continued sessions. Yes."

We are both quiet for a few seconds, and then it comes out because keeping it inside is slowly poisoning me. If I can't tell her, who can I tell? "My best friend is sleeping with my husband."

For the first time since I started seeing her, Dr. Levitt looks surprised. She moves to write something but stops herself. She settles back into the chair to look at me.

"Val," Dr. Levitt says.

"Yes," I answer quietly, unsurprised that Levitt's put the pieces together without me having to say it, and for the second time during this session, my throat closes and rasps with tears. "Her."

"Interesting that you phrased it that way," she says.

"Instead of?"

"You might have said, 'My husband is sleeping with my best friend.'"

The difference is subtle, but I get it. I shrug without thinking and let out a low, irritated cry at the pain.

"Infidelity does not have to be the end of a marriage." Dr. Levitt says this solemnly.

I frown. "Maybe not, but it sure is the end of a friendship."

On the desk behind her, the bell indicating the end of our session goes off. Dr. Levitt puts the cap back on her pen. She smiles.

"Well, Diana, it looks like I'll see you next week."

"Unless something happens to me in the meantime," I say.

Her eyebrows raise. "Do you think something might happen to you?"

"You never know," I tell her. "Things can always happen."

CHAPTER TEN

Valerie

LAST MEMORIAL DAY WEEKEND

Diana started her annual Memorial Day weekend Girls' Getaway right after she married Jonathan. At its peak, there'd been up to fourteen women participating, but the last one was just the two of us.

We took her car, of course. That red head turner was way more fun a ride than my steady old sedan. We left after lunch, the windows down and music up. The three-hour drive gave us plenty of time to catch up and reminisce.

That three-hour drive was the last time Diana and I had been really, truly friends.

Diana's beach house was small, no more than a cottage, really, but it was only a mile from the sand, and that was better than anything I'd ever have. The first order of business upon arrival was always wine. Always Briar White. She loved it enough to stock up on it by the case when she came to the beach, because the stores at home didn't carry it. It wasn't my favorite, but when you have a wealthy, generous friend who's willing to supply the beach and booze, what kind of dumb bitch complains?

So, we drank. We got drunk. We made nachos. We smoked cigarettes.

We talked.

"I'm so glad you moved back home," she said. Her words were the tiniest bit sloshy. "But I know you hate it there. I'm sorry, Val."

48

"As soon as I get back on my feet, I'll be moving back to the city. Or somewhere else. Anywhere else."

I think we both knew it wasn't likely I'd be back on my feet any time soon. I'd been sending out resumés for months, with no bites. Without a new job, there was no way I could afford to move.

Diana waved a hand around the interior of the living room. Vaulted ceiling. Creamy paint. Comfortable furniture and tasteful art. "I love this house, Val."

"I love this house too." I refilled both our glasses.

"Does it make me a bad person? To love this house more than I love my husband?" She didn't wait for me to answer, but drank a long drink and kept going. "Although this house is easier to live with than he is. I love his mother, but she really made a mess of her son."

We both drank then. Drained our glasses and refilled them. We moved outside to the front porch, and we lit up again.

"It's like she never let him grow up," Diana said then in a low voice. "I get it, you know? Harriett's always been there for me ever since I met her. More than my mother ever was. So, I get it. He likes being taken care of and catered to. He's grown to feel entitled to it. But oh my god, whatever makes him mommy's little boy does not make him, in any way, shape, or form, a good husband."

I'd heard the stories over the years. Jonathan was clueless, selfish, self-centered. He expected to be coddled. He was indecisive while also being stubborn. Arrogant, too rough in bed, patronizing. Never wrong. Incapable of apologizing. He sounded like every guy I'd ever fallen for, if I was going to be honest with myself.

I might be jealous of my friend's beauty and the privileged life she led, but still . . . she was my best friend. I hated seeing her so unhappy.

"It's easier to divorce a mama's boy than it is to change him." The words rose to my lips without me knowing quite where they came from.

Diana was silent for a moment. "I can't just divorce him. We have a prenup. We leave the marriage with whatever we came into it with, and for me that is definitely not this house—or the one in Pennsylvania either. His mother gave him both before I even met him. He'll keep them both, and we'll have to split everything else. Unless one of us cheats and the other has proof. If he does, he loses . . . well, just about everything."

"Does kissing count?" I asked. "Or does he actually have to put his dick in someone else?"

She laughed but didn't answer.

And I confessed.

"Jonathan kissed me. At Christmas," I told her. "I . . . I kissed him back."

Diana swallowed the last of her wine. "People get giddy at parties. They do dumb things. Christmas is a terrible time."

"There was nothing else," I said. "I promise."

For a long time, we sat in silence while we drank our wine. My heart was pounding—I remember that. Diana and I . . . we'd been through a lot. More than even the best of friends could usually say. We were each other's ride or die. We'd carried each other's secrets and scars. A few seconds of drunken Christmas party stupidity shouldn't have ruined that . . . but you never know what will bring things to an end.

"But if there *was* something else," she said finally, "if there was, then I could get rid of him. Couldn't I?"

* * *

She never reminded me that I owed her. She didn't have to. I could never forget what Diana had done when we were sixteen. What she'd done for me when I could not.

It wasn't the kiss that destroyed our friendship, one that had, I can say without hesitation, saved both our lives.

It was Diana who did that with what she asked me to do.

It was me who agreed.

We both did it, but I'm the one who's now left broken by it while she gets to pretend it never happened.

CHAPTER ELEVEN

Diana

"Happy Turkey Day!" Harriett's voice rises, high and shrill.

She clasps her hands together, her eyes lit with the sort of manic holiday fervor I've never been able to match. My holidays are Memorial Day and the Fourth of July. Beach holidays. Labor Day too, but that's a sad one because it means summer's over.

Jonathan lifts his glass. "Happy Turkey Day."

I don't lift mine, only because I can get away with pretending it would hurt too much. I don't feel like toasting, especially not under this pretense that we are a happy family. I slowly sip a glass of my favorite chardonnay.

"Harriett, you've outdone yourself," I tell her with genuine appreciation.

It's the right thing to say. Harriett has indeed outdone herself. She's been fluttering around my kitchen for hours, probably at least since five or six AM. Dinner's on the table precisely at noon. That's the Richmond family tradition. A golden turkey. Homemade gravy. Mashed potatoes. Corn, green bean casserole. The works. I pluck a dinner roll from the basket and tear open the softness to spread it with softened butter.

"You really didn't have to do all this," I say after a bite. "So much work."

"It was really no effort," Harriett says, seated at the head of the table. "I'm more than happy to cook for my kids. And you might scold me, Jonathan, for not listening, but I do."

Jonathan has his own little vegan spread. Mushroom gravy. Potatoes mashed with margarine and soy milk. Harriett has even put together a tofurky type of thing, sliced tofu with soy sauce and other seasonings to mimic a real bird. Basically, Harriett cooked twice the meal to accommodate her son, and he's barely acknowledged her efforts.

"I just meant that we could all have eaten the vegan meal. You didn't have to go to all the effort of making double. That's all." I give my husband what I hope is a significant look, but he doesn't seem to notice.

We eat. Her food is amazing, as always. She and Jonathan keep the conversation going, mostly gossip about family members he hasn't seen in years. I concentrate on my meal. In past years, we've had guests for dinner. A few of Jonathan's local cousins. Sometimes, people from work.

Val.

Not every year. Thanksgiving is the day her mom went into the hospital and never left. It's a rough time for her, and she often travels during it. Exotic places. Bali. Prague. *Where is she traveling this year?* I think as I watch my husband shovel food into his face like it's his job. I won't ever know. We aren't friends anymore.

After our confrontation, such as it was, at the Blue Dove, I'd been angry. But what am I now? I haven't been able to stop thinking about the texts I saw. Scrolling, scrolling, through the heart emojis and provocative selfies, I'd felt sick to my stomach.

All I have ever wanted for my best friend was her happiness, and it seems as though her happiness is my husband.

Jonathan is unusually loquacious, probably because of the wine. He tells funny stories until Harriett has to wipe tears of laughter from her pink cheeks. Her lipstick is smeared. Is my lipstick smeared? I blot my mouth with a napkin. Am I wearing lipstick? When did I put lipstick on?

I'm dizzy.

"You're not eating very much, Diana." Harriett says this with concern. "Are you hurting again?"

I am the opposite of hurting in my body, which feels light and buzzing, but my heart is aching, for sure.

Jonathan washes down his mouthful of food with some wine. "Babe, are you all right? You look bad."

"Tired," I say. "A little woozy."

"You've overdone it on the wine. You really shouldn't be drinking while you're taking your meds," Harriett says, this time with a bit of disapproval in her tone.

I instantly feel bad about disappointing her, but I haven't, though. I haven't taken any pills in the past few days. I mean, even if I've been off drinking for a few weeks, a couple of glasses shouldn't be enough to make me feel this way. I try to think how much I've had to drink and can't. My glass is full now, but I don't recall filling it.

"Eat more bread," my husband suggests, totally serious, and for some reason this gives me the giggles.

I raise my glass with my left hand, and I'm happy to be able to do it without wanting to scream. "To bread!"

Harriett loads my plate with more turkey and a healthy serving of gravy. I want to apologize to her and explain that I am not, truly, that drunk, but my mother's, voice when she used to make the same excuses, starts to filter out of my mouth. I fill it with food to keep it quiet. My right clavicle has started aching again, and I fumble with my knife and fork, trying to cut my slices of dark meat.

"Here," my mother-in-law offers, "let me."

And I let her because to protest would be more awkward than letting her cut up my meat for me like I'm a child.

"Fuck me," I say aloud—too loud. "My shoulder hurts."

Silence. They both look at me. I am appalled at what has just come out of my mouth.

Harriett frowns. "Language!"

"Do you need some meds, babe?"

"I think I'm out."

"No," Harriett says. "I refilled them for you. Let me get you some."

It seems like a bad idea, although in the moment, I can't think of exactly why. Then I remember. "No. Can't. Wine. Which, bonus, helps. Can also barely feel my face."

Cleaning up after dinner is a blur. I fumble with my plate, clumsily. I spill it on the kitchen floor as I'm trying to get it into the dishwasher. I feel bad about the mess, but Harriett shushes me.

"Go lie down on the couch, honey," she says.

I stare at the TV for a while, feeling glassy-eyed until she comes in. Harriett pats my arm. Looks into my face.

"Thanks for cooking," I say.

"What will I do," Harriett says, "when you're all better and don't need me anymore?"

She pats my arm again, squeezing my bicep. When she tucks the blanket in around me, she presses down on my arm. Her weight sends a shard of pain inside me, deep. I cry out. She murmurs an apology.

"How careless of me," Harriet says. "That must have hurt quite a lot. Are you sure you don't want some medicine?"

My mother was fond of mixing pain meds and booze. I shake my head. I am not my mother.

I don't know how much time passes before I need to haul myself up off the couch and into the bathroom, but when I come out, the dining room is spotless, as if we'd never eaten a meal in it. The kitchen, too, except for Jonathan standing at the counter with a plate of turkey swimming in gravy and a guilty look on his face.

"Oh," he says, "Mom went home."

"You're eating my food," I tell him.

"It's Thanksgiving," Jonathan replies, like that makes a difference.

This guy. He cheats on his wife and his diet. Holds onto this ideal of veganism like it makes him special, except when his desire for meat trounces it. That's who he is.

On the counter next to him, his phone buzzes with a text. Neither of us looks at the phone. We look at each other. The phone buzzes again, the sound of an angry wasp trapped in a glass jar. It would sting me just the same, wouldn't it, if I picked it up?

He puts the plate down. Fork across it. He doesn't answer the phone.

Sometime later, and I'm not quite sure how, I'm upstairs in the bedroom, where I fall back onto the bed in what feels like slow motion. I want to get up and take a shower, but I can't rouse myself enough. The bed is soft. I'm warm and drowsy. I giggle to myself, and the sound becomes more like a sob.

I should let her have him, but where would that leave me?

"You okay?" Jonathan asks from the doorway.

"Date. Grandy. No, switch those. Fine," I tell him. "I'm just fine. It's hot in here. Did you turn up the heat again?"

Jonathan laughs. "I haven't touched the heat."

I roll onto my side and snag my phone from the nightstand, almost dropping it as I thumb the screen to pull up the app that controls the thermostat. With a triumphant "ha!" I show him the number on the cartoonish dial. "Eighty!"

"I told you, I haven't touched it."

I slide my finger over the screen to get the temperature back down to sixty-eight.

"Haven't seen you this drunk in a long time," Jonathan says.

"I'm not drunk."

"I think *I* am," he says, sounding surprised.

"Maybe you'll get lucky." I crook my finger and shoot him a grin, but I'm instantly confused. I don't know why I said that.

"We shouldn't. Your shoulders," he says, taking a step back. "Won't it hurt?"

The rejection stings. The fact I do not want to have sex with him is irrelevant in the face of his refusal. I struggle to get upright, waving away his timid offer to help.

"I'm going to take a shower," I add with as much dignity as I can muster.

From the bathroom, I hear him murmuring into his phone, but I let the water cover up his words so I can't understand what he's saying. When I come out, he's asleep, with the lights still on. His phone buzzes again from his nightstand, but I don't pick it up to see who's texting him.

*　*　*

Later, I wake in the darkness. I'm cold, the covers thrown off me. Jonathan snores beside me, one arm flung over his head. He's naked, but the blankets are pulled to his chest.

I can't find my phone. I must have left it downstairs. I make my way in the dark, gripping the railing hard to make sure I don't fall down the stairs. I reset

55

the thermostat, which is set at fifty-eight. I make a mental note to see if there's something wrong with it. I'm thirsty and pull a glass from the cupboard, to fill with cold water from the sink.

Something moves outside the French doors leading to the deck. The glass slips from my fingers, and I brace for the crash, but it only bounces. By the time I get to the doors to look out, I see nothing. The motion-activated floodlights didn't come on, so it was probably a raccoon or a possum. Maybe a fox.

From this angle, I can't see Harriett's apartment. Just the faint glow of light coming from her windows. It goes out a few seconds later. It's so late even she has at last gone to bed.

I still can't find my phone, but I will have to look for it in the morning. My mouth is dry as dust, despite the water. My stomach mutters uneasily, but I'm not exactly nauseated. I press a hand to the place just below my ribs on the right side, out of instinct and memory, but I don't have anything there except scars.

I finish my water, rinse the glass and put it in the dishrack. It could have shattered when I dropped it, but it didn't. Compared to it, I am far more fragile.

CHAPTER TWELVE

Valerie

I didn't think much of Jonathan the first time I saw him. Their wedding day. Diana had come to visit a few times, but I'd avoided going back to small-town Pennsylvania for years.

He wasn't my type. Long and lanky. Salt-and-pepper hair. We shook hands after the ceremony, but he was distracted by his mother tugging his arm, needing his attention, and we never really got the chance to talk.

Diana looked beautiful, as always, but more than that, she looked happy.

It wasn't the first time I'd ever been jealous of my best friend. It wasn't the last. But at least then I was happy for her, even if I hated her decision to settle down in our shitheel little town. I didn't understand it then. How he could make her so happy. I understand it now.

There are also times when I can see how easy it was for her to start hating him.

Times like now. It's my birthday, and Jonathan isn't here. Having a birthday this close to Christmas usually sucks, but because we weren't together on Thanksgiving, he promised me he'd bring a cake. Champagne. Takeout Thai food from that place close to where he works, the place we used to meet in the beginning, during his lunch breaks, before he was too afraid we'd be seen.

He's late and he hasn't texted. This isn't normal for him, or at least it wasn't. Of all the boyfriends I've ever had, the only one who was the most consistent about getting back to me right away has been the one with the wife.

I check my phone again. The last message I sent him is still showing "Delivered" and not "Read." He'd mentioned being swamped with work today, but I can't help feeling a little worried. Like something else has come up. Something, maybe, like Diana.

I don't want to think about that now. But by the time Jonathan is an hour late, I've started pacing in front of my living room window, my phone clutched in my hand. Refreshing my text message window. Gritting my teeth hard enough to make my jaw hurt.

At an hour and a half, I say out loud, "Fuck this noise."

I don't bother texting him about where I'm going. I throw my coat on over the pretty dress that is way too fancy for staying at home. My Ryde is there within ten minutes. Jonathan had ten extra minutes to text me and stop me from going out, but he didn't, so I get in the car and I have it take me downtown.

On a Thursday night around here, the only action is in a downtown bar. If my dress is too much for a night at home, it's not much better for a night out in one of these places. Unless I want to drive another thirty minutes, though, I'm out of luck, because the only bars this piece-of-shit town has are dives. I get dropped off on the corner of the main drag and step out into the frigid weather, not caring that my shoes are too fancy for this crumbling sidewalk, dotted with greasy puddles.

It's my birthday, and I will be fucked sideways if I spend it alone.

Inside, the bar is overheated, and I wish I'd thought ahead to leave the coat at home. I'd have been cold on the short walk from car to bar, but now I'm stuck holding it unless I risk checking it. I think about it. The coat's not new, and it wasn't expensive, and it probably won't get stolen. Even if it does, I can replace it, and I am not immune to the knowledge that although I'm not living the high life like I'd once been, I am in a much better place than I'd thought I'd ever be when I was growing up, or even a year ago. A place where I can afford to risk losing a coat because buying another one won't keep me from paying my bills.

I'm finally in a position where I could get out of this town, the way I'd been planning since I came back. Instead, I've been staying. Why?

Love.

First, for her. Now it's all for him. I wish I could hate them both, so I could just pick up and go, but it's starting to feel like I never will.

At the coat check, I rustle in the coat pockets just to make sure there's nothing in there I do care about losing. I pull out a handful of receipts and a few dollars. A movie ticket. I tuck all of it into my purse except the ticket.

Diana and I had gone to that movie together, in the fancy theater with the leather recliners and the flavored popcorn. It had been one of our "date nights." Dinner first. Coffee after. I had not yet started fucking her husband. Now, here I am in a dive bar on a weeknight, ready to get drunk because I'm angry that he stood me up.

I sidle up to the bar and order a vodka tonic. I keep my attention on the drink. If I look around, I'm sure to see someone I went to high school with. This was a bad idea, and another flush of anger, this time mixed with the threat of tears, rushes through me. I blame Jonathan, when, in reality, I am the one who decided to come here. Once again, I find myself in a place I am not proud to be in, and it's my own fault.

"Why do you do it?" I can hear Diana ask me in my head. I can picture her expression. I can taste the beer we both drank too much of. Later, I'll be sick and she won't. "I don't get it, Val. You know better, and you do it anyway."

Back then, she was talking about the way I would antagonize my dad. I hadn't been able to describe to her how attracting his anger seemed the only way to diffuse my own. She wouldn't have been able to understand it, even if I'd found the words. Diana had never understood the complexities of loving and hating the same person. Of how love and hate are not opposites, but sides of the same coin. How it was better for my father to hate me than to ignore me. She didn't know what that was like. If she'd ever loved her mother, I couldn't remember it, and I didn't think she could either.

The drink is too strong, and I turn my grimace into a smile for the bartender's sake. I find a seat at a high-top table near the wall. My phone is on the table in front of me. My drink is in my hand. I wish I'd kept my coat so I could put it on the other chair. Maybe it would keep someone from trying to sit there. Except if I'm not here to get someone in that other chair, why am I here at all?

To punish Jonathan? He won't even know, and maybe, just maybe, he won't even care.

You can't ever trust someone who says they love you. People lie about everything, but especially about love.

I text him a selfie. Dim lighting, nothing to identify the location, but definitely showing it's a bar. I look sexy and dangerous and pissed off.

Within minutes, his reply: *Where are you?*

I don't answer. I sip my drink. I scroll through my Connex feed, checking for friend requests from hometown people I can delete. I even check my email. A minute passes. Another. He'll have seen that I read the message. He will be wondering why I'm not answering.

This *is* a game, isn't it? A stupid game, and it makes me feel sickly twisted up inside.

"*I am not that girl.*" That's what I'd told Jonathan the first time we went out for lunch, both of us knowing there was more to it than friendship.

I'd texted him something bold about how I hadn't been able to stop thinking about the Christmas party. That if he was up for a "drink," he could always text me. He'd said he wanted to get to know me, and I was totally down for letting him. It had been blunt and forward, my intentions clear, and I was still was surprised that he'd agreed to go.

I started it, but Jonathan was the one who started texting me more often. Wanting to meet once a week, then twice, then more. He's the one who told me he couldn't get enough of me. Of this.

Of us.

What was meant to be one month became two.

He started checking in constantly, little texts asking me how my day was going. Asking for pictures. Flirty emojis. I was doing this for her, and at first I thought it would be hard for me to want him.

Then, I thought I would be able to stop.

"*No games. No drama. I am not that girl.*"

I wasn't, then. A dozen relationships in as many years, and if there'd ever been drama, it hadn't come from me. I was the one who got chased, not the one who clung. I was the one who broke hearts.

Not the one whose heart got broken.

I was not that girl, but here I am. I don't want this drink. I don't want to be here. My phone lights again with another text.

I'm sorry I was late. Where are you?

There is a moment when I consider not answering at all, ever again. I can call myself another car and get a ride home. I could pick up a man and go home with him. I can ghost Jonathan, block him, never see or speak to him again. I have options. I am not stuck in this thing. But . . . all I really want is to be with Jonathan, drinking champagne and eating Thai food in my house.

I am not imprisoned by this love, but I do choose it.

I have chosen it every time, and I need to remind myself of that, because I will continue to choose it. I will keep choosing him. People lie about love, and so do I, but I won't keep lying to myself about this.

Downtown Lounge

The instant I send the text, the message is read. In the next, three tiny bouncing dots show me he's replying. I wait, the taste of vodka harsh on my tongue.

Be there in 10

A shiver runs through me. I've often joked with Jonathan about him "going cave man" with me, but there's no denying that it turns me on. What's too rough for someone else turns out to be just right for me. There've been plenty of men before him who tried asserting their ownership of me, and it never worked out very well for them. But with him . . . everything is different.

I gather my purse and pick up my coat. Out front, I wait on the sidewalk for his car. This time of night, downtown is all shut down except for the Lounge, but there are plenty of cars passing. None of them belong to Jonathan.

I'm getting cold. And now, pissed off again because it's been a least ten minutes since he said he would be here. He's late. Again. Five more minutes pass, and finally his charcoal Volvo rolls up.

I get in.

The light is red, and Jonathan twists in the seat to glare at me. "What the hell, Val?"

"I waited for two hours." I cross my arms and stare out the window so I don't have to look at him. "It's my birthday."

"Ah, shit. It was my mother." The light turns green. Jonathan heads out of town, toward my house.

"I'm supposed to believe that?"

He glances at me. "Yes."

"You didn't answer any of my texts. You could have at least told me you were going to be late." I sound too accusing. Too nagging. Too upset. I bite my tongue, literally, to keep myself from saying more.

"I'm sorry, baby. Believe me, I'm sorry. I couldn't help it."

He pulls into my driveway and shuts off the engine. I get out of the car and head for my front door. I fumble with the keys. He's behind me. One long arm goes up to the door. The other around me. He presses against me. His mouth finds the back of my neck.

I'm lost.

The door opens, and we spill into my front hall. My coat and purse go flying. The door slams as Jonathan kicks it closed. I'm in his arms, and his mouth is on mine, and then I'm on the stairs, with him between my legs. He pushes up my dress.

Fervent. Eager. Demanding. Possessive.

I think about fighting him. My hand comes up to slap him, but he grabs it. The fingers of his other hand hook into my panties and tug them to the side so he can dive between my legs. His mouth, hot, sweet, finds my bare flesh, and my head falls back. I groan.

The wooden stairs are hurting my back and my neck. The ridge of the one I'm sitting on digs into my ass. I can't move. I can only open myself up to this fierce pleasure, this violent ecstasy.

I come, hard. With a shout. My entire body jerks hard enough to slide me off the step and down to the next one, banging the back of my head in the process.

I'm crying.

Jonathan gathers me into his lap at the base of the stairs. He cradles me. I close my eyes and let him hold me until the steadiness of his breathing calms me.

"My mother needed me to stop by her apartment and fix something for her. I couldn't tell her no."

I unfold myself from his lap and head for the kitchen. I need a drink. Something cold. He follows me, watching without a word as I fill a glass and swallow half of it without looking at him. For years, I'd have given anything to be able to do something nice for my mom again. How could I fault him for it now?

"What could I tell her, Val? That I can't stop by because I have plans to spend the night with my mistress? That it's her birthday?"

It sounds so ugly when he says it that way, but it's the truth. I put the glass on the counter, and then both hands, still facing away from him. My shoulders slump. I feel worn out. The back of my head hurts.

"You could have texted me to say you were going to be late. That's all."

He moves behind me, and I let him pull me back against him. He nuzzles the side of my neck. "I'm sorry, baby. I should have."

"I thought . . . Never mind."

"What?"

"I thought you forgot." My words are stiff. My body, stiffer. I don't pull out of his embrace, but he moves back a step, leaving me where I stand.

"I wouldn't," Jonathan says, "forget your birthday. Ever."

So it has to be all right, then, doesn't it? Because he's here now, and the champagne and Thai food are both getting cold out in his car. Everything between us needs to be fine, now, unless I want to ruin my own birthday.

At the table, I pour us glasses of fizzy liquid, and Jonathan dishes out the food from the takeout containers onto the plates I'd set out earlier. And then, there's a gift bag. A small one, decorated in hot pink and black, with ribbons tying it shut.

I am expecting lingerie, but instead I pull out a piece of paper. Confused, I turn it over. I stare. I shake my head and smile uncertainly.

"A plane ticket to Kansas City?"

"I know it's not Punta Cana, baby, but hear me out," Jonathan says hastily, holding up his hands as though I've made some kind of protest. I haven't said a word. But my insides are twisting, and I'm trying to keep my face from doing the same. "I have to go there the end of January on business. I want you to come with me."

He's right. A conference center in Kansas City is no goddamned all-inclusive resort in the Dominican Republic, which is where we were supposed to go in October. But I'm not upset about that.

I fold the ticket carefully and tuck it into the bag. "You want me to go with you to Kansas City on your business trip?"

"Yes. I'll have to be in meetings all day, but there is a spa . . ." He looks hopeful.

I can see by his face he doesn't quite understand. I will have to spell it out for him, and even then, I suspect he won't get it. What is it with men anyway? Why are women so hard for them to figure out?

"When we go away together, I want it to be a real vacation. Not some tagged-on business trip. The two of us."

He looks uncomfortable. "You know that's not possible right now."

"When, then?" I demand and toss up my hands as I move away from him. "When, Jonathan? How much longer do you think we can keep doing this?"

"I don't know."

"Wrong answer," I tell him. "I think you should leave."

He tries then to plead with me. To placate. To woo. I'm not having any of it. I'm finished with patience, with his reluctance and excuses. With all of this.

I might finally even be finished with him.

"We fucked. You're done. Get out. And take your plane ticket with you. I'm not going to fucking Kansas City." I toss the bag at him.

"What the hell do you want from me?" He's pissed off.

Good.

"I want you to figure out what you're doing, Jonathan. I want you to decide where this is going, what you want from it. What you want from me. Us, I guess." The fight's slipping out of me. This isn't how I wanted to spend my birthday.

"I can't do anything until after the holidays. Okay? I just . . . I can't leave her at Christmas."

I bark out laughter. I know it, and he should too, that Diana does not and has never given a rat's ass about Christmas. When I tell him this, he looks uncomfortable again. He runs a hand over his hair, longer than he usually keeps it. I told him once that I liked to be able to sink my fingers into it, and he remembered. I want to think that's his reason, not that he's simply been too busy to get a cut. I want to think it's because of me, but right now I simply can't make myself believe it.

"Will I see you? On Christmas, I mean."

He says nothing, which is the answer I already knew.

"It's going to break my mother's heart, Val. I just don't want to be the guy who ruined the holidays for everyone because he's left his wife."

I draw in a long, shuddering breath. "But it's okay to ruin my Christmas. And my birthday too, I guess. It's okay to ruin me."

"I don't want to ruin you, baby."

"You might not want to," I tell him, "but you are."

CHAPTER THIRTEEN

Diana

"I already asked Jonathan to do this for me," Harriett frets behind me as I pull down the folding staircase that leads into the attic space over her apartment. "Just wait for him to get home. He'll do it."

She's worried I'm not strong enough to pull down the boxes of decorations, but it's been three months since the accident, and I'm finally out of the slings. Honestly, between the two of us, she's the one more likely to get hurt. She's frail that way. I hear her muttering but ignore it as I find the first bin of Christmas junk and tug it forward from beneath the eaves.

"Be careful!"

"It's fine, Harriett."

The space above her apartment is lofty, almost big enough to be another floor if not for the steep slant of the eaves. The big house has limited attic space, so we've taken to storing things over here. My husband, I've learned over the years, seems incapable of getting rid of things. He wants to save it all, even if it's broken. Especially, it seems, if it's broken.

That's probably why he hasn't left me yet.

Despite the huge amount of empty space, everything we've put up here is easily accessible within an arm's reach from the stairs. I tug one plastic bin labeled "Xmas" toward me, testing its weight. It's heavy, and I have to concede that Harriett was right—if I'm not careful, I just might mess up my collarbones again.

"Let me help." She's on the ladder behind me, grabbing at the plastic tote. It's either fight her for it or let it go, so I do. I'm surprised but relieved when she doesn't drop it or fall off the ladder, but manages to wrestle the bin to the floor. She's stronger than she looks.

If it were up to me, I wouldn't be bothering with any of this. It had taken Harriett mentioning wistfully several times over the past week for me to get the hint—she wants Christmas. In past years, she's been content with minimal decorations, but at least there was a party. I'm not up to hosting one this year, and I can tell she's disappointed. So, after all she's done for me, putting up a tree seems the least I can do for her.

I pull out the second bin, this one bigger but lighter. Those two are all we have. A tree and ornaments. No door wreaths, no nativity, no angels or candles or Santas or snowmen. I don't have some grand reason for this. No *Gremlins* sort of story, like my dad tried to play Santa and got stuck in the chimney. I've never liked Christmas because it's the time of year where everyone pretends extra hard to care about each other, and it never lasts. If someone loves you, they ought to do it all year round and not use a holiday as an excuse to make an effort they're not going to keep up.

Before I can manhandle the bin through the hole, something else catches my eye.

"Hang on a second," I say over whatever she's asking me.

My fingers brush stiff canvas. When I pull it from the shadows, my stomach lurches in recognition. At the same time, another plastic tote shifts, tipping on the beam so the lid pops open. I can see papers inside.

"What's going on?"

"Just a minute," I tell her and push aside the Christmas tote so I can climb the rest of the ladder and get all the way up into the attic.

I crouch there, hesitant. The small canvas is one of my mother's oil paintings. I thought I'd gotten rid of all of them. I don't recognize it. On the back, it says "For Diana."

The rest of the tote is full of stiff and crinkly pages. Watercolors. My mother always worked in oils. I shove them back into the tote and put it on top of the bin of Christmas junk, then push them both through the hole in the floor, keeping hold of everything and moving down the ladder fast enough that Harriett has to get out of the way or be pushed out of the way.

I let everything fall onto her living room floor and bite back a groan. The pain's not as bad as it would have been even a few weeks ago, but it's still there. I ignore the Christmas tote and open the one with the paintings in it.

Harriett cranes her neck. "What's that?"

"I don't know." I sit back on my heels to sift through it all.

My mother never called herself an artist.

She was a *painter*. In her good moods, she talked about colors and techniques, but in the bad ones, she'd lock herself in her room, chain-smoking and painting. She painted and she was good at it, but she painted ugly things. There was no commercial success for her and no artistic triumphs either.

The painting I've found is different from the ones I remember. Broad strokes, with layers of paint creating texture. Still surreal, but not ugly. This painting has an odd sort of beauty and a sense of peace I would never have associated with anything my mother ever did. She'd meant it for me, but I've never seen it before.

On the other hand, the watercolors in the plastic bin show little talent. In their soft lines and pastels, they are at least pretty. Landscapes. Still-life of apples and pears, vaguely fruit-shaped smears. Nothing inspired. None of it is *art*, and none of them were painted by my mother. My gut clenches. I don't recognize any of these paintings, but I know the signature at the bottom.

It's mine.

My phone tinkles with Jonathan's text tone.

I'm home. Where are you?

"Jonathan's home," I tell her.

I get to my feet with a glance at the small clock on the wall. He's been getting home at his usual time for the past week. Since the day after Val's birthday, as a matter of fact.

With a backward glance at the newly discovered cache of paintings I appear to have created, I follow her out of her apartment and into my own kitchen, where she talks about dinner. She pulls out a package of ground beef and also one of tofu from the fridge. She turns with both in hand and a broad grin. "Tacos?"

I can't remember the last time my husband and I had a meal together that his mother didn't cook. "That sounds terrific, Harriett. Jonathan, can you come next door with me to carry over the bins of decorations?"

In Harriett's living room, I show him the plastic bin of art. "I made these."

"Yeah?" He looks confused.

"When did I paint these, Jonathan?" I already know the answer. It has to be sometime during the blank in my memories. But I want to hear it from him.

"Over the summer. You had so much free time after you quit your job, you signed up for a class downtown at the rec center."

Signing up for a class at the rec center does not sound like me at all, but I can't argue or deny it since the apparent proof is staring right at me.

Pay RC

Rec center. I haven't been able to throw away the list I found in my nightstand drawer months ago, just in case I remembered something. At least one of those mystery entries on the list makes sense now.

"Who put them in the attic?"

"You did," he says, then pauses. "I mean, I assume you did."

"Why would I put my artwork away in the attic? And when did I do that?" I sift through the pile, pulling out a few pieces to look at before shoving them all back inside and putting the lid back on. They're nothing. Fruit, flowers, what is meant to be a tree—nothing scary about them, but looking at the paintings, most particularly my signature, unsettles me.

He shrugs, hands on his hips. He's getting the tiniest bit of pudge around his middle, and I know why. Instead of going to the gym, he's been getting another kind of workout.

"I don't know, babe. You never seemed happy with anything you did in class. Maybe you just . . . I don't know. Decided you didn't want to look at any of them."

I find it hard to imagine myself signing up for a painting class in the first place, but it reminds me of something more recent. "Dr. Levitt told me that maybe I should think about taking some kind of creative class."

Jonathan has lied to my face about working late when he has plans to meet his lover, and yet I've never seen him look this guilty. "Uh . . ."

I get to my feet and wince, hard, because I've used my right arm to push upward. "What does that mean?"

"I . . . well, when you first started seeing her, she asked me about you, about the last year or so and stuff. What you'd been up to. What you'd been like before the accident. If there was anything about your past that might help her understand you better."

The idea that my own psychiatrist could not understand me without my husband's input infuriates me.

"So, what did you tell her?"

He doesn't answer at first. My husband, the coward. Mr. Nonconfrontation. It had been something I liked about him when we first met, how easy he was to get along with. I started hating it about him about a year into our marriage, when I discovered that having someone say yes all the time, even when they had no intention of following through, was so, so much worse than an honest no.

"Jonathan!"

"I just said that your mother had been a painter."

Everything inside me goes cold. "You told Dr. Levitt about my mother?"

"Well . . . yeah . . . and that she'd basically abandoned you when you were in middle school, but that two summers ago, she came back around and you thought maybe you'd be able to patch things up with her, but she up and disappeared again. And then she died. It kind of fucked you up even more."

I can't get the words out. I have no air. Ten years married, and this is how my husband describes me to someone else? "Is that what you think of me?"

"No, of course not," Jonathan says, but in a way that means yes. "I mean . . . she asked if there was anything that I thought she ought to know about you, about what might be keeping you from regaining your memories—"

"She said—" I put a hand to my chest and feel the pounding of my heart. I force myself to speak when all I want to do is scream. I already know my husband is a liar, but has my doctor been lying to me too? "She said that the amnesia was not trauma related, that it's from the anesthesia, and it's a common thing, and that they can't be sure anything will work—"

"Babe, babe," Jonathan cuts me off, moving toward me as though he means to embrace me. "It's okay."

I step back so he can't touch me. The thought of it repulses me, that he could even think I would allow him to touch me after what he's done. "It's not okay. If I'd wanted to talk to her about my mother, I would have. You had no right. *She* had no right!"

"It's not a big deal. I just told her you'd taken the class last summer as a way of connecting with your memories of your mom and a way of making your peace with her and all that."

I am silent for a moment, almost incapable of processing this. "What. The. Actual. *Fuck?*"

The vulgarity of that profanity burns, a bitter taste. He has pushed me to being what I swore I would never become, and I want to drop to my knees with sudden, furious grief. I might not be able to remember hating him enough to want to actually leave him, but it's clear to me now that even if I didn't before, I do now.

"Shit, Diana, I don't know. Okay?" He tosses up his hands. "I thought it would help her to help you! I did it for you."

The one and only time Jonathan met my mother, they'd made polite small talk in a coffee shop. Two weeks later she was dead, strangled on her own vomit in a cheap roadside motel. He had never known her, and it's very clear now that he's never really known me.

"But that's not even close to the truth! I would never . . ." I have to swallow hard, both to keep the rush of sour spit from pouring out my mouth and to stop myself from spewing forth some violent words.

We stare at each other. The first time we ever made love, in bed together after the orgasms had faded and our sweat had cooled, Jonathan had pushed the hair off my face and traced his fingertip over each of my eyebrows. Along my jaw, my chin. He'd brushed it along my lower lip, opening it for his kiss.

"Are you happy?" he had asked me then, and in that moment, in the cocoon of our new and unexpected love, I had answered yes.

I don't remember when I stopped being happy, only that one day I woke up and realized that I wasn't. No one thing had led to it. No one thing, I think now as my throat closes, ever does.

He gives me a cagey look. "You told me something like that. You just don't remember it."

"I told you that I was going to take a watercolor class at the local rec center because I missed my mother?" My voice rises, high-pitched like a teakettle whistle.

He doesn't answer me. His expression says it all. "You just . . . don't remember, babe," he finally whispers when I don't say anything.

I refuse to believe that. He will never be able to convince me that it was because I was trying to connect, in any way, with my mother.

My lip curls. "Levitt can't talk about me like that to you, can she? Isn't that a violation of something? Doctor–patient confidentiality or something?"

"I think that only applies to things you've told her that she can't relay to me. Not the other way around."

I want to smack that smug look off his face. He's probably right. Still, I am betrayed and disgusted at the idea of the two of them talking about me. It's worse than the thought of him and Val discussing me, because I expect that to happen. I thought my doctor was . . . well. I thought she was mine, unlike my husband and my ex–best friend, anymore.

"She was trying to get a handle on your situation, that's all."

"The point of talking to her about my 'situation' as you put it, is that *I* am the one who talks to her. Not you." I catch sight of myself in the decorative mirror Harriett has hung by her front door. I stare at my reflection, expecting that I'll look angry, but I just look sad.

"Babe . . ." He sounds frustrated but not apologetic. This is something else I've grown to despise about him.

Jonathan Richmond is never, ever wrong.

"Never mind." I bend to gather up the crinkly papers and shove them back into the tote. I gesture for him to pick up both it and the ones with the decorations. "Can you take these next door, please?"

"If the paintings bother you so much, maybe you should toss them."

"Clearly," I say, "they meant something to me if I decided to keep them."

"Yeah, but you put them in the attic," Jonathan says.

I'm not sure I believe I was the one who did that, but again I can't argue with him about it because I really don't know. Without a word, I leave Harriett's apartment and cross back to my own house. The smell of browning meat wafts from the kitchen. My stomach rumbles.

Jonathan puts all the decorations in the den, where Harriett will have to sort through them after dinner and put them up. I plan to claim pain as a reason why I don't want to bother. The truth is, I have some legal research to do on my laptop.

Happy belated birthday, Val. You're going to get exactly what you want.

Before that, we sit at the dining room table and eat the tacos my mother-in-law has expertly prepared.

"I'm going to have a glass of wine. Who else would like one?" I decide this out loud, looking at each of them like an invitation, although it's not, really.

Harriett's brows raise. "You know I don't drink."

"Jonathan? Or are you planning on going to the gym later?"

He looks quickly at the wall clock, instinctually, and his mouth gets tight. "No. I'm not. And I only drink red, babe."

The bottle of my Briar White in the fridge is chilled, which is perfect; it's three-quarters empty, which is not. I have backup bottles, of course, in the basement fridge. I should have at least two cases left. Except that now, when I go downstairs to get one, I see four bottles in the fridge and only one box of others.

I can't remember how many had been in there.

I don't remember drinking most of the open one upstairs.

I grab one of the bottles and take it with me. I fill my glass with what's left from the open bottle and put the other in the kitchen fridge. Jonathan and Harriett both look up when I come back to the dining room.

"*Babe*," I say slowly, carefully, the endearment flavored like rotten meat, "have you been drinking my wine?"

"I just told you, I only drink red." He shoves a tofu taco into his face and says, "Mmm."

I keep my eyes fixed on him. "I'm just asking because I thought I had a lot more down there. You know. From when there was that case discount sale."

For a long moment, his gaze holds mine.

Val drinks white.

"I haven't been drinking your wine, Diana."

Jonathan scrapes the remains of his dinner into the trash and excuses himself for his traditional after-dinner constitutional. I finish my tacos and the glass of wine. I keep hold of my empty glass when Harriett reaches for it.

"I'll keep this. I might have another in a little while."

Her mouth purses in disapproval, and her eyes go to the recycling bin next to the back door. Then back to my face. "If you need to."

I follow her gaze. The bin is full almost to overflowing. Taking out the trash is Jonathan's job. Garbage is picked up every week. Recycling, every other.

From here, I can see the necks of three wine bottles poking up from the rim of the green plastic bin. I don't move toward it. I shift my gaze back to Harriett's, expecting her to say something. She doesn't. She doesn't have to, really. I can tell what she's thinking from her expression.

"It's not about needing to, Harriett. It's about *wanting* to." My words slip out, sounding mushy, like my tongue's gone thick and unwieldy. That one glass of wine feels like four. Or five.

"I'll clean up the kitchen, honey. Why don't you go rest on the couch?"

"I actually have things I have to do upstairs," I say and grab the bottle opener from the drawer. It takes me a long minute or so to open another bottle with my too-clumsy hands. I pour a generous glass and watch the pale yellow liquid shimmer.

"We could watch our show," Harriett says in a trembling sort of voice.

Runner. I've been a fan since the show first aired. It was canceled for a brief time, but the fans rallied for it to come back. It's in season fourteen now. Harriett and I started talking about it when we worked together at Sunny Days, and then later, watching it together every week.

In the early days of our relationship, before Harriett introduced me to her son, she and I spent a lot of lengthy lunches working together for the charity events. I confided in her then about the lack of my mother in my life, and all the reasons why. The booze, drugs, the unreliability. I confessed my fears that, despite the fact that I shared no DNA with her, I was still too much like the woman who'd agreed to, but had barely, raised me.

"You aren't anything like her. So don't you let yourself think you are," Harriett always told me.

She and I had once been so close.

Now, everything she does sets me on edge, and I can't figure out why.

74

"Another time," I tell her. "I have a lot of stuff to catch up on."

"I'll just unpack the bins then, I suppose. When Jonathan comes back down."

Upstairs, I grab my laptop just as Jonathan comes out of the bathroom. "Your mother's waiting for you to help her unpack the decorations."

"Don't spill your wine," he says in a tone so snide and snarky that I actually have a second's respect for him. Then he pushes past me and out of the bedroom.

In the small room down the hall I use as my office, I pull open the filing cabinet where I store all my important papers. I sort through them quickly. A copy of the deed for the house stops me, my fingers curling and almost wrinkling the paper before I can stop myself. My name isn't on it, but I knew that. Jonathan's name is on it.

So is Harriett's.

So much for her giving the house to him, I think. This means she still owns half of it. Another quick search shows the same thing for the beach house.

With a sinking heart, I sit back and study the deeds. I hadn't considered this. It changes everything because now, even if I get all the requirements to break the prenup, I'll still only be entitled to half of both homes. Even if I was awarded his entire share, I'd still own them with Harriett. I'm not stupid enough to think that would work out very well.

I quickly make copies of the deeds and put the originals back in their place. When I search further for the copy of the prenuptial agreement, I come up with nothing. It's not in any of the folders, and I look through them all. Then again. I can't find it anywhere. I remember the gist of it all, but not every detail. I recall there was a specific protocol and list of items required to enact the part about divorce on grounds of adultery, and I need it if I'm going to move forward.

My head is spinning far too much for having had only a single glass of wine. The second sits, still full, on the small side table next to me. I force myself to focus.

I haven't used my laptop very much since getting out of the hospital. I'd never used much social media. I usually check my emails from my phone, and it had simply been too painful for so long. My fingers feel unwieldy on the keys.

First, I look up "PA divorce law." Then, a few minutes after that, "How to legally bypass or break a prenup." Without the details, I can only gather information, but I bookmark a few sites to go back to.

I have one more task to complete. It takes me a bit of searching for the lawyer's website, only to discover that the one who worked with us ten years ago is no longer practicing. There is no information about how to get in touch with him or how to access any copies of anything from him.

I'm looking up internet advice on how to handle that when the laptop dings with an email notification. I pause to check it. The message has come in on an account I don't have set up on my phone. It's the one I've had the longest but now use the least. The new message is just junk, but when I scroll up a little bit, I see a familiar email address.

Dated in August just a few months ago, Val's message is brief. I can't remember getting it the first time, but I'm sure I was as devastated to read it then as I am now.

Never contact me again.

What happened in August?

But no matter how far back I scroll, there are no other messages to tell me. I type a quick message to Val. *We need to talk. Please.* I hit "Send" before I can stop myself, but it doesn't matter, because within a minute I get an error message telling me the email was undeliverable.

Dizziness rolls over me, relentless as a storm. Nausea follows it. I manage not to vomit, but I'm clammy and shaking. Dr. Levitt told me this might happen—trying to remember what happened during the blank spaces might trigger physical reactions. Another rush of dizziness hits me. My entire body buzzes and hums with a weird electric sensation like a really rough high. All I can do is breathe through it.

Whatever happened in August doesn't matter right now. Whatever I asked Val to do and whatever she has done will have to wait. All I can do right now is breathe.

CHAPTER FOURTEEN

Valerie

HIGH SCHOOL

"Get up, Val. C'mon. Wake up."

I didn't want to wake up, but Diana's voice wouldn't let me stay asleep. She shook me, too, and I flailed out of bed in a tangle of sheets and blankets and my own sour sweat. My mouth tasted like an ashtray.

"God. I can smell you. Come on."

Before I could figure out what she was doing and stop her, she dragged me out of my room, down the hall, and into the bathroom. She flung open the shower curtain, and even I turned away, repulsed. Nobody's cleaned it in weeks. Months, maybe.

Not since before Mom . . . died.

Diana started to pull my T-shirt over my head, but I stopped her without much effort. "I'm fine. Leave me alone."

"I'm not going to do that."

I scowled and, catching sight of my reflection in the mirror, turned away. I didn't need to see what I looked like. It was bad. I could feel it, but I couldn't care about it. I couldn't care about anything.

"Look," she said next in a softer tone. "I lost my mom a long time ago. I know it's not the same—"

I interrupted. "No. It's not. I loved my mother."

She was silent for a moment, then nodded. "Yeah. I know you. But right now, you stink."

"So let me stink!" The shriek rose up, up, and up and out of me, hurting my throat.

Diana backed up. I thought she was going to leave, and that was good—it was just fucking perfect. I wanted her gone. Out. I wanted her to leave me alone to just . . . I wanted to be alone.

"Fine," she said, "don't shower. Smell like ass and puke. Whatever, Val. But even if you won't clean yourself up, you're still coming out here with me."

She gripped my arm with a grip like iron, and even if normally I could fend her off, I hadn't eaten in . . . well, couldn't remember when I ate. I tried to pull away, but I couldn't. Diana marched me down the hall, through the living room, out the back door to the deck. Into the yard. She let me go and I stumbled forward a few steps in the too-high grass.

We were in front of the shed that had been falling down for years. When we were little kids, we played house and fairy castle in there, and when we got a little older, sometimes we took the boys in there to play kissing games. We still played kissing games, but now we did it in other places. Private places, for private things.

Diana went inside the shed and came out with a cardboard box. It rattled. She put it down in front of me. It was full of old mason jars without lids. Mom didn't can anything after she got sick. She must have taken these old jars out to the shed to make room in the kitchen.

"She was always making sure to keep stuff neat. She hated clutter. She hated things being dirty." The words barked out of me, hoarse and harsh. "She didn't deserve all that pain. I'm glad it's over. I'm glad she's dead. I'll never feel bad about what we did. Never!"

I started to shake. Diana pulled a jar out of the box and pressed it into my hand. I didn't know what to do with it. She took one for herself. Held it up. She looked at me.

She threw the glass as hard as she could. It shattered against the side of the shed. The crash was spectacular, loud and shocking, and the glitter of broken glass reminded me of fallen snow in the summer's green grass.

"Now you," she said.

I threw the jar as hard as I could. Then another. Another. She went into the shed and brought out another box, this one bigger. Mason jars are heavy glass. Thick and hard to break. Together, we shattered every single one.

After, panting and sweating, she hugged me hard. She breathed into my hair. She whispered in my ear. "When you hate so much you can't feel anything else, Val, break something you won't miss."

* * *

I've thought of the day by the shed hundreds of times since, and of Diana's advice. *"Break something you won't miss."* I don't want to miss her. I do want to break her.

My ex–best friend, my lover's wife, is not made of glass. For fuck's sakes, she survived a car accident and then an emergency surgery to take out an organ that was so close to rupturing she might have died. That bitch is not so easy to break.

I've known Diana for more than half our lives. I should know her well enough to find her weakness. To break her in other ways. The thing is, my dear friend Diana's weakness and her strength have been two sides of the same coin. Need to put someone toxic out of your life, even if you love them? They're gone. Need to defend someone you're loyal to, even if they're in the wrong? Done. She is both fiercely emotional and dispassionate.

I mean, look at the way she cut me out of her life, just like that. Anyone else would have fought me, at the very least. Instead, she used me and then dumped me as easily as she'd unzip a dress and step out of it to leave on the floor behind her. I was nothing more than the means to an end.

"We need a rock-solid case," Diana had said. She'd been wreathed in smoke on the front porch of her beach house, several glasses of wine deep. "Incontrovertible proof. Harriett's lawyer wrote that prenup like he wanted to take it to the prom. If I want to put the adultery clause into effect, I have to file first. If he does, I can't come back with that after the fact. But it'll be worth it to you, Val. If we can break that prenup, I'll have enough money to make sure you can move wherever you want."

She'd laughed drunkenly. "We'll get a place in New Orleans. Share a cute little place near Bourbon Street. Have cats. The way we always talked about."

"What if I can't get what you need?" I'd asked her. She had a whole list of specifics required by the prenup. "I mean . . . what if I can't make him *love* me?"

Diana had scoffed. "He doesn't have to really love you. We just need to get proof of him telling you he does. Whether or not he really feels it doesn't matter."

So, when did it become love? Was it the night he brought me ibuprofen and a heating pad, a bottle of wine and a box of chocolates because I'd complained about a rough period that had laid me flat? The night we didn't fuck, but instead cuddled in my bed and watched classic movies until I fell asleep? I woke to find him gone, but a note on the pillow. In it, he called me beautiful. Was that when it happened?

Or was it the weekend in August when we stole away together to New York City while Diana went down to the beach by herself? A real dinner date. Dancing after. I'd imagined him, tall and lanky, dancing like one of those blowup mascots you see waving outside of car dealerships, but Jonathan danced with the ease and grace of Fred Astaire, if he'd done his routines to hip hop. When Jonathan danced for me, yes, then, that's when I fell in love. Three months, that's all it took for me.

But for him?

I have no idea.

I have not been answering his texts the way I used to. He was always the one who got to decide when and where and how we could be together, but now I have a say in that too, and right now I am choosing not to see or talk to him. I turned off the function that allows him to see if I've read his messages. Now he can sit with a "Delivered" for hours, not knowing if I've even seen it.

I need this distance from him, and if I don't force it, I won't get it. He will woo me with his flirty words and compliments. With the promises I do believe he wants to keep but that he cannot bring himself not to break.

His tone in my voicemail is pitched low. Furtive. I imagine there's some hesitation, some anxiety.

"*Please*," he says. "*Just call me back, Valerie. Okay? Call me.*"

I don't.

You can't prove whether someone really loves you, but it can be possible to prove that they've told you they do. He has never said he loves me, never in person or on the phone or in a text or a message. That's the one thing I know she needs in order to divorce him the way we'd planned. If I get what I want, Diana gets what she needs.

But I'm going to do my best to make sure she really gets what she deserves.

CHAPTER FIFTEEN

Diana

First, there is darkness. Then, light. It blinds me. I am running in the rain, cold and wet, icy slaps of clawed fingers from a monster I can't see.

My mother's face. Twisted. She is shouting. I hit her with a closed fist. Again. Again.

Again.

She falls.

I am running.

There is pain in my knees and on the palms of my hands; there is going to be blood. I taste it in the place where I bit my lip. My hair obscures my vision.

I see trees.

I am close to home. I see my house when I twist back, I see the house, I see the lights on inside the house, the lights that blinded me at first have gone dark, but in the house there is a shape. A person. In the window. Watching. Then gone. Maybe not there at all, maybe a shadow, maybe curtains, maybe I am insane and running, running through the night and the dark and the cold, and I fall to my hands and knees again.

My fingers sink into the earth at the base of a tree, and I dig. A nail breaks; there is more pain. I am digging, and the sound of my breath is loud in my ears, and the world is shifting and turning upside down, and I am on my back with the rain dripping into my open eyes.

Rain, like needles.

A man is with me.

"Are you all right? You're going to be all right. Don't you worry, Diana. You're going to be all right."

*   *   *

There are some nights without dreams. Seamless and black. After those nights, I wake with a dry mouth, hair plastered to me with sweat and no idea what day it is. Somehow, the nightmares are better.

The one I had last night is the closest I've come to what feels like a real memory.

Not the part about my mother. I'd never actually punched her in the face, although I'd thought about it many times. No, it had been the man's voice. That, I think was real. From the night of the accident. But is this really a memory or just another dream? I don't know.

I hate him for being right, but Jonathan was, at least about this. What happened with my mother last year really did mess me up even more than I'd already been. We'd been supposed to meet for coffee, part of her efforts at returning to my life. She didn't show. It took authorities two weeks to track me down as someone who needed to know she was dead. I was devastated. Not because I'd missed a last chance to connect with her, and not because she'd succumbed to an addiction she'd told me she'd beat.

I was destroyed that I'd allowed myself to trust her again. Still, that's my baggage to deal with, on my own terms. Jonathan had no right to blab about it to Dr. Levitt. She had no right to talk to him behind my back.

I didn't speak to Dr. Levitt directly when I canceled my next appointment. I politely told the secretary I was not interested in rescheduling. I was not expecting Dr. Levitt herself to get in touch with me, definitely not on Christmas Eve, so when her name popped up on my phone screen yesterday, I didn't answer it.

Her voicemail message was brief, her voice calm.

Diana, I'm concerned that you haven't made any new appointments with me. If you're intending to stop our sessions, please let me know. I can refer you to another doctor if you like, but you do need someone overseeing your care, if only for the sake of monitoring your meds. Please call my secretary . . . No, just call me directly. You have my number.

I'm not going to call her back. The idea that she and Jonathan discussed me, my mother, my issues, that all along she knew about it without so much as raising an eyebrow when I deflected . . . I'm not totally sure if that's unethical or immoral, but it certainly feels like it should be.

I haven't told Jonathan I'm not going back. It's possible he'll ask me, but honestly, it's been so long since he seemed to have any sort of clue about what's going on with my life, I doubt it will occur to him that I'm not seeing her anymore. As for her concern about my meds, the last time I checked, every single bottle still had plenty left in it, so I don't care if she won't renew the prescriptions. Besides, I don't need them . . . even if I sometimes want them.

My internet searching taught me that January is "Divorce Month" because so many people try to stick together through the holidays but can no longer stand it once the new year comes around. Will he do it then? Is he waiting until after the holidays? More importantly, what will I do if he doesn't?

If I leave him for any reason other than his infidelity, I will lose almost everything. If I go after him for having an affair, I need to have everything documented and proven in a specific format, or it won't hold. Until I can track down that prenup document, I don't know everything I need, and I can't tip my hand before then. The one who files first has the advantage.

Standing at the master bathroom sink to wash my hands, I have a clear view into the back yard. Although the temps have dropped to freezing and we had some snow in November, there's been nothing but ice since. The trees in the back yard are coated in it, their branches weighted and probably ready to break. Beyond the deck and the huge backyard shed is the small slope of yard that goes up into the trees.

It is the scene from my nightmares. That view, from a slightly different angle because of where I'm standing now. It takes the water scalding my hands to shake me out of just standing there staring. With a hiss, I run the water cold and rinse my hands. The back of one hand is red already fading to pink. My skin will be fine.

My mind, though. What about that? The nightmare comes back to me, the sense of running. Falling. I turn my palms up to look at them, scanning for any signs of scars, but of course there are none. Only the lines crisscrossing and making hashmarks.

A palm reader in New Orleans had told Val and I that we'd be friends forever. She'd traced a series of curving lines on both our palms. *Friends forever.* We got matching tattoos, small hearts outlined in black and red. Hers on her left shoulder, mine on the right. It doesn't escape me, the irony of that being the place of my worst injury.

What does my husband think when he presses his mouth to the ink on her body that matches mine?

From downstairs, I hear the clatter of dishes in the kitchen and the low murmur of voices. It's not quite eight on Christmas morning. It's the earliest I've been up without an alarm in months, so it makes sense that Harriett looks startled when I come downstairs and find her and Jonathan at the kitchen table. Mugs of steaming coffee are in front of them, and he has a bowl of creamy oatmeal.

"Merry Christmas," he says.

"You're up so early," Harriett chimes in as she gets up. "Let me make you some eggs, dear."

"Merry Christmas," I say to both of them but put up a hand to stop her from going to the stove. "Oatmeal looks great, Harriett. I'll just get some from the pot."

She keeps moving. "It's no trouble, Diana."

"It's Christmas, Harriett. The last thing in the world you should be doing on Christmas morning is cooking for me. Sit. Relax." I try to keep my voice jovial. Festive. It's Christmas, after all. Everyone's supposed to be happy and nice on Christmas.

She looks uneasy. "It's really no trouble at all. Are you sure you don't want eggs and bacon? You need your protein . . ."

Instead of filling a bowl, I just pour myself a mug of coffee. "You know what—I'm not really even hungry. Hey. Why aren't we opening presents?"

This is what she lives for, I swear, and so, distracted, Harriett beams and claps her hands. The three of us go into the den, where the tree has been set up.

Lit with plain white lights and strung with pearl garlands, hung with what are mostly Harriett's "heirloom" ornaments, it's pretty, but it's not mine. Beneath it is the modest pile of gifts I'd ordered online for them both. They'd arrived already wrapped, since I wanted them to look nice and not like something a demented monkey with a glue stick and safety scissors had put together.

In contrast, the towering stack of exquisitely wrapped boxes with gift bags and coordinating ribbons and bows is clearly Harriett's work. As always, she's done too much. It used to make me uncomfortable, but I'm used to it by now. There will be packages of new underwear and socks. Bath products. Trinkets. Books. Scented candles. It's like she can't stop herself.

"Oldest to youngest," she says with another clap of her hands.

It takes her a few minutes to unwrap each gift, and she takes the time to try on each item or marvel over it. Or worse, as in the case of the leather-bound daily planner that Jonathan got her, cry over it. I mean, it's a nice planner and all, but the woman spends her days cleaning and cooking in my house. I don't know what she needs to plan. It's the sort of gift that's so typical of him, though. Expensive, high quality, practical, but not necessarily . . . right.

Like the car.

It's my turn to open presents. In the driveway is a silver sedan. A Volvo. It wears a broad red ribbon on the hood.

"What's this?" I shiver in the frigid December air, but it's not really the cold making me shake.

"Merry Christmas!" my husband says, as pleased with himself as a man can be.

Next to me, Harriett clasps her hands to her bosom. "Oh my goodness. A new car?"

This car *cannot* be for me. I'm well aware of beggars and their ability to choose, but the fact is, I'm not a damned beggar, and I did not choose this . . . this vehicle. It's safe, reliable. It's boring.

It is the complete opposite of my Camaro.

"I . . . wanted slippers . . ." I whisper. Neither of them hear me.

"It's time you get back to driving yourself around. You can't expect to rely on Mom or friends forever," Jonathan says.

"I never minded driving her," pipes up Harriett. She sounds reproachful. "You make it sound like it was a burden on me, Jonathan."

I haven't been in the driver's seat since that last memory I have, rolling down the highway the Friday before Memorial Day in my cherry red baby with the radio on and the wind whipping my hair while Val and I sang along with the radio. I can't recall the accident, but my body does. Dry mouth. My throat convulses. The burn of acid sizzles the back of my tongue. I blink and blink and blink, trying to force away the hazy tinge of red around the edges of my vision.

My shoulders and back are so stiff, he practically has to force me to bend so I can get into the car.

Jonathan slides into the passenger seat. In the next second, Harriet gets in the back. They're both gabbing on and on about the car, but all I can hear is an effervescent hum. I close my eyes. Grip the wheel. My body tenses and clenches, bracing for an impact I am happy not to recall.

". . . got it because it has the most safety features on the market," Jonathan says.

He hated my red car. He hated that I drove it fast to places I went without him, but most of all, he hated that I'd bought it without any input, financial or otherwise, from him. He once called it "ridiculous," and he was right. It had been ridiculous, but it had been mine.

Jonathan told me he'd had the car towed away. I'd never even asked to see it, my poor broken baby. I'd been broken enough.

This . . . this is the kind of car he thinks I should drive. Not the kind of car I want to drive. If that doesn't say it all about our marriage, I don't know what does.

I hate this car.

"C'mon, babe. Let's take it for a spin." Jonathan jangles the keys toward me.

I decline, shaking my head. "No, not right now. I'm not dressed, I'm not wearing shoes—"

"Go grab a pair." He's excited, eyes shining.

For a moment it's so easy to remember why I fell in love with him. This is something I wish I could forget. I shake my head again and force a smile.

"It's cold. Icy. I'm not ready."

Jonathan looks disappointed, but Harriett understands. She bustles us back into the house for cinnamon rolls and coffee, and to unwrap more gifts. When she uses the bathroom, he and I sit in silence.

"You're not going out?" I ask at last.

"It's Christmas," he says. "Where would I go?"

CHAPTER SIXTEEN

Valerie

All of this was meant to be over by now. He would leave her, filing before she could so he could block the prenuptial agreement he's never mentioned and which he might believe I didn't know about. We would spend Christmas celebrating the birth of our new lives.

Instead, about twenty-two hours before our plane was supposed to leave for Punta Cana, she ended up in the hospital.

This is the last Christmas I am going to spend alone.

The text is sent before I can change my mind, but once it's gone, I have no desire to take it back. I meant it. The message is delivered, but not read.

He's with her, of course.

No way to get out of it. How could he explain to his mother that instead of an all-American Christmas with his wife and mother, he's going to spend it with his side piece? Any woman who's fucking a married man and thinks she's going to spend any holiday with him is a dumb bitch.

I might be a bitch, but I ain't dumb.

That's Diana's line, and it's perfect, and right now I hate her more than ever. For finding him first. Frankly, for being *given* him first. For keeping him long after she stopped wanting him. For getting injured so that he feels guilty about leaving her.

I hate her for not admitting that she wanted to let him go.

I was going to travel this long weekend to New York. Treat myself to a hotel room, a Broadway show from the discount tickets booth, some really good ramen. But haven't I been hoping, uselessly and stupidly, that Jonathan will at least . . . try?

I see that he's has read my message, but he doesn't reply. The last couple weeks we've spent without seeing each other, barely texting, and speaking only once every few days have not been the most terrible of my life. I won't say that, even to be dramatic. In fact, in some ways, they've been easier than talking to him every day, if only because I can convince myself I'm getting over him.

People lose their minds over having a white Christmas, but this year it's more like a black one. Freezing temperatures, warnings about staying off the roads because of patches of invisible ice. I have turned off the radio so I don't have to hear "Last Christmas" one more damned time. I roasted a turkey with all the fixings, but I'm drunk by the time it's ready, and I pass out on the couch instead.

Hours later, I wake in the dark. I check my phone immediately, but there's no message from Jonathan. I curse his name. Softly. Then louder. I don't have Diana's expensive tastes, and my white wine is cheap. My stomach is sick from no food, too much wine. I'm sick with heartache.

In the car, I shiver as I wait for it to warm up. My breath plumes out in smoky trails that make me wish for a cigarette. It takes only ten minutes to drive to the house in the woods that Jonathan shares with Diana. The roads are curving, twisty, and the houses are all set apart from each other. Trees in between. Privacy. When I lived in Brooklyn in a brownstone, there was no such thing as not knowing what your neighbors were up to, and I never minded. But back in my childhood home, with houses so close on either side, I swear I can hear the people inside them breathing, and I am suffocated. If I lived in Diana's neighborhood, I would never complain about feeling isolated, the way she does.

I park at the end of the long, sloping drive leading to the detached garage and the mother-in-law apartment. I get out of my car. My fists clench.

I should not be here. This is everything I never wanted to be. But the hate is welling inside me, and the loneliness, and the love—that fucking shovel to the face. My love for Jonathan is like nothing I've ever felt or ever thought I would feel. It has ruined me for anything else.

Moving closer, I catch sight of Harriett through her living room window. She's crying and drinking white wine right out of the bottle. My heart seizes. I know how she feels. Her husband died. The thought of losing Jonathan has bent me over more than once. If she wants to double-fist her drinks because she's alone at Christmas, I don't blame her.

Swiftly, I climb the narrow concrete stairs into the yard and the curving stone path to the main house's front door, which I avoid. Instead, I duck around the back and along the side, where I can see right into their bedroom. The lights are on inside, but dim, as though coming from a different room.

There he is.

My fingers are numb with cold, but the bite of my nails into my palms is fierce. So is the tang of blood on my lower lip where I've bitten it. Jonathan is naked. Hair rumpled. Do I imagine the gleam of sweat on his lean body? Do I see evidence of something between them that's not there?

Oh my god. He's been fucking her. My teeth chatter, but I am an inferno. I text him quickly.

I see you.

The floodlights come on.

I *am* a dumb bitch. Of course I should have remembered their security system, the motion-activated lights and cameras. Home security was Diana's entire career, after all. I move back, out of the light, glad I thought to tuck my hair inside a wool beanie cap and pull my hood up to shield my face, grateful for the baggy pants and oversized hoodie I'd thrown on because it was all I could bear to make the effort for.

I'm at the top of the stairs to the lower drive when the front door of the main house opens. No outside lights have come on from Harriett's place, and I have time to make it to the bottom, convinced I'm going to trip on the uneven stairs, no railing to catch me, before Jonathan makes it to my side.

"The fuck are you doing?" He grabs me by the arm so hard I twirl and fall against him. He grabs my other arm to keep me upright. He's backlit, face in shadow, but I see the gleam of his teeth. He's wearing only a pair of low-slung pajama bottoms, feet and chest bare. His voice is rough, the words a little slurred.

"Are you drunk?" I demand. That would explain it, maybe. If he got drunk on Christmas Day with his wife, if something happened between them because he'd been drinking and I'd been ignoring him for days.

But that's not an excuse.

He grips me harder. "No, I'm not fucking drunk."

"You sound it."

"I had a couple glasses of wine at dinner, that's it. Fuck, Valerie, it's freezing out here. What are you fucking thinking?"

I know he's drunk. He never swears that way unless he is. His fingers dig into my arm even through my sweatshirt; it feels like I might even bruise.

"Let me go." I bite out the words and pull away from him.

I think he's going to. At least, I make it halfway down the driveway before he catches up to me again.

He snatches at me again, barely catching hold. "You can't be here. You can't come here like this. What's wrong with you?"

We're far enough away from both the house and the street that it's unlikely anyone could overhear us, but still, he keeps his voice pitched low. It's dark here, and I'm glad for it. If I had to see his face, I might scream. I don't hit him, but I want to. In the frigid air, it is impossible to smell him, but I imagine the warm waft of his body. His breath, the taste of it and of his skin. I am shaking.

"Val . . ."

"I'm leaving."

Jonathan snags my sleeve again. I let him turn me. He must be freezing. I tell myself I don't care. He deserves frostbite.

"You just . . . you can't do this, baby."

I force a few words from between my chattering teeth. "I. Was. Alone."

"I know, I know. I thought you were going to the city." He tries to pull me close. His skin is cold. I stiffen to keep him from embracing me.

"I didn't go. I would have been alone there, too." I want to ask him if he was fucking her, but I don't want to hear him lie. I don't want him to tell me the truth either.

We are both silent.

"She doesn't have access to the security notices anymore," he says abruptly. "She turned off the app notifications, and I changed the account information, so I know she can't log back in. She won't know you were here."

I have nothing to say about that. I don't care if she knows. My car is no more than a minute's walk. Every step I take away from him is like walking on broken glass, only the glass is in my heart. By the time I get there, I am gasping. In the driver's seat, I grip the wheel and try to catch my breath.

He doesn't come after me again.

I drive away.

As I pull into my driveway, my phone lights with a text, an answer to the one I'd sent earlier.

It's the last time you'll have to.

In the dark, my car still running, I clutch the phone to my chest and let out a single barking sob. I want to believe him, but the truth I have to face is that no matter what he says, he's never going to leave her. The thought of living without Jonathan honestly makes me feel like I want to die, but it's seeming more likely that the only way we'll ever be together is if Diana does, instead.

CHAPTER SEVENTEEN

Cole

Sunlight breaking through storm clouds. That's the sight of Diana there in the coffee shop. For four months, I've made it here every day and pretended to work on something important when all I'm really doing is scrolling through a bunch of forums and listings, looking for my next gig. You know how it feels when you've been waiting so long for something that you've started to believe it won't ever happen? That's me, stunned and grateful and disbelieving and relieved.

It's all I can do to stop myself from getting up and greeting her. I know better, though. Unless something has changed drastically since that day in the hospital, Diana isn't going to remember me. It was hard enough to realize that when she was covered in bandages and stoned on pain meds. I'm not going to make a scene about it here and now.

So, I watch her. God, she's beautiful. She carries an oversized leather purse with her left hand, but moves so cautiously that it's clear she's still in pain—or at least expecting to be. She wears skinny jeans tucked into knee-high brown boots with a leather jacket the color of rust. Her hair, so black it sometimes looks highlighted in blue, hangs to the middle of her back, pushed off her face with a simple plastic headband. She used to wear it in a braid or a bun.

Diana orders her favorite: a brownie with fudge icing and a bottomless mug of coffee. She seems uncertain about how to carry both items to a table without putting her bag over her shoulder. Her grimace says a lot. I'm on my feet, then.

"I can help." I gesture toward the table next to mine. "I'll grab your stuff."

"No, you don't have to . . . Ah, you know what? Yes, that would be great. Thank you. Thanks," she says again as I pull out the chair for her.

She settles herself in the chair with a low, long sigh. It's just after New Year's, but the coffee shop hasn't yet taken down their Christmas tree. It's hung with multicolored lights, and they reflect rainbows in her hair. I put the plate with the brownie in front of her, then offer to fill her mug from the small self-service bar behind us. Again Diana looks like she might refuse, but then smiles and nods her permission. I fill her mug and set it on the table, making sure not to splash it on her bag. She's looking at a thick catalog I recognize as the rec center's class listings.

"Thank you so much. I broke both my collarbones a few months ago," she says. "I just got permission to be out of the slings a while ago, but I still have to watch what I'm doing, or it hurts all over again."

I slide into my own chair at the table diagonal from hers and nod sympathetically, like I have no idea about the accident. I'm a liar. I've always been a liar, and it's likely I always will be. "Ouch. Broken collarbones are a bitch, I hear. Take a long time to heal."

"You hear right." She shifts her right arm a little bit and gives a small nod. "I tend to overdo it, then regret it later. Anyway, thanks again for the help. You must've been an Eagle Scout."

"Nobody's ever accused me of that before." I laugh because that's the damn truth. I gesture toward her table and drop the next question all casual. "So, were you doing something crazy like skydiving or . . .?"

"Oh God, no. Never. Car accident. I was lucky. It could've been worse. The worst part is I lost my car. I loved that car." Diana frowns and shakes her head, looking sad.

"What kind of car was it?" I ask, although of course I already know.

"It was a . . . bitchin' Camaro." She laughs softly, referring to the song by the Dead Milkmen.

I lean back in my seat to make a show of checking out the parking lot through the coffee shop's huge plate glass windows. "Camaros rock. Where is it?"

"It was totaled."

Surprised, I say, "Totaled . . . as in scrapped?"

"Yes. I guess it doesn't take much to total a Camaro."

That doesn't make any sense. I'd seen the accident photos. Small-town news stations still cover that sort of thing. The car wasn't in that bad of shape. "Maybe you can get another one."

"I hope so." Diana leans forward with a small conspiratorial smile that reminds me again of that first light after darkness. "I got a replacement car, and I hate it."

I think about making a joke, some light words to tease her with, but they dry up. We've spent hours laughing together, but I think if I made her laugh now, it would break me.

She gives me a curious look. For a moment I have the bitter hope she's going to ask me if we've met before. Not sure what I'd say if she does, but turns out I don't have to worry. There's no hint of recognition in those blue eyes, and that does fucking slaughter me.

She shakes her head, and her smile goes away like time clouds covering the sun. She turns her attention deliberately to the catalog. She sips her coffee and turns the pages.

I get the hint and focus again on my own task, or at least I try to. There's no paying attention, not even to find work, with Diana sitting so close to me. It had never occurred to me that seeing her without being able to talk to her, really talk, would be worse than never seeing her again.

Her phone hums from her purse, and she pauses to dig it out with a wince. "Hi. Yes, I am. Sure. No, I'm fine. Really. No problems. It was fine. I came over to the rec center to sign up for a class . . . I didn't know you'd want to come with me. I'm sorry. Yes, I'll be home soon. No, I don't know what time he'll be home."

She slides her thumb across the phone screen and lets out a disgruntled sigh.

"My mother-in-law," she says, catching me staring. "She's . . . needy. This is the first time I've left the house on my own since the accident. I didn't tell her I was going anywhere. I guess she panicked a little. I mean, I'm an adult woman.

I shouldn't have to tell her where I'm going or why, right? If I want to take a class, I don't need her permission."

"What class are you taking?"

She gives me another of those head tilts, eyes narrowed, looking me over. She *has* to know me, even if she doesn't remember, but all I see is a vague suspicion. I've been too nosy.

"Intro to watercolors. It's every Wednesday at four."

"Sounds fun."

Another assessing look. "It could be, I guess."

The urge to tell her the truth is pretty hard to squash, but I manage it. She turns back to her food, and I have no more excuses to make conversation, so I go back to my laptop. She doesn't say goodbye when she leaves, but I'm not worried about it.

Now I know where to find her every week.

CHAPTER EIGHTEEN

Diana

The instructor greets me with a friendly smile. She wears paint-stained jeans, and there's a smudge of what must be clay on her men's button-down, but her smile is sincere, and she looks happy to see me. I can't tell if she knows me or not.

"I'm Diana," I say.

She nods. "Welcome. I'm Mary. I saw that you took this class last summer? You might get a little bored, repeating the beginner class, although I do have a different approach than the former instructor. You might still find something new to work on."

"Oh. It wasn't you? I mean, the class I took before wasn't with you?"

Mary gives me an odd look, and who can blame her. "Nope, according to the records, you took Introduction to Watercolors with Betty. I'm sorry to say she's moved down to Florida, so I took over. I do have room in the advanced class, if you like."

"Oh, I'll be fine," I say cheerfully. "I don't remember anything from the original class."

Mary dimples. "I'm sure it will come back to you."

"I hope so," I say and tell her about the accident, my surgery, and the amnesia.

Her surprise looks genuine. "So . . . you don't remember anything at all?"

"Nothing for a certain time period. Nope."

I'm still cheerful. I have been since breakfast. Harriett's egg, bacon, and cheese quiche had been waiting for me when I got up. The coffee had been brewed. Lunch was chicken and dumplings, left for me in the fridge. Yet Harriett herself was notably absent, which meant I got to shovel food into my gullet all day long while I read clickbait articles on my phone without having to have a conversation. It was glorious, and all day I've been feeling euphoric.

"That must be very strange," Mary says.

I laugh. "You said it, sister."

I've never said such a thing in my life, but it's seems the sort of thing someone like Mary would like to hear, and I add a couple of finger guns. *Pow, pow!* We both laugh then, and it feels good. I like it. I like Mary. I like this class. Hell, I might even like watercolors, I don't know. The world seems bright and magical right now, and anything is possible.

Why have I signed up for another class in watercolors? I don't expect to get any better at it than I was before, and I can honestly say I've never been a fan of the way they look even when painted by someone with skill.

The truth is, I'm hoping that somehow, some way, something is going to get pulled free from the swamp of eternal sadness that is my brain. I want to remember why I signed up for that class last summer. Hell, I want to remember anything at all.

The class fills up with ten students, each of us in front of an easel hung with fresh paper next to a tray of paints, brushes, and of course a mug of water. Mary spends the first few minutes demonstrating techniques. Then she walks around the classroom offering help.

I have a grand old time. My painting sucks, but whatever. Mary's a good teacher, but you can put a pig in a pair of high heels and never get it to dance. Thinking that, I laugh. It was something my mother said, but today, not even that memory can make me feel sour.

Toward the end of the hour, my right shoulder has started humming. My mood is dimming.

In the parking lot after, I'm trying to juggle my purse, which is too damned big—why do I need such a big purse?—also my keys, and the fresh painting, still damp. A fresh, bright flare of pain bursts through me as I attempt and fail to hit the correct button on my keyless remote. I drop my bag, which hits the asphalt with a crunch. The picture tries to float from my grip, and clutching it tighter makes it all hurt worse.

I mutter a curse and lean against the car with one hand. My picture crumples. I'm about to do the same.

"Hey, are you okay?"

I don't want to turn at the sound of a concerned male voice. I'm embarrassed. Then I see it's the guy from last week. The one I met in the coffee shop next door to the rec center, and an inexplicable sense of relief washes over me. I'm still mortified, but I don't mind so much.

"I overdid it. My shoulder's really hurting, and I'm trying to get my car unlocked. I feel so stupid."

He shakes his head and bends to pick up my purse. Gently, he holds out a hand for the picture, which I hand over. This gives me the chance to use both hands to press the remote to unlock the car.

"Driving home's going to be the real bitch," I tell him.

"Hope you have some good pain meds or at least a nice glass of wine waiting for you, then," he says and shifts both my bag and the watercolor into the same hand with an effortless ease I envy. He offers his hand to shake. "I'm Cole, by the way. I don't think we introduced ourselves the last time."

"Diana. Thanks again. I promise you, I'm not usually so helpless." I don't owe him an explanation, but I guess it's not for him. It's a reminder for myself.

Cole grins. "I wouldn't have thought so. We all need a hand now and then."

We stare at each other for a minute or so. Too long. I'm embarrassed again. He's easily ten years younger than I am, with that purposely unkempt style I usually find so pretentious, but on him the faded jeans, battered black work boots, and matching leather jacket work. So does the long reddish hair he's got pulled back, not quite in a man bun, but something close to it. Cole's eyes are the color of bittersweet chocolate, and they hold mine until I look away.

"It's this car. I'm not used to it yet." I'm forcing my voice to remain casual, light.

"Ah. The car you hate, right?" He steps back to look it over.

I know what he sees. A steel gray Volvo. Brand-new, shiny. Expensive.

"It's not awful," I say for him.

Cole tips a smile my way. "It's no bright red Camaro."

"Okay. It's awful. It's new—that's the best I can say about it. My husband picked it out. It's just like his, only slightly less nice." I pause. "How'd you know it was red?"

"Lucky guess. You look like a red car kind of lady."

For a tiny, indulgent moment, I think that maybe I shouldn't have mentioned a husband. Cole might be younger and scruffy and not my type, but he's also good looking, and to be blunt, the last few months have left me feeling anything but desirable. There's nothing wrong with looking, I think, then frown, hard, at my justification for something nobody could ever really argue is even bordering on being unfaithful. Thoughts are nothing without action.

"Thanks for the help," I add when it becomes obvious he's not going to say anything more.

Cole nods and steps back. "Any time. How's the class going?"

"You should take it and find out." I'm not sure why I'm being so bold.

"Maybe I will. You need any more help?"

I decline and watch him walk away, half-hoping he will turn around to wave goodbye and relieved when he doesn't. I'm still thinking about him when I get home, fifteen minutes later than expected, because my arms and shoulders are aching so much I had to drive slower than usual.

A quick glance in my rearview mirror shows only my eyes. My makeup is a little smudged, and the crow's feet are undeniable, but there's a light in my gaze that I try to quell. I'm not a cougar, I tell myself. I'm not in the market for a boy toy. I'm not in the market at all.

I don't announce myself as I come in through the laundry room. I mean, it's my house. Why, then, does my mother-in-law whirl around looking like she's expecting a serial killer in a hockey mask to be attacking her with a machete?

"Diana! You startled me. What are you doing here?"

"I . . . live here. What are *you* doing here?"

From here I can see a platter of pasta glistening with what my nose tells me is garlic and oil. There's also a basket of dinner rolls, still steaming, and a big bowl of salad. A pan simmering on the stove smells like meatballs.

"Making dinner."

"I wasn't expecting you." Slowly, carefully, trying not to show that I'm aching, I put my purse and coat on the hook by the door and affix my watercolor to the fridge with a magnet Jonathan and I got on our honeymoon. I look at the magnet for a moment longer than necessary. It's a reminder of what we had when we started out, which is nothing close to what we have now.

But all the same, we do have something. Don't we? His boots are still in closet, as my grandmother might have said. He's here now. Nothing is ever ended until it's over.

And why isn't it over?

Jonathan has still been coming home at a normal time since the beginning of December. There've been no late-night, furtive phone calls that I've overheard. No buzzing texts calling his attention away when he's home. I'm still trying to track down a copy of the prenup, but that's as far as I got. I think he and Val might have ended things . . . and I think that's why I have not.

"What's that?" Harriett is trying to get into the fridge, but I'm blocking her way.

"I made it in Intro to Watercolors."

She whirls, eyes wide. "What? You're taking a class?"

"I told you the day I registered."

"You didn't tell me! You told me yesterday afternoon you'd be out with Trina tonight. After your appointment with Dr. Levitt."

"That was weeks and weeks ago. I don't even see Dr. Levitt anymore."

Harriett's eyes narrow. "What? Since when?"

"Since before Christmas."

"I didn't know." Her voice hitches. "Now that you don't need me to drive you around anymore, I guess I just don't know anything about your life."

I didn't tell anyone about quitting Dr. Levitt, but I did tell her about the painting class. I'm sure I did. Didn't I? Is not being able to remember the same as forgetting?

Chilly fingers trip up and down my spine, and my bones throb. I was feeling so good earlier today. So up. I'm crashing now.

"I guess you just don't need me around at all," Harriett says in a tearful voice.

Before I can tell her that's not true, Harriett engulfs me in a hug. Her face burrows against my neck. The heat of her tears splashes my skin. The sudden embrace rocks me, and I have to take a step back to keep from staggering.

"Harriett—"

She sobs. She shudders. Worse, she squeezes. Hard.

I gasp out a curse. Harriett lets go of me, stepping back, swiping at her face. She turns away to grab a dishtowel to wipe her eyes. I'm reeling with nausea from the sharp pain arcing through me after being manhandled.

"If you had children, you'd understand," Harriett says, "how hard it is to let go."

It's been over a week since the last time I took any pain pills, but I need to get ahead of this. The bottle in the cupboard doesn't rattle when I shake it. It's empty. "When's the last time you refilled these?"

"I thought you quit taking those," she says.

The nausea is fading. The ache is no longer sharp, but experience tells me it's just settling in. "I'm trying to."

"You overdid it today," Harriett says firmly. "You sit. I made meatballs for you. We'll have a nice dinner, and after we can snuggle up on the couch and watch *Runner* together, the way we used to. I'll run out and get your refills tomorrow for you."

"See?" I say, but weakly. "I do still need you."

And then I burst into tears.

Immediately, she launches into "mom mode," bustling me into a kitchen chair, murmuring words of comfort, handing me a tissue. I tense when she puts a hand on my shoulder, but her touch is deliberately light and brief. She pats my hair a moment after that and leans to smile at me.

"You'll feel better with some food in you, and my goodness, you need some meat on those bones. You sit tight," Harriett says from the oven as she bends to check the meatballs.

"I'm not happy." The words slip out of me, too late to call them back.

Without turning, she answers, "Healing takes time."

"No, Harriett. Listen to me . . . it's about Jonathan." I draw in a breath, trying to find a way to tell her about everything that's been going on. I've shared my deepest sorrows with her in the past, but those were about my mother. Not about Harriett's son.

Harriet straightens. Faces me. Her cheeks are blotchy and pink from the heat of the oven or from her earlier tears.

"You know, Diana, out of all the women he's ever dated, you're the only one I've ever loved."

How do I break her heart?

I need a glass of wine for this. In the fridge I find a bottle of the Briar White with only an inch or so of golden fluid inside. It looks like even less poured into the glass. A few swallows at most. How could I have finished that much of the bottle without noticing?

Both of us look up as the door to the garage opens.

"I'm"—Jonathan pauses like he's surprised to see us both—"home."

"Just in time for dinner," Harriett says. "Why don't you run downstairs and grab Diana another bottle of her wine. She seems to have finished the one that was up here."

When the door to the basement closes behind him, Harriett says, "When the two of you got married, I was so thrilled to have the chance to be the mother you've always deserved. If something were to happen with the two of you, Diana, I'm not sure what I'd do. The two of you were made for each other. Absolutely made for each other."

I don't have to time to answer her. Jonathan's footsteps on the stairs alert us a second or so before the door opens and he appears, bottle in hand. Harriett turns back to the stove, pulling out the pan of meatballs and fussing with the bowl of pasta.

We are all seated at the table some minutes after that, and I've said nothing. Jonathan has poured himself a glass of red wine, and I have my white, both in the crystal glasses Harriett pulled quickly from the cupboard. Our wedding crystal. When's the last time we even used them?

So. Awkward. So, so weird.

Harriett also has a glass from the crystal set, hers filled with sparkling water. She lifts it. "To family."

"Pinkies out." Jonathan lifts his glass.

104

That's mine and Val's saying. Did he hear it from me? Or from her?

"To family," I say as our three glasses clink.

Harriett beams. Jonathan smiles at me across the table, and for the first time in a long time, it feels good to be here with him. We share a look, and if there's something like guilt in his gaze, I look away before I have to admit it.

I don't want my marriage to be over.

All the years, the small and subtle slights, the chronic and grinding wearing down of love. And still, I don't want us to end. We were never perfect, but I loved him once. Now, here, even though I know it's over, I do not want it to end.

Harriett ladles pasta onto Jonathan's plate and then does the same for me, adding a few meatballs.

"I always loved your meatballs," Jonathan says wistfully and acts like he's going to stab one with his fork.

His mother slaps his hand away. "I made those for Diana!"

"She won't mind," he says but withdraws his fork.

"I mind," she says firmly with a nod and a smile at me. "If you're going to suddenly start eating meat again, you let me know, and I'll make enough for you both. But right now, tonight, these are just for her."

She pats my hand.

By the time I've eaten my third meatball, the single glass of wine has started me spinning. That warm buzz. The glow. It's so easy to fall down this rabbit hole, but when Jonathan offers to refill my glass, I wave him away. He pours one for himself and waves the bottle in front of his mother, who huffs and puffs but doesn't seem too offended that he's trying to give her some.

"You know I don't . . . Jonathan! You're so naughty!"

She actually said *naughty*, which makes me laugh, and then he laughs, and we're all laughing. In this moment I'm happy. It's not all perfect, but it's what I have.

Later, Jonathan comes into the bedroom. His kisses taste like ground beef. His hands roam. I push him away.

"You sneak," I tell him. "You ate my lunch for tomorrow!"

"Don't tell my mom," he whispers, and his hungry hands and mouth devour me.

His hand on my breast, thumb passing over my nipples. His hardness pressing my thigh. My world has gone lazy, hazy, blurry. Syrup. Sweetness. Kissing. His hands on me and mine on him.

We are naked. Touching. Stroking. The sex is rough and fast. He takes me from behind. Pulls my hair a little. This is never how I liked it, but when he pushes me back against the bed, I let him. His thickness, pressing inside me. I gasp his name. He covers my mouth with his, muffling my cries. I don't come; he does.

As Jonathan starts to snore, my mind fills instead with images of Cole's smile. His eyes. The sound of his voice.

What would I do if I could be in the market, after all?

CHAPTER NINETEEN

Cole

I signed up for Intro to Watercolors, and it was worth it to stand there in front of my easel with fifty bucks worth of brushes and supplies, because when Diana walks into the room, all I can see is her. Yeah, I know it's kind of fucked up. Kind of like being a stalker. I don't have an excuse for it.

She doesn't notice me at first, which is fine by me. I'm playing it cool, you know? Yeah, she's the one who suggested I take the class, but now that I'm here, will she think it's weird? She takes a spot closer to the front of the room and pulls out her paints and brushes from her bag. She looks like she's having a little bit of trouble with the paper, which is on a large roll attached to the top of the easel. Her arms, I think. Her shoulders are still hurting. The instructor comes over to help her. They laugh at something Diana says, and in that moment she glances over her shoulder and catches me staring.

What can I do but smile and lift a brush toward her? She smiles back, then returns her attention to her easel. The instructor goes back to the front of the class and starts talking. I figure I'd better pay at least a little bit of attention.

After fifty minutes, we've all shared our pictures. We clean up, and the instructor takes a few minutes with each person to talk about our progress. She likes my picture all right, and I am not surprised. I paid my money. It's the rec center. Pretty much anything is going to get positive feedback.

I am taken aback, though, when Diana waits as the class files out, to take a look at what I'd done.

"Nice," she says. "I like the way you've used the colors."

She points. I look at my picture, still attached to the easel because I haven't yet torn it off the roll. What I've done isn't any better than anyone else's, but I give her a grin anyway and make a show of buffing my nails against the front of my shirt.

"Some of us are born with natural talent," I say. "Let me see yours."

She snorts soft laughter, and I'm undone. I'd make myself any kind of fool to see that smile again. She looks hesitant, then holds out the paper. We're all painting the same still life, a couple of pears and an apple, but Diana's picture is . . . different. She lets me look at it for a few seconds before laughing self-consciously and pulling it back.

"I don't know why I painted it like that," she says. "All sort of wavy and distorted."

"Maybe that's what makes it art. You know. A different perspective," I offer.

She tilts her head to give me an assessing look. "You think?"

"Maybe?" I know my grin is charming. It's worked on women since I was thirteen and discovered I was getting hair around my dick.

"I don't know. I was feeling weird about it. I'm sort of feeling weird in general."

I have to stop myself from touching her, because charm or no, I do know how not to be *that* sort of asshole. "Weird how?"

"Just . . . out of sorts. I almost didn't come today." Diana waves a vague hand and laughs again, a little embarrassed.

The instructor is pointedly waiting for us to leave the classroom.

"Want to grab a coffee, maybe a brownie?" I ask Diana.

She gives me a look that is equal parts wariness and gratitude, but nods. I stand aside to let her pass me out the door, and we walk side by side down the rec center's long, sloping hall. The rec center used to be an elementary school, and they changed very little about it other than adding the coffee shop at the front. We pass a couple of classrooms, most of them dark. Watercolors is one of the last classes of the day.

The coffee shop, though, stays open hours past the rec's closing. This afternoon, they're setting up in a far corner for an open mic night. Beat poetry, according to the flyers.

"I hope we're out of here before that starts," Diana says with a lift of her chin toward the sign announcing the night's entertainment.

"Not a fan?" I know so much about her, but I didn't know this.

She looks apologetic. "No. Are you?"

"Hell, no."

We both laugh. It's easy and natural, and I bask in that moment. I order us two mugs of self-service coffee and two brownies with fudge icing. She gives the brownie a funny look when I set it in front of her.

"My favorite," she says.

"You had one the last time we were here."

"The day we met," Diana says.

"Yeah," I tell her, the words so smooth they don't even seem like a lie. "The day we met."

CHAPTER TWENTY

Valerie

LAST SUMMER

There had to be rules to the game Diana asked me to play. The first was that she was never allowed to ask me anything about what her husband and I did together. The second, the one we never actually said aloud, was that I was not supposed to fall in love with him. Yet here I was, in bed with Jonathan Richmond, and all I could think about was how much he made me laugh.

If it wasn't love, it was as close to it as I'd ever been.

"I have something to ask you," he said.

For one incredibly foolish minute I thought he was going to pull out a ring. I rolled onto my side to face him, my heartbeat thundering in my ears. He smoothed my hair over my shoulder and kept his hand moving down my bare arm until he settled it on my naked hip. Our legs tangled beneath the edge of the sheet we'd kicked off in the August heat.

"I want to take you away somewhere," he said, "for a week."

The tap of his toes on mine should have irritated me, but it only made me shift closer. Belly to belly. "A week's a long time."

"A few nights here and there aren't enough. Is it enough for you?" He sounded anxious, his brow furrowed with the question.

I had to be honest. "No."

"So you'll go away with me?"

"What will you tell her?"

The rule with Diana was that she and I didn't discuss her husband. The rule with Jonathan was that we didn't discuss his wife. But I had to ask.

"I'll tell her it's business. She never goes along with me on business trips," he said.

I knew that was true, just as I knew that even if she did, she would have declined whatever trip he was talking about now. That was the plan, wasn't it? Give him the rope to hang himself with?

"Where will we go?" I kissed him.

"Someplace warm," he told me. "With sands and beaches and fruity drinks with umbrellas."

I laughed and kissed him again, soft and sweet and slow, and then, suddenly, hot and full of yearning. I had to gasp out my next question. "When?"

"October," Jonathan said.

Months away. What more proof could there be that this was something more permanent? It was all we needed . . . no. It was all Diana needed.

I'd discovered I needed so much more, and I wasn't going to let her stop me from getting it.

CHAPTER TWENTY-ONE

Diana

Time moves in minutes, days, hours, weeks, months. It's only been six weeks since the first time I met Cole. Time bites itself into pieces you can chew, but that doesn't always make it a meal. Sometimes you end up still hungry.

We've just finished our last class and head outside to the parking lot.

"You'd think I'd have gotten better at it by the end. Plus the fact I've taken the class before." I wave my damp paper around in front of Cole's face and step back before he can grab it.

He wears his hair loose today, red-gold strands hanging from beneath the dark gray and black beanie cap. He holds up his paper. "I'll show you mine if you show me yours."

We both laugh.

"It's colder than a witch's icebox out here. February is the worst." My teeth chatter for a moment, and I dance in place.

"Yeah, but you get Valentine's Day right in the middle. That counts for something, doesn't it?" Cole says, then pauses with an arched brow.

How did this become so easy between us?

I started taking this class because I hoped it would help me remember something, anything about last summer. It had become immediately clear in the first couple sessions that it never would. Why, then had I kept going? One reason.

Cole.

"Coffee?" I look toward the coffee shop.

For a split second, I hope he says no, but why should he? We've been meeting for coffee after every class. This will be the last time, I tell myself.

"Sure. Coffee." The way Cole says it makes it sound like more than coffee, and I shiver again, but this time not from the cold.

It's just coffee.

"They should have an entrance that connects directly from the rec center to the coffee shop," I grumble as I step back to let Cole open the door for me, "so we don't have to go outside into this frozen hellscape first."

He laughs again. "No shit. Grab a table. I'll get us some coffee. Brownie?"

"Oh man. I want one, but"—I pat my stomach through the heavy winter coat—"I'd better not."

"What are you talking about? You look great." He scoffs, his eyes meeting mine.

I was so cold my teeth were chattering, but now I am warm. I settle into the table at the back, the one that by default, without discussing it, has become "ours." Of course that's ridiculous. Cole and I have no "us" or "ours." We barely know each other . . . except that every week for the past month, we've had that watercolors class together and coffee and pastries after. Six weeks. Six meetings. That's all it's been.

Moments later, he slides a plate with a fudge-iced brownie on top of it in front of me. Then, while I'm still half-heartedly protesting, he fills our mugs with coffee from the self-serve tankards on the counter behind him. He puts one in front of each of us and takes his seat with a look of feigned innocence.

"What?"

"You're a bad influence." But I'm not going to turn down the brownie. I do cut it in half, though, and push the plate between us. When I look up, I catch Cole's gaze. Neither of us looks away.

Finally, he reaches for the brownie and bites into it. I sip coffee. We don't say anything for a minute or so, and the silence is not awkward or strange. It's the comfort of not needing to fill every space with noise that happens between friends, and I think, *Is that what we've become?* Just like that?

"So," Cole says, "last class today. Are you signing up for another one?"

I've already told myself I won't be, but I shrug like I haven't decided. "I don't know. I'm not very good at it."

"Let me see." He takes my painting and looks it over with a frown. Hands it back. "Yeah. You suck."

Our laughter turns heads, and I don't even care. I make a show of crumpling up my painting and tossing it in the garbage pail next to the coffee station. Cole, laughing, tries to stop me, but it's truly no loss. I have others, and Cole's right. I do suck.

"Don't do that," he tells me, laughter fading but his smile still broad. "Think of how much better you make the rest of us look."

I groan. "Ugh. Mean."

"Sorry. But . . . are you going to take another class?"

"I don't think so. What about you?"

"Not sure. I might look into pottery." He sounds serious, but I can't be sure he's not setting me up for some kind of joke.

I tilt my head, looking him over. "Interesting. Clay pots?"

"Something like that. Who can't use a nice, lumpy clay pot?"

"You might really be good at pottery, Cole."

"Well, not to brag, but I am pretty damned good with my hands."

He holds them up. Long fingers, broad palms. One of his hands could engulf both of mine, and I am suddenly greedy, looking at them. I want those hands on me. Desire sends a shiver through me I try to cover up by shifting in my chair. I can't look him in the eyes, or I'll give myself away. I'm not ashamed of this wanting, but I don't want to offer anything I'm not prepared to give.

"Maybe calligraphy," I say to cover up the sudden silence between us that is no longer so comfortable. "Write fancy greeting cards. Stuff like that. It's like a lost art. I mean, who handwrites anything anymore? We all use our phones."

Like I summoned it, his phone hums in his pocket, and he pulls it out, stares with a frown at the screen, and puts it back. I am desperate to know if that text was from a girlfriend or, worse, a wife. He doesn't wear a ring. That doesn't mean anything, I think. I do, and I'm still here. He could have someone calling him home the way my husband no longer ever calls me.

"Oh, before I forget." I pull my purse onto my lap to dig for my wallet. "Let me get you some cash for the—"

"No way." Cole shakes his head. "Forget it. My treat."

I shake my own head, keeping my gaze averted.

"No. I invited you," I tell him stubbornly.

I dig without luck through my bag, setting items on the table. A small leather-bound daily planner Jonathan gave me that I always forget to use. A lipstick. Some loose change. At the bottom of the bag, three prescription pill bottles, labeled identically with the name of my old pain meds. They don't even rattle—all empty. And at the bottom, finally, my wallet.

Cole helps me gather up the junk from my purse. When he grabs the pill bottles, I flood with heat, rising up my throat and into my face at what he must be thinking. More, a tingling rush of it, when he looks at the labels before handing them to me.

"From the accident," I tell him. "I don't actually take them anymore. I guess it shows you how long it's been since I cleaned out my purse. I didn't even know they were in there. Anyway, I told you, I got this. You can pay the next time."

"So long as that means there will be a next time," Cole says.

Another long silence. My face is still hot, but the warmth is trickling through every other part of me. I know it's wrong to want this. I'm not sure I care, really. But I do know.

Time moves in heartbeats, in sighs. It moves from one breath to the next. It moves in the breaking of friendships and hearts. It moves in letting go.

I want there to be a next time, but really, I don't want this time to be over. With Jonathan in Kansas City, I don't even need an excuse to rush home. "I'm just going to use the restroom real quick. Be right back?"

"Sure," Cole says. "I'll be here."

CHAPTER TWENTY-TWO

Cole

I'm the guy you go to when you want something done that you don't want to do yourself. It wouldn't make my mama proud, but it pays the bills. I like the freedom of being my own boss and making my own schedule. I like the ability to just bug out whenever I want, spend a month driving cross-country. Pick up a job or two along the way to cover beers and burgers. Before I met Diana, I'd never spent more than a couple weeks at home base before heading out again.

After I met her, everything was different.

The past few weeks have been a glimpse into what it might have been like if we'd met in a conventional way, but today was the last class, and so that means an end to these weekly coffee dates. I should let it go, right? I should be the good guy, not the bad one.

The people who pay me to find out if their husband, wife, boyfriend, girlfriend, or whoever is cheating on them don't want to know how I attained the information they're paying for. They just want proof. Because I'm the guy who does the things you don't want to, I have a number of resources at my disposal. Most of them are shady. Pretending to be interested in your wife so you can see if she's willing to cheat. Adding key loggers to computers. Adding GPS tracking to phones. And of course, figuring out passcodes on devices.

Like phones left on a table while the owner uses the bathroom.

I know how to find out where people are going, when, and with whom. I know how to blend into a crowd so they don't figure out they're being watched.

Like Liam Neeson says in *Taken*, I have a particular set of skills, and I don't always need to be paid to use them.

Sometimes I do it for myself.

By the time Diana is back from the bathroom. I've cleared the table of our trash and made sure everything that she took out of her purse is back inside it, including her phone. I stand when she returns.

We walk together to the parking lot. We stand by her car. I shove my hands into my pockets. Her teeth chatter, but I can't be sure if she's shaking because of the frigid air blasting us, or because of what I hope might be nerves. Maybe desire.

We haven't had nearly enough time together, but I can't think of any more excuses to linger here. I hold out my hand to take her cold fingers in mine. I don't want to let go. "Well, Diana, it's been great getting to know you. I hope I see you around."

"Same. Yes. Maybe pottery." She shakes my hand and lets it go quickly.

Before I can do something really fucking stupid, I pivot on my heel to stalk off toward my car, parked on the opposite side of the lot. I drive a battered black Mustang with rust on the bumpers and patches of gray primer on the back panel. It's no showpiece, but it purrs like a dream. I listen to the engine rumble while the car warms up, and I watch her boring silver sedan exit the parking lot. In my hand, my phone app shows a small blue dot, moving away from me. It doesn't matter whether or not she takes another class.

I will always know where to find her, wherever she goes.

CHAPTER TWENTY-THREE

Diana

By the time I get home, I'm ready to put on comfy clothes and veg out on the couch. The buzz I got from the coffee shop treats is wearing off. Well, who am I kidding? The buzz is from being around Cole.

I'm tired, and the house is too hot again, set at nearly ninety degrees. This is ridiculous. I reset the temperature to something reasonable, pull out my phone, and place a call to the local HVAC company we use. I get the voicemail, so I leave a message. I also make a quick phone call to the number of another lawyer, trying to track down who's got the files I need.

I need more coffee. I'm not too proud to microwave the dregs leftover from this morning, but putting on another half a pot seems like a good idea. The maker doesn't turn on, even though I've filled it with fresh water and changed the filter. I mutter a string of curses. It's been acting up for some time, but I think it's possible the damned thing has finally died. I almost want to stroke it like an old, faithful dog that has at last passed away in its sleep.

The microwave beeps, and I turn to fetch my reheated coffee. I drink half of it while I mess around with the recalcitrant coffeemaker, which I can't seem to bring back from the dead. At a sound behind me, I turn and scream at the sight of the figure standing there. "Oh my God!"

Harriett shakes her head. "What on earth are you doing?"

"Trying to make coffee." Also, now, trying not to wince in pain at the way I yanked my arms around, making my shoulders ache. I am not surprised that

118

she's here, although I am startled by her presence. She must have come in through the front door. I really need to remember to turn on the motion alert notifications on my phone again. "What are you doing here?"

"I told you yesterday I'd be by this afternoon to make dinner, since you'd be coming late from your class," she says.

"You didn't," I tell her. I know she didn't. Yesterday afternoon I binge-watched half a season of some BBC show and fell asleep on the couch. I finish the rest of the coffee and rinse the mug, putting it back on the counter.

Harriett purses her lips. "I came over to check on you. You were watching that show about those two young men solving mysteries. I told you I'd be over. You said it would fine."

I'd been watching something else entirely, but still, I wrack my memory to recall any kind of conversation with her. She's staring at me expectantly. I gesture with frustration at the coffeemaker. I feel on the verge of tears and woozy, tired despite the mug of coffee I just finished.

"Thank you. But I really don't need you to cook for me. I'm just going to maybe take a nap and make a sandwich later."

"Well," Harriett says, "if you don't want me . . ."

"That's not what I meant."

"No, no, it's fine. I understand. I'll just go. I just thought with Jonathan out of town this week, you might want some company. But if you'd rather be alone, that's fine. I'll make myself a nice grilled cheese sandwich in my own apartment and eat it all by myself. That will be fine."

Now I've gone and done it. Harriett does make an amazing grilled cheese sandwich. And although I'm nowhere close to lonely with Jonathan out of town, it's very clear that my mother-in-law is.

"Harriett, no, please. You're here. Stay. It's nice to have company." I grit out that last bit through a smile she doesn't seem to know is fake.

"Why don't you go up and have a nice shower. Change into something comfy. Wash your face," Harriett adds.

The idea of a hot shower and comfy clothes is appealing, but something in how she mentions washing my face gives me pause. "What do you mean?"

She looks surprised. "About what?"

This is not the first time I've sensed a less than subtle reproach from my mother-in-law, but I can't put my finger on what exactly is annoying me about it. "Is my face dirty?"

"Oh my goodness. It's not dirty. But you are wearing an awful lot of makeup. Aren't you?"

I'd spent too long this morning second-guessing my mascara, shadow, the shade of my lipstick. Heat floods my face now. I'm self-conscious.

"Am I?"

"You look more like you were out standing on a street corner than taking a watercolors class," Harriett says. "But what do I know about fashion these days? Maybe that heavy-handed look is 'in,' as they say. What's wrong? You look upset."

"I'm not upset." This is sort of a lie. My coffeepot is broken, the thermostat isn't working right, and I've just been vaguely called a whore. I'm not upset only because I'm too tired to be. Too lazy to make much of a fuss about anything.

"You go on upstairs," Harriett says gently. "I'll make us some dinner. All right?"

Upstairs, I strip out of the clothes I'd chosen so carefully. Too fancy for a watercolors class at the rec center. I'm thinking of Cole again as I step into the shower and tip my face into the water. I open my mouth to fill it, letting it overflow with warm water. I'm warm all over. I wash my hair, waiting for the ache to rise up again, but it seems fine. Everything seems fine, actually. Warm and fine and fun, and I'm hungry now, and I also feel giddy and giggly. The water's too hot, so I dial it back, letting it wash over me, trying to chase away this thick feeling in my head.

I have to admit that Harriett was right. Scrubbed and clean, everything does feel better. I pull on leggings and a tunic top, drag a comb through my hair. I'm a little dizzy. The edges of everything have gone fuzzy.

When I come back down to the kitchen, Harriett has set the table with a plate of chicken-salad sandwiches and fruit salad. Also, more coffee.

"You got it working? What was wrong with it?"

Harriett shrugs. "Nothing. I pushed the button and it started up."

I had also pushed the button, several times. I frown and study the coffee maker, but indeed, it seems to be working fine. "Huh. Weird. Maybe it's time to replace it."

"That would be a waste of money. That one still works."

"This one's ancient. I wouldn't be surprised if it was on its way out." My mug is missing from the counter, so I pull another one from the back of the cupboard. It has a pinup mermaid on it and the name of the New Orleans restaurant Val and I went to when we celebrated our thirtieth birthdays. When she and I were still best friends.

I fill the mug anyway, but the coffee is more bitter than I'm expecting.

Harriett watches me add sugar. "I thought you took your coffee black."

"Usually, yes. But today the coffee tastes off. Maybe I'll just go shopping, pick up a new coffee maker. Oh, that reminds me, I need to see if the furnace people have called me back." I look around for my phone, which I remember leaving on the counter.

"What's wrong with the furnace?"

"The thermostat schedule keeps getting messed up. Have you seen my phone?"

"Have you lost it?"

Still looking around for my phone, I pause with the mug halfway to my mouth. I finish sipping before I answer. "I had it earlier, but I can't find it, now."

"You should be more careful, Diana. You've had two new phones in the past few months. With only one income in the house, you ought to be a little more careful." Harriett takes her place across from me at the table and nibbles gently at the edges of her sandwich.

I burst into surprised laughter. "Harriett, you're kidding. Right? I lost my phone in the car accident. Just one phone."

She is clearly not kidding. My laughter fades. *New phone.* I think of the list in my nightstand. I sip more coffee, still too bitter, even with the sugar. I could blame the coffee maker, but I think it's probably the mug and its memories. I contemplate what Harriett just said while she fusses with the food on the table.

"And that was your newest one. You're always getting the newest phone," she says. "And with you not working . . ."

"You do know I took an extremely generous payout during some company restructuring, don't you? And then I had a car accident and emergency surgery, so I haven't exactly been fit for work, have I?"

"I'm sorry you're offended, but there's no need to raise your voice."

I had not raised my voice, but I took an extra breath before answering her, anyway. "I appreciate your concern, Harriett, but Jonathan and I are not in financial difficulties. I hadn't planned to go back to work right away, even before the accident. He knew that. We discussed it. Together."

"It's none of my business, I suppose. I just remember how it was when I first met you, how worried you used to be about making ends meet when you were on your own. You certainly wouldn't have replaced something that was still working, just because you felt like being fancy. Back then, you were certainly far more worried about stretching that paycheck."

I find myself blinking rapidly, both at her statement, which is not untrue, but also at a fresh rush of dizziness. I put a hand on the back of the kitchen chair to center myself. Harriett frowns.

"Are you all right?"

"A little dizzy. That's all."

Her smile grows wide, and I am uncomfortably reminded of the Grinch's curling grin. "Is there something you want to tell me maybe? Some good news?"

"About what?"

Her gaze drops briefly to my stomach before returning to mine.

I'm so stunned my tongue trips and tangles on my reply. "Oh God. No. That ship has left the station. The train, I mean. No, whatever, no, I'm not pregnant."

"A touch of the flu then? You look exhausted. Are you still not sleeping? Maybe you should go upstairs and lie down. Don't bother with the kitchen— I'll clean up."

"I sleep. I just have bad dreams." I hesitate, but right now, Harriett's the only one I have to tell this to. "I've been dreaming about my mother. Hurting her. Her hurting me."

Harriett makes a low noise of disgust. "Oh. Her. You shouldn't waste your time, Diana. She's not worth it."

I am allowed to think that, but hearing it come from Harriett's mouth somehow sets my teeth on edge. "Well, when you've figured out a way for people to control what they dream about, let me know."

"Oh, honey." Harriett tuts, shaking her head, and gives me a sympathetic look. "They're just dreams."

"They feel so real. I feel . . . guilty," I admit, not wanting to, but unable to stop myself from confiding.

Harriett narrows her eyes. "You have nothing to feel guilty about. She was a drug addict and a whore, and you're better off without her in your life. She wasn't even your real mother!"

The words hit me in the gut, worse than a punch. What makes someone your "real" mother, anyway? Is it how you feel about her? Or how she makes you feel about yourself?

"That doesn't matter, Harriett. I've started thinking that there's something about her, something I know but don't remember—"

"Maybe it's better that there are things you can't remember," Harriett snaps. "Maybe there's a good reason for that!"

"It's not better for me!" I shout. Too loud. Too fierce. I lower my voice. "It's not better to have a huge blank space in my brain, Harriett. Even if the memories are painful, I should still get to have them. No matter what they are."

"You should go upstairs," she says. "Take a nap."

I don't think it's the flu, but I am very tired. I grab my purse from the back of my chair to take it upstairs, glancing inside it as it gapes. And there, inside . . .

My phone.

"Harriett. Did you find my phone?"

She straightens from putting our plates in the dishwasher. "No. Was it lost?"

"I misplaced it. I told you that. But now it's in my purse." More wooziness rushes over me.

"You haven't mentioned your phone. It's that oversized handbag," she says lightly. "My goodness, no wonder you can never find anything in it."

I rustle through it, sorting past the leather appointment book, the loose change. The pill bottles are gone. I feel her gaze on me as I go to the cupboard where I've been keeping all the pills.

The orange bottles are lined up. Each is full. One is for anxiety. One for pain. One for nausea. I have no way of knowing if they are the same as what was in my bag or different. I gather them in fumbling hands.

"Are you all right?" Harriett asks.

"I don't need these anymore." I shake the bottles and look inside one. It's full. So's the next I try. "Harriett, when's the last time you refilled these?"

"I'm not sure." She attempts to take them from me, but I pull back. "Diana, what's going on?"

"I don't want you to fill them anymore. I'm going to stop taking them. All of them."

She watches as I toss them all into the garbage. I take a deep breath. My hands are shaking.

Harriett shakes her head. "I see. It's just . . ."

"It's just what?" I ask, irritated.

"I'm a mother. I'm allowed to worry."

"You're not *my* mother," I say before I can stop myself. "And I don't need you to keep fussing so much over me!"

Silence.

I've wounded her, but I want to be alone. Is that so much to ask? That I just have my own house to myself? I used to love spending time with Harriett, but my God, it's been nearly nonstop for months.

"Oh all right, then. Well." Harriett draws herself up and lifts her chin. "I'll just go on home then."

I follow her to the front door to make sure she actually leaves. "Be careful on the walk. There might be ice."

I watch her until she gets inside her apartment. I close my front door. I lock it. I lock all the doors.

Upstairs, tucked into my bed, I bring up the app on my phone that allows me to monitor the outside cameras and security system. My thumbprint won't open it. I log in using the credentials I remember, but that doesn't work either. I try to reset the password, but it says the email address I'm trying to use isn't associated with the account.

I'm the one who designed this system, chose the equipment, set up the app, all of that. It makes no sense that I'm now locked out of it.

Jonathan and I used to video chat with each other when he went away on business, but I'm not dumb enough to do that without warning him first.

Although I suspect that he and Val are no longer together, I'm not one hundred percent positive he's alone in that hotel room. I call, instead.

"What's up?" He sounds wary.

"I'm just checking in with you. How's Kansas City?"

I hear a rustle like cellophane. "Boring, but productive. How are things there?"

"Fine. Cold. I think we're supposed to get snow. Hey," I drop in casually, like it means nothing, "I can't log in to the camera app."

A pause. "Babe, you logged out so you wouldn't keep getting all the notifications waking you up. Remember? Are you okay? You sound . . . tired."

"I do remember. But that was months ago. I want to log back in. I mean, with you gone and everything. I want to be able to get the notifications again. I'll feel better. Safer." I'm laying it on a little thick, but I'm not exaggerating the sudden tremble in my voice.

Jonathan crunches something, speaks with his mouth full. "You're the one who set all that up."

"I know I did. But now it won't accept the password, and it says the email address isn't associated with the account. Did you change it?"

"Why would I change it?"

"I don't know. Did you?"

There's silence. When he does speak, it's slowly, carefully, and infuriatingly placating. "You know I don't mess with that stuff. That's all you, babe. Have you been drinking?"

My heart thumps rapidly. I feel like I'm swimming up from the depths of a deep, dark lake. Panic builds at the thought I might drown before I can reach the air.

"I'm going to request a new password using your email address." I speak as carefully and slowly as he did. "Let me know if it shows up."

"I told you, I didn't change it." Now he sounds sharp. Irritated.

"I might have changed it to your email address by accident or something," I say with him on speaker as I tap away into the app. I hold my breath for the few seconds it takes after I enter the email address, but that one also comes up as not associated. "Shit. That's not it either. Are you still getting alerts?"

"No. But you know I never got it set up on my phone—that was always your thing. Listen, could you have, I don't know, deleted the account instead of just logging out of it?"

"No. I mean, why would I do that?"

"Maybe," he says, "you just forgot."

I want to scream a curse at him for that, but I bite it back. "That makes no sense. I wouldn't have changed the email address to something else or deleted the account. I just logged out so your mother would stop waking me up every morning."

"Calm down."

I sip at the air. My hands are shaking again. My stomach feels sick, seriously twisted, like I might actually vomit. "I've got to go. I don't feel well."

"Are you—"

"I'm really going to be sick." I disconnect, toss the phone onto the bed, and flee to the bathroom, where I fall in front of the toilet, gripping it hard enough to send a shockwave of pain through my barely healed bones.

I don't actually throw up, although I wish I could. Instead, I hang over the toilet for a minute or two, heaving. When it's clear nothing's going to come up but sour spit, I sit back and concentrate on my breathing. At the sink, I splash cold water on my face, then draw some in the glass and sip at it. I wait there in the dark, and after a few more minutes, the sick feeling fades.

What is happening to me?

CHAPTER TWENTY-FOUR

Valerie

What the hell do you think you're doing, Valerie?

Jonathan's voicemail starts off without even a greeting, and although I should be pissed off about that, or intimidated or something, instead I feel that rush of heat that comes when he shows me how strong he can be . . . when he wants to. Maybe I shouldn't have texted him the link to my house listing.

You put your fucking house on the market? Where are you going? Call me. Now. A pause. A sigh. Then, softer. *Please, baby. Let's talk about this. Call me. I'm in Kansas City until next week. You can call me any time.*

It's been weeks since we spoke, but I haven't forgotten that he offered me a chance to go on this trip with him, such a sorry replacement for what had been meant as a romantic getaway. Proof of our relationship being more than a fling. I could've been with him now in Kansas City, but instead he's calling me with a tone of desperation in his voice that I've never heard before.

I don't call him back. I dial another number instead. I think it's time Diana and I have another little chat. Maybe this one will jog her memory. Maybe she and I will finally get some things squared away between us. But the call goes right to voicemail. I don't leave a message. I call back. Again, right to voicemail.

That bitch has blocked me.

CHAPTER TWENTY-FIVE

Diana

The bullshit with the security camera system and app has knocked my feet out from under me. I haven't been able to shake the feeling that I was, in fact, the one who deleted the account, but I can't find a record of doing it anywhere. No cancellation email, no nothing. The only solution is to reset the entire damn thing with a new email address and login, but I just . . . right now, I just can't.

I'm caught up in a syrup of lethargy. Everything takes an effort. It's only been three days since the watercolors class ended, but I haven't had the energy to do much beyond watch TV all day. Jonathan won't be home until late tomorrow night. Harriett has been nursing her hurt feelings by not speaking to or cooking for me, which doesn't feel like as much of a punishment as I'm sure she means it to be. This is the longest I've been alone since the accident.

I don't feel depressed, but maybe I am.

Waking up Saturday morning, though, I feel the best I have since coming home from the hospital. Sure, there are still some residual aches, but I'm clear headed. No upset stomach or dizziness.

When Trina calls and invites me to go out dancing at the newly reopened place downtown, I'm happy to say yes. Not so thrilled to hear that she left her husband of twenty-some years right after Christmas—Divorce Month is a thing, after all. But it makes me all the happier I agreed. Trina has been a good friend to me in the aftermath of the accident, so now it's my turn.

"Who knew this place could shine up so nice?" I look around at the interior of what used to be a dingy dive bar but has been transformed into a hipster version of the same bar. By this I mean they still serve Pabst Blue Ribbon and Genesee Cream Ale, but you can also get a glass of sort of pricey wine. No Briar White, not even Briar Red, but the selection is decent despite that.

Trina looks over the menu. "I haven't been out like this in forever."

"Me neither." I don't ask about her separation. If she wants to bring it up, she will.

"I'll take a glass of pinot grigio," Trina says to the very young, very cute server who arrives to take our order.

"Chardonnay for me, please."

When he leaves, she giggles and waggles her eyebrows at me. "Gah, I'm too old to be looking at that."

"Shut your mouth. Never too old to look." I shift on the high bar stool. My skirt rides up. My legs are still cold from the walk from the Ryde that dropped me off at the front door of this bar. I'd been smart in advance, not wanting to risk driving home even if I have only a couple drinks. The way wine's been hitting my system since the accident, I don't want to take any chances.

Trina twists to get a look at the dance floor, still mostly empty except for what looks like a bachelorette party. "Wish there'd been a place like this when we were younger."

"I wasn't really sure they'd be playing good dance music. Now I'm rethinking the heels. This place has really upgraded."

The server is back already with our drinks. I sip the chilled wine with a small grimace. It's not the best, but it'll do the trick. Trina and I clink our glasses together. We people-watch for a bit. The bar's getting crowded. I'm glad we got a table when we did. We both have another glass of wine.

Trina has to raise her voice over the crowd noise and the music now. "It's so weird being single again. At first, I felt like I should wait to get back out there, but . . . why wait? I was miserable for years. My marriage was over long before I told him I wanted out."

"I'm sorry I didn't know."

"What would you have been able to do about it?" Trina shakes her head. "Nobody knew. Hell, he's claiming even *he* didn't know, just so you know. No wonder we're getting divorced."

"I want to leave Jonathan."

Trina doesn't even blink. She just lifts her glass and waits for me to clink mine against hers. "Get a good lawyer, that's all I have to say. Divorce is expensive, but I took a look at the calendar and my life, and I decided I couldn't just wait around for him to die."

The warmth from the wine is flowing through me. I drain my glass and nod at the passing server for another, making a small circle with my finger to indicate he should bring Trina one too. "Did you want him dead?"

"Not enough to kill him," Trina says. "But I guess there's always next week."

"Listen, I want to apologize."

"I already told you—"

"No." I shake my head. "About how I kind of just . . . well, when Val moved back home . . ."

"I get it. She's your bestie. And honestly, Diana, I was in a bad place for a while. It wasn't just you not reaching out. I was kind of holed up in my own little world."

"I should have been there for you."

"You're here for me now," she says.

Fifteen minutes later, Trina and I are in the middle of the dance floor. It's been so long since I moved this way, easy and free. I'm expecting to feel drunk after two glasses of wine, but unlike the past few times I've indulged, I'm no more than slightly buzzed. If anything, I feel a clarity I haven't had in ages.

The music thumps, and my body moves. My husband out of town and my best friend is somewhere else. And I . . . I can let them both go. Not yet sure exactly when or how I'll do it, but for the first time since I got home from the hospital, I feel like I can start moving forward instead of staying stuck in one place.

A young guy moves up behind Trina so smooth there's no way anyone could call her the cougar. He's clearly the predator in this case, but he's charming about it. Hitting on her hard. His friend, shorter, not as cute, looks a little sheepish as he tries to dance with me.

"I'm Matt," he yells over the music.

"Dee," I yell back, because I'm not giving him my real name. No way.

I'm up for the dancing, but Matt and I aren't meshing. Matt tries, bless his heart, by putting his hands on my hips. But we don't move together. He tries to go right, I'm twisting left. I try to let him lead, but he's not very good at it.

Trina and her guy are grinding. I mean, so is almost everyone else, and I'm not sure when that happened, but it's that magic time of the night. The tipping point when everyone's had just enough to drink and it's close enough to closing time that suddenly finding someone to go home with becomes more important than who that person is.

I look for Trina in the crowd. She's sucking face with her dance partner. I wave Matt away when the song changes and push my way through the crowd. In the shadows around the back edge of the bar, I take a breath of cooler air. I type a text to Trina to let her know where I am.

They say in dreams you can't read or make out numbers, and if you ever wonder if you're asleep and dreaming or awake, just try to read something. *So, am I dreaming,* I think as I hit the small arrow to send the message to my friend. I must be dreaming, because I look up to see the shadows move and shift next to me, revealing someone standing there.

It's Cole.

CHAPTER TWENTY-SIX

Cole

I'd been watching Diana for the past hour or so. Drinking with her friend. Then dancing. I wanted to punch that little punk in the face for trying to make the moves on her, even though I couldn't blame him. I hadn't intended to approach her tonight, just watch, but when she made a beeline for me, I figured it was fate. A swath of red and blue light washes over us for a moment, lighting up her face.

"Cole," she says, loud enough for me to hear her over the blast of music. Her teeth shine purple-white. "Hi!"

I lean close enough to say into her ear, "Hey, Diana. Fancy meeting you here."

"I'm out with my friend!" Her breath is warm, fruity with wine.

"Hey!" Her friend, breathless, appears and gives me a look, but only a quick one. She turns to Diana. "Are you all right?"

"Yeah, I'm okay. Where's your boy toy?" Diana says with a grin.

Her friend gives me another swift glance. "He's waiting for me."

"Go," Diana tells her. "I'm going to head home. Oh, Trina, this is Cole. We took a painting class together."

Trina's gone in the next minute, leaving me and Diana alone.

Diana's lips move, but I can't hear her. She tries again. "I asked you if you're here alone!"

"Oh. Yeah. My buddy just left. I was about to leave too." The lie slides out of me, smooth as silk, so neatly I should feel bad about it, except in the case of lies, I never really do.

I follow her outside, where our breaths make smoke. Her teeth chatter. She's only wearing a thin top and a short skirt. I shrug out of my jacket without a second thought and hang it gently on her shoulders.

"I was going to call for a car. You know. A Ryde." Her voice is loud out here. Echoing.

"It'll be a twenty-minute wait for a car. I'll drive you," I tell her. "I only had one beer before my buddy had to go. Really, Diana, it's freaking freezing out here. Let me give you a ride."

She nods then and follows me to the Mustang. I turn the heat on high to stop her shivering. We sit in the parking lot, staring toward the front entrance of the bar. I can smell her perfume and the wine on her breath.

"I don't want to go home," Diana says.

CHAPTER TWENTY-SEVEN

Diana

"Where do you want to go?" Cole asks.

"How about your place?"

Is it the wine buzz that's already fading? Is it the way he smells, the cologne I've grown so used to, the faintest hint of cigarettes? Is it the coffee-not-dates and the way he makes me laugh?

Is it revenge?

I don't know my reasons for asking this of Cole, but he must have his own reasons for agreeing because he puts the car in drive and heads out of the parking lot without so much as a raise of his eyebrows. I lean forward and twist on the radio. I expect classic rock, but I get classical.

"Schubert? You listen to Schubert?" I lean back and look at him.

Cole glances at me before looking back at the road. His fingers tighten on the wheel. "Yeah. It's a CD. It was a gift."

"I love Schubert," I say and fall silent as the sounds of the cello fill the car. "The cello is my favorite instrument."

Grit spatters the underside of the car as Cole drives. Schubert's melody surrounds us. I can't blame this on being drunk, and really, I don't want to have an excuse. I'm making this choice. I know where it's going to lead. I should feel bad or guilty about it, but I don't.

Cole lives in a double-wide trailer on a large lot a couple miles out of town in the opposite direction from my house. Probably about twenty minutes away, longer if you get stuck at the train tracks with a train going by. I haven't been on this side of town in years, and I tell him so.

Cole's laugh is rough as he turns off the ignition. "No reason to visit the wrong side of the tracks, huh?"

As if on cue, the train howls. We both laugh. With the heat off, the car is getting cold fast. I have a moment in which I think about asking him to turn it back on, to drive me home instead. But then he's got his car door open, and the cold is rough, like a slap, and I've got my door open too.

Then we are inside his house, and it's warm, and before I can think about stopping myself, I let him close the door behind us, and when he turns, I grab the front of his shirt with my better hand and pull him closer. I push up on my toes to offer him my mouth, so I can't be sure who starts the actual kiss, only that it goes on and on and on, until Cole lets out a low moan and pushes me back against the door, and I cry out. Not so much because it hurts . . . but because it could.

"Oh shit, Diana. I'm sorry." He pulls away from the kiss. His face is flushed, his eyes bright. His mouth is wet, and the sight of it sends sparkling sizzles all through me.

"It's okay. It just aches if I'm not careful."

We stare at each other. I'm breathing hard. So is he. I want him, and I'm not going to pretend otherwise.

"Can I get you a drink?" He backs up a step.

The moment is getting lost, but I'm not about to force it. I don't know how to navigate this business of beginning an affair, and to be honest I'm not sure I intend for this to be more than a single night. Can you call a one-night stand an affair? I have no idea.

"Sure. Water, please." My laugh is self-conscious, and I realize I don't want him to think he's taking advantage of me.

I take the chance to look around his place as I follow him through the tidy but sparsely furnished living room and a small, equally neat but empty dining room. His galley kitchen is decorated in hues of beige and forest green, with red accents in the wallpaper border.

"Roosters?" I ask with a small chuckle.

Cole looks at me over his shoulder as he opens the fridge. "They came with the place. I keep meaning to redecorate, but then I always figure I'm not going to be here much longer, and I never get around to it."

"Oh, you . . . you think you're moving? Away?" I take the cold can of seltzer he hands me. Pink grapefruit. That's my favorite.

"Always thinking of moving away," he says.

I crack the top of the can and sip, meeting his gaze before I speak. "But you haven't."

"Haven't so far, nope."

"What keeps you around?" The seltzer's fizz is crisp and delicious.

Cole doesn't answer me at first. He leans against the counter, both hands gripping it behind him. He licks his lower lip like he's tasting me on his mouth. The idea of it sends another series of shivers through me. I don't want anything else to drink, but suddenly I am so, so thirsty.

"A job?" I ask, to break the silence. "Family?"

He doesn't answer.

"A woman," I say with a small hitch in my voice that I hate because it gives away too much.

"It's always a woman, isn't it?"

I put my can on his small kitchen table. I want to step closer to him, but now I'm a little too shy. "If you have someone, why am I here?"

"Because you asked me to bring you here," Cole replies in a low voice.

Tension crackles between us. Only one, two, maybe three steps at most would put me in his arms again. Neither of us moves.

"What would she think about that?" I manage to say.

Cole's lips press together, like my question gives him a pain. "She wouldn't give it any thought at all."

"You broke up?"

He's silent.

"She broke it off?"

"It ended," Cole says, "but neither of us wanted it to. It was circumstances. Shit luck. That's all."

"My husband is sleeping with my best friend." I want him to know this. I want him to understand that I have a reason for being here, that I'm not the sort of woman to have an affair without justification. "I keep waiting for him to leave me for her. I think he would have already except that I had the accident, and now he feels obligated to stay. That's how it feels to me anyway. Maybe that's just my own projection."

"Why don't *you* leave *him*?" Cole's tone is rough.

"I used to think it was because I loved him. Isn't that why people usually stay?"

"What about now?"

Now? Now I'm not sure I have an answer, especially standing here in another man's house far too late at night while my husband is out of town.

"Money. Some people stay for the kids. I stayed for the bank account." I can't tell by his expression if he's disgusted with me or sympathetic. "Here's what the bridal magazines never tell you. You can be alone *in* a marriage, or you can be alone out of one. Sometimes, the only difference is where you get to go on vacation. I have a very comfortable life, financially, and I used to think that would be enough."

"But you don't anymore?"

"I'm done, but I can't leave yet. If I can prove that he's maintained a long-term physical and emotional relationship with someone else, I can clean him out. I don't yet have all the proof I need." I don't say this with any kind of pride. I signed that prenup thinking it would protect me. I never dreamed it would end up like this.

Cole's face is still impassive, but at least I don't think I've repulsed him. "And if he decides to leave you before you get it?"

"Then he wins," I say. "I have to be the one to bring the first accusation."

"What if he finds out about this?"

"This," I say as I take a step toward him, "is no proof of an emotional relationship, and it's not at all long term."

Cole takes the next step toward me. "And what if that changes?"

"I'm here now. That's all I can tell you, Cole. That's all I can think about right this minute."

We each take that final step. The kiss this time is softer, sweeter. His hands go easily to the curve of my hips, where they fit just right. When he breaks the kiss, he lets his forehead rest on mine. His eyes are closed. Mine aren't, and I swear I can count each of his eyelashes, so much darker than the hair on his head or even the red-gold scruff of his beard.

"Open your eyes," I whisper.

He does. They are the color of whiskey in a crystal glass held up in front of the light. A thin rim of green surrounds his pupils, gone wide and dark. Cole's eyes are beautiful, and I lose myself in them.

"Bedroom?" he asks.

I nod. For a moment I'm convinced he's going to sweep me off my feet and carry me there, and as romantic and sexy as that sounds, my entire body tenses at the thought of how it would hurt. I sigh, relieved, when instead, he guides me by the small of my back through the dining room and living room, and down the hall toward a big bedroom at the end of it.

The only light comes from the hall, but I can see a king-sized bed, neatly made. Pleated shades are drawn over the windows. A mirror set over an antique dresser reflects light and our shadows as he leads me to the bed. He whisks away the comforter to reveal white sheets. Flannel, I feel when he gently, gently lays me down.

We work together to get out of our clothes. He is careful of my arms and shoulders, and I am conscious of how much he's paying attention to make sure that nothing hurts me. When we are both naked, he tugs the comforter up and over us as he settles between my legs. I feel the hot length of him against my belly.

We are kissing, kissing, kissing. It's sweet and hot and delicious. His mouth traces a pattern of kisses along my jaw, my throat, over my breasts. I gasp at the tug of his lips on my nipples. Lower, Cole slides his tongue along my ribs. Over the scars from my surgery, which are still pink and ugly but no longer hurt. He pauses to touch the one directly beneath my ribs with his fingertip.

"Gallbladder," I say in a low voice. "The night of the car accident, I was driving myself to the hospital with a gallbladder attack."

He kisses me again. Harder this time. One big hand moves to my rear, and he tugs to slide me beneath him again. His hand moves between my thighs, where his questing fingers find the perfect spot without effort.

Everything Cole does is perfect. He has me on the edge in minutes. He moans into my open mouth. I want him inside me, but before I can so much as mention it, he rolls off me and fumbles in the nightstand. He kneels in front of me to tear open the condom and put it on. Then he's between my legs again, filling me, and I gasp at the surprise and pleasure of it.

Time slows as the desire builds. I'm not sure how exactly he's managing it, but he's moving inside me while kissing, and his hand is between us, stroking in perfect time. I am mindless, but not without a voice, even if I can only manage gasps and groans and finally, at the end, his name.

We finish together, and I am astounded at that and how good it was. Cole's face is buried against my neck. He's holding his weight mostly off me, which I appreciate, but I put my arms around his back anyway to hold him close. He's warm and smells like sex, and in that moment, I am fully content in a way I haven't been in a long, long time.

When he finally rolls to the side to lay on his back next to me, I'm so lazy and comfortable that I don't want to move. I have to, though. I need the toilet and I want to rinse out the taste of stale wine from my mouth. And even though I know I'll be going home to an empty house, I would like to take a shower before I do.

"Towels are in the closet," Cole says sleepily. "Do you want me to get you one . . .?"

I lean to kiss him lightly. "No. I'll be fine."

His bathroom is clean, something I note and appreciate. In the small closet tucked between the shower/tub and the wall, I find a stack of plush navy-blue towels. I pull one out, shifting the pile, and a crinkly manila envelope shifts with it, tipping forward. I catch it before it can fall off the shelf, but not before the contents begin to slip free of the flap.

Money.

Lots of money.

Embarrassed, I look over my shoulder to make sure Cole hasn't suddenly materialized behind me and caught me snooping. I heard the low rumble of a snore, but my heart's still racing. I tuck the money back inside as neatly as I can and push it back into the place alongside the towels.

I don't wash in the shower so much as rinse. I'm done in a few minutes and dry myself quickly. At his sink, I use my finger and some of his toothpaste to brush my teeth, and then I cup my hand beneath the faucet to catch some cold water. I take several swallows. I'm not buzzed anymore, but I can't tell if the hangover is starting or if I'm just exhausted because it's so late.

I stare at my reflection, trying to see if I look like something's changed. Side to side, I turn my face. I don't look any different.

But nothing feels the same.

CHAPTER TWENTY-EIGHT

Cole

I ask Diana if she wants to spend the night, but I'm not surprised when she asks if I'm okay to take her home instead. She does let me make her cinnamon toast, though. Her hair is a mess, and her mascara is smudged under her eyes, but she's still so gorgeous it makes me want to take her back to bed again. It makes me want to tell her everything, all the truth of us.

"I love cinnamon toast," she says.

I know she does. The same way I know her favorite seltzer. Her favorite classical composer. The scent of her perfume and the worst thing she ever did in her life, and so much more.

"Cole," Diana says, catching me daydreaming. "This wasn't a mistake."

"I didn't think it was. I thought maybe you would, though. Glad to know you don't."

She finishes the toast and dusts her hands into the sink. Her lips glisten with sugar, and when she licks them, my cock twitches. She rinses the sink when she's finished, and even though I hadn't even come close to forgetting it, at her consideration of my space I am stunned once again at how fucking much I love her.

"But I don't want you to think that I think it's okay to be unfaithful," she says.

I know she doesn't. She'd said the same words to me already, after the first time we went to bed together. I guess nothing has changed.

"No. Of course not. But sometimes it's justified," I tell her.

Diana frowns. "You can always justify your own bad choices. That's what people do."

"So . . . we aren't going to see each other again, then? Is that it?" I keep my voice calm, even though I think it will kill me to have touched her only to lose her again.

"No. We're going to see each other. If you want to. I'm a big girl. I make my decisions. I'm just not promising you anything, that's all. I mean, if there was anything you even wanted me to promise." She lifts her chin, her voice a little strained. She meets my gaze head-on, though.

She's going to hate me when she learns the truth, but for now, I can just . . . have this. Can't I?

"I'll take you home now," I tell her, even though I don't want to. I want to keep her here with me.

Forever.

CHAPTER TWENTY-NINE

Valerie

AUGUST, TWO SUMMERS AGO

I'd stayed in this motel before. Back in high school, the kids with the fake IDs would rent a couple of adjoining rooms, and we'd party with wine coolers and cheap beer. Someone would lose their virginity. Someone would pass out in the tub. The motel hadn't changed very much since then, but it was both cheap and the only option in town, especially since I didn't want to stay at my dad's house even for the day or two I planned to stay.

I didn't want to be there at all, but when your dad calls and says he's dying, you either rush to him because you love him and want to spend time with him or, in my case, so you can hope to be there to see it happen. As it turned out, he wasn't as close to death as he'd wanted me to believe, but it had come out that he didn't have a will or an executor, no medical power of attorney, or any of that. I'd finished the final paperwork with him earlier that day, and I'd be heading back to Brooklyn the next, as fast as I could go. He claimed I was just there to make sure I got his money, what little was left of it. He was right.

When I headed outside to get some ice from the machine tucked into a narrow alcove between two of the rooms, I saw a woman going into the room next to mine. I hadn't seen her since I was in middle school, but I recognized her anyway. Diana's mother. For a second, I almost called out to her, but she'd already closed the door.

Diana had told me her mother had come back around a few weeks ago, asking for, if not a fresh start to a relationship, at least forgiveness for the way she'd treated her in the past. We'd traded texts about it, but I'd been so busy dealing with what was going on with my dad, traveling back and forth, and also with my job, that we hadn't managed to connect beyond that.

She'd been happy, though. Cautious, but willing to see what might happen if she gave her mother a chance. I made a note to give Diana a call in the morning, before I left town. If I couldn't make at least an hour or two for my bestie, I'd be a really shit friend.

Shouting from the room next door woke me in the middle of the night. Two raised voices, both female, but before I could rap on the wall and tell them to shut the fuck up, they both went quiet. I was so exhausted even the hard motel bed couldn't keep me awake, but a thought jolted me out of sleep—Diana was next door.

I couldn't be sure it was her voice. I'd been thinking about her when I fell asleep, and maybe even dreaming about calling her. The thought wouldn't leave me, though. I got out of bed and pressed my ear to the wall.

Nothing.

Moments later, the door slammed hard enough to rattle the pictures on the wall. I jumped back, my heart pounding, and went to the window to pull the curtain aside—just enough so I could see out, but not enough that anyone could have seen me watching.

The parking lot was narrow and angled, with one-way entrances and exits. The dark sedan pulling out onto the highway looked boxy, but I couldn't be sure what kind it was. It might have been a Volvo, the car Diana drove, but it also might not.

I'd turned off my ringer, but my phone vibrated with a call. My dad was dying. I should come right away. I packed myself up as fast as I could and got out of there.

He didn't die that night.

But, as it turned out, Diana's mother did.

CHAPTER THIRTY

Diana

Running.

I am running. Branches slap at my face, bruising. I can't bat them away. My hands are full of something I can't risk dropping.

Running. I am not running—my burden is too heavy. I am dragging. Step by step, through the night. I can't see anything but the trees.

The smell of earth. The taste of rain. On my hands and knees, I dig and dig and dig. I make a hole.

I put something inside it.

I cover it up.

Pain. Burning. Ripping. I am doubled over, gripping my side, upright. It's my heart. My heart is breaking, I think. No, I am dying.

I am dying, and it's not fair. I'm not ready to go. I just found . . . something. I just got here, where I am, and now I am going to die.

The pain means I'm going to die, and I scream out.

* * *

Screaming, I wake.

The blankets are tangled around my feet. I've sweated through my boxers and tank top, and my hair is a sticky, soggy mess. My mouth is dry, but the bitter acid taste of the orange juice I gulped down at five this morning when Cole brought me home lingers at the back of my tongue.

The house is quiet. Jonathan isn't due home until late tonight. I hear a ticking clock. Beneath the warm blankets, in my cozy cocoon, I don't want to get out of bed. I did not wake up feeling as though I'd been dumped in a ditch. Nothing hurts. I luxuriate in this simple feeling of *no pain.*

Because that's what it comes down to, isn't it? Until we have pain, we don't truly know how to appreciate the lack of it. I'm still tired, but no wonder. The clock tells me I've only had about three hours of sleep. When I swing my legs over the edge of the bed, it takes my feet a few seconds to find the floor. I yawn, hard, and rub my eyes. I think with longing of my pillow and falling back to sleep, but there is a kind of tired that lends itself to dreams, and then there's the sort that is better suffered until you can get through it. That's this kind. But nothing actively hurts in this moment, and if anything, I'm in a happy kind of daze. Maybe it's the shift I felt last night, that I'm finally ready to take the next steps. Maybe my injuries, at last, are healed enough for me to get back to a normal life.

Maybe it's Cole.

I wait for guilt, but feel none. Only a rising warmth that spreads up my throat and into my face. I put my chilly hands on my cheeks to cool them and allow myself to think about last night for as long as it takes my heart to stop thumping. That's a few minutes, at least. It's cold enough in the room to help, too. I use the app on my phone to check the thermostat, which has been set to fifty-eight degrees. The HVAC guy said both the furnace and the thermostat were fine, so I check the program, which somehow has been scheduled to swing between freezing and broiling temperatures without any seeming regard to time of day or year or anything that would make sense. Then I take a minute to scroll through the app's history.

There's no way to tell if someone's been changing the program or resetting the temperatures, either manually or remotely. All I can see is how many hours a day the furnace ran. For good measure, I change the pin code to something unguessable and random.

No smell of coffee greets me, which tells me that Harriett is still giving me the silent treatment. I have enjoyed the past few days without her, but I'm going to have to patch things up with her sooner or later. No matter how irritated I've been, she's the only mother I have, and I don't know how much longer I'm going to have her. Once I leave her son, she will probably never speak to me again.

My stomach rumbles. I'm craving pancakes. They're usually too sweet and rich for me, but something about a sugary carb overload appeals to me right now.

On my way to the fridge, my feet go out from under me. Liquid on the floor, cold and slippery. I try to catch myself on a kitchen chair, but I miss it. I hit the floor with my right shoulder and the side of my head.

I don't hear it break again, but *ohgodohgodohmyfuckinggod* I feel it.

My right clavicle is an inferno of agony. I sprawl in a puddle that soaks my robe. It stinks of white wine, and although I'm not yet able to get up from the floor, from here I can see the edge of the kitchen table and the bottle hanging over it.

A red haze threatens. When it passes, so has my sense of time. I can't struggle upright without hurting my collarbone, but I roll, gormless and awkward, as best I can toward my left. My feet swim against nothing. My fingers curl into the tiles and slip without purchase. There's an entire bottle of wine on the floor, wine I did not open and did not drink.

I make it to my left side. Then to my knees. I sag, breathing hard. The pain is not fading. It won't. It's going to rise up and up and up until it kills me this time. Or I will just wish it had. And then, after another few breaths, it eases. Still agony, but I will not let it keep me down.

Standing at the counter, my right arm cradled against me, I see a wine glass shattered in the sink. The pitcher of orange juice I remember gulping from is still on the counter. Only an inch or so of juice remains.

I did not break that glass. I did not spill that wine.

I left my phone upstairs. We have no landline. I cannot face the climb right now. I fumble open the cabinet, looking for the prescription bottles that have been in there every fucking day since October, but they are all gone. My purse hangs over the back of a kitchen chair, but it, too, is devoid of pain pills. I dig in the trash with my left hand, tossing aside junk mail and dirty paper towels, but I can't see any orange bottles. I threw them all away just days ago. Jonathan is the one who takes out the trash, and he's been gone. They should still be in there. I dump the garbage can and sort through coffee grounds and stinking leftovers. Nothing. They aren't there.

I hear the low cry I make, but it sounds like someone else. Or some*thing* else, some wounded animal. I don't sound human anyway, and it feels like that's what I have become. Something mad and feral.

The front door opens. Footsteps. Harriett, in the kitchen doorway.

"Oh dear," she says. "Diana. What have you done?"

CHAPTER THIRTY-ONE

Cole

I know I shouldn't expect Diana to call or text me the morning after. Or ever. That doesn't stop me from checking my phone when I first wake up.

Putting the tracking app on her phone was bad. Using it is so much worse, but that doesn't stop me from doing it again now. I expect the small blue dot to hover over her address, but it's moving. She's driving. I have half a hot second of hope that she's coming to see me, but that's just fucking stupid.

I close the app. Then delete it. It won't stop me from reloading it, or logging in again, but for now I'm at least attempting to not be a garbage human being. I'm a lot of things, and a lot of them are bad, but this is going too far. No matter what we agreed to in the past, this is wrong.

Diana Sparrow does not do what she doesn't want to do. I know that because I know her. So last night wasn't something I forced on her. She was on board. God, was she ever. But I did orchestrate the situation. My reasons for it are different now from they were the first time around, but does it matter?

It's all a fucking mess. I need to leave her alone, let her figure out her life and get divorced. Or not. Whatever she chooses, I shouldn't be in the middle of it.

I still haven't figured out what to do with her money.

CHAPTER THIRTY-TWO

Diana

HIGH SCHOOL

Val's house stunk like puke and piss and shit. Unwashed sheets. Food left to rot on dishes all over the house. The smell was enough to make me cough and gag as soon as I got through the front door. I hadn't been here in a couple weeks, but even so, how did it get so bad so fast?

"Val?" I called out in a low voice.

She'd missed a week of school at this point. She was going to need more than a doctor's note, which I was sure she didn't have. If she was sick, it was nothing any kind of medicine could cure.

Her dad's truck wasn't in the driveway, but I was still careful. Gino Delagatti had threatened to run me off his property with a shotgun before. I wasn't sure he'd actually do it, but I wasn't going to take the chance. He used to like me, but after Val's mom died, he started hating me as much as he hated his daughter.

"Val!"

I heard a small, shifting noise from the bathroom at the end of the hall. I didn't want to go in there. The last time I'd seen my mother, she was overdosing in the bathtub, one wrist only half slit but more than enough blood. I couldn't find Val like that. I just couldn't.

But I had to because if Val was dying, I had to stop her. So I ran, down the hall, past the open bedroom doors. I slammed open the bathroom door so hard it bounced against the wall, the knob punching a hole in the flowered wallpaper.

Val sat on the toilet, her head in her hands. She wore an oversized T-shirt. Her panties were around her ankles. I saw the splashes of blood everywhere, and for an instant, I was sure she'd tried to kill herself. But then I knew it was just her period. She got them bad, much worse than me.

"I ran out of tampons." Her voice was hoarse. Dark circles under her eyes made her look like death. "I only have those big fucking diaper pads."

"I have some in my purse. Why don't you get in the shower? I'll bring them."

She didn't fight me about it. Only nodded. Slow, like it hurt her. I turned on the hot water and waited until she got off the toilet. She stepped out of her panties and took her shirt off, all so slowly. Her body bloomed with bruises. I could count her ribs. She'd lost so much weight since her mom died, even though it had only been a few weeks. She needed to see a doctor.

I wondered if she regretted what we did. She said she wouldn't, but people don't always know what's going to happen. You do things you think you can deal with, but sometimes it turns out you just can't.

"Val." I could only manage a whisper.

She turned, stepping into the tub. The water hit her, so she winced. It splashed out beyond the curtain she hadn't yet drawn.

Then she started to cry.

I got in the shower with her. It was all I could do. My friend, my sister. The other half of me. She'd lost her mother, and I didn't know what to say or do to make it better; I didn't think it could ever get better.

"I love you," I whispered over and over. "I love you."

"Promise me that we will always be there for each other."

"I promise."

"Nobody will ever come between us, Diana. Promise!"

"I promise." I meant it. She was my best friend. How could anyone ever come between us?

* * *

This is the ER where I took Val the day we cried together in the shower. It's the same ER they brought me after the car accident. The same hospital where Val's mom died. Lebanon's not a big town, and there's only the one.

"They really should just take you right back." Harriett looks uneasily around the room, particularly at a Hispanic family trying to deal with their wailing toddler.

Agony has divested me of any courtesies I'm able to manage. I mutter a comment about how I'm not going to get cooties, and she should really just stop worrying about brown people.

"What's that?"

I shake my head. "Never mind. It's fine, Harriett. I'm not going to die."

Fortunately, that's when they're able to take me back to a room. I sit there for another hour while Harriett paces and complains, until I ask her if she'll run out and get me something to drink. I really just want her to go have a smoke already, because it's clear she's jonesing for it, and I'm about to bite her head off.

The doctor who comes in to see me while she's gone is young. Dr. Banerjee is handsome and knows it, and I'm still barely loopy enough to appreciate the way he tries to set me at ease with a broad grin. He calls for an X-ray. That takes another hour. I send Harriett out for another drink.

Right before noon, Dr. Banerjee comes back to see me. "Some good news. There's no new break."

"I felt it . . ." I shake my head. The meds have worn off. With my arm in a sling, the pain's manageable. "I thought I felt it."

"From what I can tell, it's simply still in the healing process. This is the worst of the breaks, yes?" He gestures at both my clavicles. "Common in clavicle breaks sustained during car accidents. The seatbelt, you know, where it crosses over. You were the passenger?"

"I was driving. Are you sure it's not rebroken?"

He gives me a curious look, but then smiles. Charming. "Comparing it to your previous X-rays, there's no new break. So when you fell, it looks as though it aggravated the existing injury."

"Is it going to take me another ten weeks to get out of this thing?" I point at the sling, defeated.

AFTER ALL I'VE DONE

"It might. But it might be much sooner than that. Just be careful. No more ice skating," he scolds. "Or spilling wine on the floor. That's a waste of good wine."

I manage a laugh that doesn't sound too forced. "I'll see what I can do."

"Let's get you out of here. Your mother-in-law is going to drive you home? It's going to be a bit of time before you're able to get behind the wheel again."

I groan. "Great. Yeah, she drove me here."

"I'll make sure all the papers are waiting for you at the desk." He pauses, the wide grin fading a bit to be replaced with some concern. "Mrs. Sparrow . . . you do realize that you can't drink while you're taking the medications I'm going to prescribe for you. It could be very dangerous. So if you're not going to be able to stop yourself from drinking alcohol, I'm going to have to withhold this prescription for something less effective."

My laugh fades away when I see that he's not joking. "I like a glass of wine now and then, doctor, but I'm not an alcoholic. Do you think I'm a problem drinker?"

He presses his lips together. "Your mother-in-law shared with me that she had a concern when she discovered the spill that led to this accident."

Stunned, I blink rapidly. "If I couldn't stop myself from drinking it, there wouldn't have been anything left to spill."

Dr. Banerjee nods after a moment. "I suppose that's right. Well, you take care. I don't want to see you back here again."

I flash back to being eight years old. My mother telling the pediatrician that I'd fallen off the swing set and broken my wrist. In reality, I'd tripped over some of her painting supplies, and it wasn't broken, only sprained, but she'd convinced the doctor to give me some kind of pills. I wasn't the one who took them.

"Do you think I'm faking this to get more drugs?"

It's the wrong thing to say. If he didn't think so before, he probably does now. But Banerjee is an overworked ER doc who sees drug-seeking patients all the time. He has to know I'm not that.

"If I truly thought you were drug seeking, I would not prescribe you more," Dr. Banerjee says kindly. "But I'm happy to give you some information on support resources, Mrs. Sparrow, if you think you might need some."

"I'm fine," I snap, then repeat it more softly. "I'm fine."

At the desk, I sign a stack of papers. I pull out my credit card to take care of the co-pay. It's declined. Embarrassed, I offer my debit card. It, too, is declined. When I get the fraud alert text seconds later regarding the credit card, I reply with a bold "YES" to indicate that the charge was in fact mine.

"Try it again, please."

The credit card goes through, no problem. I'm disturbed about the debit card, though. I rarely use it. In fact, I rarely use the account it's linked to. I've had access, of course, but Jonathan has always paid the bills and kept control over the accounts. As with every other freaking app on my phone, my thumbprint isn't opening the one for the credit union. I'll have to wait until I get home to log in on the laptop.

"Let's just pop into the pharmacy and pick up your pills." Harriett glances at me as we leave. "You look upset."

"It's my debit card—never mind. It's okay." I'm not going to get into my finances with her again.

At home, I suffer her fussing, but because I haven't been to the grocery store, there's nothing much for her to make for the lunch I don't really want to eat. She settles on canned soup and saltine crackers. She puts the bowl at my place on the table, along with two pills and a glass of water. She'd already mopped up the spill for me before we left for the ER.

"You should take your medicine with food," she says, "so you don't upset your stomach. I'll go to the store for you. You might have mentioned it while we were out."

"I just wanted to get home, Harriett."

She nods. "Of course, honey. Eat your soup and take those pills. Then take a little nap. I called Jonathan to let him know what happened, but he didn't answer."

I take the pills but manage only a few bites of the soup before I excuse myself to go upstairs to grab my laptop. She doesn't follow me up there, thank God, but calls up the stairs that she's going to the store. For me to take a nap. She won't bother me when she comes back. She'll just let herself in.

Of course she will.

It takes a few minutes for me to log in to the credit union account, longer than usual because I can type only with one hand, I'm fuzzy with pain meds, and I have to reset my password.

My checking account has only the minimum balance in it, which is why the card was declined at the hospital. I haven't looked at this account in months, and why would I? Jonathan deals with it. There's supposed to be plenty of money in it. I check the savings, the money market, the vacation shares. There's money there, but not as much as I would have thought.

There's his paycheck, regularly deposited. Utility bills paid with auto-payments. The mortgage, the credit card, our streaming accounts, all there. I glance over the cash withdrawals with a frown. Of course he uses cash for all the things he doesn't want me to see listed on the credit card bills. So, where's the money?

My payout isn't there.

To be honest, I can't remember if the payout ever hit my account. That would have happened sometime in June, during the months I can't remember. It's just the sort of screwup I'm used to from GenTech.

I toss off a quick email to my contact in payroll at GenTech. It bounces back within seconds. No longer with the company and no forwarding information. Damn it. I'm going to have to do more research into who to contact, because they owe me that money, and it should have been deposited months ago. I'm not surprised I might have to chase them down, though. There's a reason why I left instead of moving along with them during the restructuring, and it was just this kind of thing.

Jonathan won't be home until at least midnight tonight. A little less than twelve hours away. Harriett thinks I'm napping, and I can't drive myself anyway, so I thumb open the app to call for a Ryde.

I can't stay in this house right now.

It takes me a couple tries to get the message just right, no typos. I send it.

I'd like to see you again.

In seconds, three little dots appear. Cole is typing. I hold my breath, waiting.

Anytime.

Now?

Please, comes his answer. *Yes.*

CHAPTER THIRTY-THREE

Cole

"Tell me about the first person who ever betrayed you," she says.

This isn't the sort of question I'm used to being asked in bed. Or anywhere. The women I used to get with usually aren't much for asking questions that have any kind of depth to them. I sit up to look at Diana, but the sight of her naked body has left me unable to talk for a few moments.

"Cole," she says and pushes my foot with hers.

Her breast, the one I can see beyond the sling, jiggles a little. My dick twitches again. Does she know what she's doing to me? She has to, but she doesn't seem to notice.

"The first person who ever betrayed me? Hell. I don't know. You mean like a girlfriend?"

Leaning, I pull open the nightstand drawer and take out a pack of smokes and my pop's old Zippo. It's older than I am. I don't light up. She doesn't like the smell. But there's a comfort in having the habit right there next to me, where I can at least look at it.

Despite the mid-February cold, my bedroom is sweltering. My furnace is old, but it works hard. I can taste the sweat on my upper lip. See it beading on her forehead. I should get up and turn on the overhead fan to get some air stirring. I can't make myself get off the bed, though. I don't want to move away from her.

"It doesn't have to be a girlfriend. Anyone. Mine," she says, "was my mother. What a cliché, right?"

"The reason things are cliché is because they're true for a lot of people."

She tilts her head. "Yes. You're right. Sometimes I think I tolerate my mother-in-law more than I would otherwise because I'm just not sure what's normal for a mother to do. You know? I mean, mine was pretty awful, but at least she had the decency to get out of my life when I was in sixth grade. She did try showing up again later. By that time, I was married. And—stupid me—I gave her a chance, and surprise, surprise, she went and messed it all up again. Just up and disappeared without a word. It was weeks before I found out she'd died of an overdose."

"But I thought—" I cut myself off before I can finish.

I lost my mom in middle school. She'd told me that, very specifically, a couple times. I had assumed her mother had died and that it wasn't much of a loss. But then, I'm not very sympathetic toward druggie winos who abuse their kids. Once, she'd even told me she'd found her mother during a suicide attempt. Maybe Diana had been deliberately blurring the facts. Maybe she'd just flat-out lied. The thought is unsettling, but I have to remind myself that she's completely capable of it. I'd just always thought it would be about me, not *to* me.

Diana gives me a curious look. "What?"

"I thought maybe you didn't like your mother-in-law. You know, because she was annoying you the day we met."

"She's been better to me than my own ever was. I mean, my own wasn't even my own. I was adopted," Diana adds with a harsh, self-conscious laugh. "Of all the people in the world who could have adopted me, I got stuck with that one? So not-fair. It really wrecked me."

"You don't seem like you're wrecked to me."

She smiles. "No?"

"Nope." I lean forward to kiss her. "Definitely not. Anyway, we all have damage."

Her tongue teases mine. Her breath tastes sweet. She moves away to study my face for a few seconds.

"I worry that I'm still too much like her, no matter how much I don't want to be. How much is nature versus nurture, you know? It's why I decided never to have kids of my own. What if I screw them up as bad as she screwed me up? Or worse." Diana shakes her head. Her voice is low, her gaze shadowed. "I've thought about trying to find out who my birth parents were, but I never have. Even when I worked for Sunny Days and could have looked up my adoption records, I didn't. You want to know why?"

"Tell me."

"I'm afraid my birth parents are even worse than she was," Diana tells me, "and I'd rather not know. Anyway, you haven't answered my question. Who's the first person who ever betrayed you?"

"I guess the first person who betrayed me was a buddy of mine who stole my girl. We were in fourth grade. She was in fifth."

"So," she teases, "you've always had a thing for older women?"

I chuckle. "I guess so."

She leans a little and offers me her mouth. I kiss her. My hands slide over her warm skin.

"Did you forgive him?" Diana whispers.

I'm too caught up in the taste of her to figure out what she means at first, but then I say, "Yeah. I mean, it's not like it mattered in the long run."

"I don't forgive people who betray me. There's something hard in me," she says. "Always has been. Once you've crossed that line, that's it. We're done."

"Is that a warning?"

She looks surprised. "Oh. No. Well, I guess it is, but I didn't mean it as a threat. I was just thinking about what I'm doing here and why I don't feel bad about it. That's all."

There goes the moment when I had intended to look her in the eyes and walk her through all the things she doesn't remember. Plus all the things she never knew. I already have betrayed her, but she doesn't know it yet, and if I'm lucky, she never will.

"Cole," she says in that low, teasing voice with a small smile, "do you plan on betraying me?"

I kiss her again so I don't have to answer that.

"I really like you," Diana whispers against my mouth.

I close my eyes. "I really like you too."

The breath she lets out is a shiver, a shudder, a sigh. "I need to get home. He's due back soon."

Stay rises to my lips, but I swallow it. She can't stay. I should never let her come back here, but I know I will. If she wants me, I won't be able to say no.

CHAPTER THIRTY-FOUR

Diana

The lights are on inside Harriett's apartment when I make it home just past eleven PM. I hold my breath, sure Jonathan's car will be in its bay, and I will be caught out, but I've made it back before him. For all I know, he's gone straight from the airport to Val's place to greet her before coming back here.

At some point, is he just not going to come back here at all?

My fridge is bursting with food, courtesy of my mother-in-law. I'm not hungry. Cole fed me well before driving me home. Both my stomach and my soul.

Anyone who says really good sex can't fix what's wrong has never had really good sex. I went to his house anxious and unsettled. I left it relaxed, feeling like I could handle whatever else life decided to toss my way.

I'm not dumb enough to think this is going to end well. Things like this don't, do they? I'll be caught, and my marriage will end. Or I won't get caught, and Cole and I will come to an impasse, and I'll have to make a choice. Or he'll get tired of me and break my heart. That's the most likely scenario, but right now I'm not going to dwell on that. Right now, I'm tired and I plan to be long asleep before my errant husband gets into bed beside me.

* * *

Blood on my hands. Blood and mud. The stink of it fills me.

160

I did this. I did this thing, this bad thing. And it's going to catch up to me.

I can't get away with it.

* * *

I wake screaming, this time not from the nightmare, but the pain in my shoulder as Jonathan shakes me. "Stop!"

"Sorry, babe. Jesus. What's the matter with you?"

I struggle to sit and point at the sling. "What do you think's the matter with me?"

"Why are you wearing the sling again?" He looks befuddled.

I can see this because he turned on the light. If I were coming home late to my sleeping spouse, I'd leave the light off so as not to wake him up, but I guess that's just me. I work up the spit to say something nasty but swallow my words.

"I slipped this morning. Yesterday morning. Whatever," I say. "Didn't your mother call you to tell you she had to take me to the ER?"

Befuddled, now guilty. "I . . . ah, shit. I saw she called, but you know how she is. I just figured it was something I could hear about when I got home. Are you okay?"

"No. It hurts." I run my tongue over my teeth. My mouth is gummy, sticky, gross. My eyes feel gritty.

"I'm sorry I shook you. I didn't know. You were whimpering," my husband says. "Another nightmare?"

I lean against the headboard and take a few deep breaths. "Yeah. A nightmare."

"Same thing?" He sits on the edge of the bed.

"Yes. No. They're all kind of the same, but different sometimes. It's fine. It's fading now. I can't really recall it. Can you get me a drink?"

"Sure, babe. Sure." He pats my leg gently through the covers and disappears into the bathroom.

I snag my phone up from where it's charging on the nightstand and make sure to mute text notifications from Cole. I'm just setting the phone back when

Jonathan brings me the glass of water from the bathroom. It's cool and welcome, and I thank him.

"What time is it?" I ask, although I was literally just looking at my phone and should have noticed.

"Almost one."

"You're a little later than you said." I don't mean for this to sound accusatory, but it does.

He shrugs. "We got in a little late. The baggage didn't show up right away. I needed gas on the way home."

"It's not an interrogation," I tell him, although I guess maybe it was. A little.

"I'm wiped. I'm going to bed. Do you need anything else?" He pauses. "What did you slip on?"

"Wet patch in the kitchen."

He nods but doesn't ask anything else. Harriett will fill him in, I'm sure. I listen to him in the shower and try to doze back to sleep, but I'm still wide awake when he comes back. He turns off the light. Gets into bed. He doesn't try to kiss me goodnight, thank God.

In minutes, the soft huff of his breathing tells me he's asleep. I try but can't manage to get back there myself. It's not the dull, vibrating throb in my clavicle. It's not the fear of nightmares either. I can't sleep because with Jonathan in it, this bed feels more like a prison than a haven.

I don't turn on the lights when I get up. Even now, I'm kinder to him than he is to me. I take my laptop and go downstairs to make myself a mug of hot herbal tea. My stomach is a little unsettled, maybe from hunger, maybe the pain, maybe just the looming fact that I'm more likely to be divorced by this time next year than I was last year at this time.

I spend some time hunting down and emailing anyone who I think can help me figure out where my money is. Then I set up the camera app again. It takes some fine tuning to get the system reconnected to the Wi-Fi and pulled up on my phone app, but at last I can scroll through every outside camera we have. The feed shows the front door, the side yard, the back yard, and deck. The detached garage and Harriett's apartment.

Harriett is outside on her small porch, smoking. It's one in the morning, and the lights inside her place are off, but the cameras have night vision. She has to be freezing, but she wears no coat. She smokes furiously, the plume a haze in the live video footage.

Against my better judgment, I check the feed's saved footage. It only goes back a couple months. As I figured, it's mostly shots of me, Jonathan, and Harriett coming and going, with the occasional package drop-off. The mail is delivered to the bottom of the driveway, so no regular visit from the postal truck. I find the couple clips of me arriving home too late for explanation and delete them.

Then, from a night weeks ago, a figure in a hoodie creeps along the side of the house, from Harriett's driveway. No car that I can see. I can't see their face but I don't have to. The shot of Jonathan leaving the house to chase after them tells me enough.

Val came to my house in the middle of the night, my husband ran out to meet her, and I had no idea. On Christmas night. A shiver runs through me, twisting my stomach.

What else happened that I don't know about?

I scroll through everything else, all the way back to the first saved video. There's nothing unusual. Back to more recent clips.

Wait. Something I almost missed. In this clip, there's a hint of something moving by the back deck, going inside the house. Definitely a person, although I can't see what they're wearing, the gender—nothing. They navigate the yard by creeping around the house without setting off the motion-sensitive floodlights—so they must know what they're doing. They go in but don't come out.

Revulsion closes my throat. He's been sneaking her into our house. My house, with me inside it, sleeping. Fucking her where? On our living room sofa? In the basement, on the pool table?

As I'm fighting back a rush of sick fury, an email pings in on my phone. It's from the final lawyer I was able to track down. I guess I'm not the only one suffering insomnia. She has the name of the person who took over the archives of the lawyer who made the prenup.

Finally.

I don't plan to kill my husband, but I am going to slaughter him.

163

CHAPTER THIRTY-FIVE

Cole

LAST SUMMER

I couldn't take her money. I mean, I wouldn't take it. Diana was still talking, but for me, the conversation stopped the second she oh-so-casually dropped the line about giving me the cash.

"No." I stopped her before she could keep going.

She paused. Stared. "No? Why not?"

"I'm not taking your money."

"You already took some of my money, Cole."

"I'm not taking *this* money."

"You're not taking it. You're just keeping it for me," she said and added with that little teasing laugh I usually loved but in that moment despised, "Payment for services rendered."

The joke wasn't funny. She apologized, but it was the first time that we both realized how serious all of this was and how seriously we should be taking it.

"You know I would never do it for the money. I'd do it for free." I knew that in the end, I'd do whatever she wanted me to do.

"I just need it to be kept safe, away from him." Diana stood at the window in my living room, where she tugged aside the curtain to stare out into the late afternoon sunshine. "What's the worst thing you ever did in your life?"

I chuckled. "I've done too many bad things to count. I couldn't tell you what's the worst."

She twisted to look over her shoulder at me. "Have you ever killed someone?"

"No." I paused. "Have you?"

She flicked the curtains shut, dimming the room. "Letting someone die is not the same as killing them."

"No. I guess it's not."

Diana drew in a breath. "I hardly ever feel bad about anything, Cole. I'm not sure if that makes me a bad person."

"You're not a bad person."

"When I was in high school, Val's mom was really sick. Cancer. It started in her ovaries and just spread so fast that they couldn't really do much for her. She suffered a lot. She was in and out of treatment, but finally nothing worked. She got sent to palliative care at the end. It really fucked Val up. She couldn't handle it. So I did."

"Sounds like you were a good friend to her. And now she's being a good friend to you," I said.

"She's in love with him," Diana said. "It changes everything."

That was why I took her money. Because everything had changed, and not just for Diana. It had all changed for me too.

CHAPTER THIRTY-SIX

Diana

I have never liked February, but this one sucks more than most. It's cold. It's dark. My not-rebroken-but-still-broken clavicle thrums and whines every time I try to lift my arm.

It's Valentine's Day, and I haven't heard from Cole since the day I had to go to the ER. I've texted him twice. The messages are delivered, but I have no idea if they've been read. It's very obvious that he's not answering them, though, and I think, *Well, fuck. So much for that.*

I'm hardly surprised. He's a young, handsome guy. Why would he want to get tangled up with an older married woman with two bum collarbones and a trunk—no, a boxcar—full of baggage? I can't blame him, but it's always worse to be the one who's dumped. So, I'm cranky. Hurt. Angry.

And Jonathan's made some excuse about a late work meeting.

"On Valentine's Day? What poor planning." I say this over the rim of my coffee mug as he's spooning cereal and soy milk into his mouth.

"I'll make it up to you this weekend, babe."

He's clean-shaven and smelling of cologne. He's wearing his normal work clothes, but that doesn't mean anything. I search his face for any signs that he's lying to me, but there are none. Doesn't matter. I know that he is and . . . I can't bring myself to care. I don't want to spend a lover's holiday with him, and it's just more proof anyway. I finally got a copy of the original prenup agreement. The more lies I can document, the sooner I can turn off the life support to this dying marriage.

He leaves. I check my phone for messages, but there are none. I wait for Harriett's inevitable visit, but this morning she seems to be taking her sweet old time.

I eat a pan of her homemade beef macaroni bake and finish the pot of coffee.

I get an answer from GenTech. The money was paid out months ago, not by direct deposit, but via check. And the check was cashed. By me. They send a screenshot of the canceled check with my signature on it.

What is going on?

In the days after I woke up, my missing memory had pushed me into overwhelming waves of anxiety. Talking to Dr. Levitt had helped, at least until I found out she'd been discussing me with my husband and without my permission or knowledge. The meds had helped too, but eventually, even if I was very aware of how much my situation sucked, I wasn't anxious anymore.

Until today. Now, I pace. My palms are sweaty, but chilly sweat trickles down my spine. I can't breathe.

I have to breathe.

I signed the check. But I did not deposit it into any account I can access. The money is gone. Where is it? What did I do with it?

I can't remember. I can't remember so much, and it's knocking me to my knees.

Where is my mother-in-law? Any other day she'd have been here at the crack of dawn, but today, the day I'm totally losing my mind, she's AWOL. I text her. No answer.

I text my husband. *Please call me.* I don't want to need him right now. It feels weak and wrong, considering everything that's been going on. I don't want to rely on him for anything.

I dial Jonathan's number, but I don't tap the screen to connect the call. I put my phone down. I pace some more. I pick it up again. I take my arm out of the sling. The humming vibration of pain feels distant and soft, there but easily ignored.

Deep breath.

Count to ten, and if I can't make it to ten, at least to five.

Count to five.

Close my eyes.

Panic swells inside me, the rising of a tide driven by a storm. I do close my eyes. I do breathe deeply, again and again. I run through every trick my pony can do, everything Dr. Levitt had ever suggested to quell the anxiety, but I can still feel my fingers curling and releasing into fists at my sides.

My phone pings with a notification. Motion alert at the front door. Harriett gasps in surprise and clutches at her heart when I fling it open before she can.

"Hi," I say. My voice isn't shaking, so there's that. "What's up?"

Harriett's brows rise. "Oh, nothing, honey. Just checking on you."

"I'm fine."

She blinks. "May I come inside?"

I was desperate for her to be here, but now I don't want her. When she gently pushes her way in, guiding me away from the front door, I fight to find the words to tell her to get out. But, defeated, my heart pounding, I just keep breathing instead.

"Are you hungry? It's past lunch." She calls this over her shoulder as she heads for the kitchen.

Food is Harriett's love language.

What is mine?

"Diana! Did you finish the entire pan of beef macaroni bake?"

I have followed her into the kitchen, step by step. "Yes."

"My goodness, that was a lot. It's good to see your appetite is back. How are you feeling?" She bustles around at the sink, starting to wash the pan I'd left in it to soak. "Did you take your meds?"

Before I can answer, she's opened the cabinet to pull out the prescription bottle. Nothing rattles inside. She turns slowly, with a strained smile.

"You've finished them?"

I didn't. I mean, I don't think I did. I can't really remember taking any, but my arm isn't hurting a lot, so maybe I did.

"Yesterday, maybe," I say.

You can see her cat-butt face from space, and I'm surprised the entire universe doesn't get sucked into the black hole she's making with her mouth. I am an awful person. Terrible. Harriett has been nothing but good to me. I am ungrateful.

I should feel bad. I do not. Why do I never feel bad about all the awful, terrible, and horrible things I do or think?

Harriett moves around the kitchen. "Hmm. Well. Why don't you let me make you a grilled ham and cheese and some tomato soup? I'll add bacon, just the way you like it. Although I don't suppose you're hungry after eating all the bake."

Actually, my stomach is empty and complaining, and I press my hand against the rumbling. "Okay."

Where is the money?

I fight another rush of panic.

I sit at the table in front of the bowl of soup and the sandwich. I drag the spoon through it, bring the rich, creamy soup to my mouth. It's good. Harriett's food always is, and I'm suddenly hungry enough to almost gobble it, along with the perfectly toasted and decadently dripping sandwich that she's made with a myriad of cheeses, including bleu. Meat and cheese, meat and cheese, just for me. All for me. I force myself to take small bites and chew thoroughly.

Harriett doesn't eat anything, but I'm used to that. She moves around my kitchen wiping at countertops and emptying the dishwasher. When she pauses to lean against the counter, the twitchy way she slips a lip balm from her pocket to slide across her mouth tells me she hasn't had a cigarette in too long.

My stomach fills quickly, long before I'm finished. When I get up to scrape my bowl into the sink, Harriett reaches to stop me. Creamy pinkish red soup splashes over the back of my hand. It doesn't look like blood, but my stomach twists hard, and I have to blink quickly to clear my vision when it threatens to blur.

"Don't waste it. You might want to eat more later." She pries the bowl from my hand and sets in on the counter so she can pull a glass container from a cupboard. "I'll just put this back in the fridge for you."

I'm not going to eat it later. The fridge and freezer are full of half-eaten meals Harriett has insisted I put away in case I want to eat them later. That doesn't stop her, but neither do I. I step back and let her tuck my sandwich into another container.

When she puts the food into the fridge, I spy the bottle of white wine. Harriett has the smokes she pretends she doesn't need. I'm suddenly craving a drink I don't want to admit I want. I wait until she steps aside, then open the fridge myself and grab the bottle.

White wine is classy, I remind myself. It's not like I'm slugging back a bottle of one of the brothers. Not like my mother. Rich bitches drink white wine with their pinkies out and their pearl necklaces strangling them.

Harriett watches me pour myself a glass of yellowish liquid. It's the last of the bottle from the fridge. I don't remember drinking the rest of it, but I know better than to say anything to her about it. Instead, I toss the empty into the recycling bin where it clinks against four other bottles I also don't remember drinking, and sure as hell not since the last time the trash went out.

I take a long, deep drink from my glass, until it's empty. Somehow, I'm in front of the basement fridge like my feet took me there while my brain was somewhere else. I pull another bottle to take upstairs, but pause. It's chardonnay, the kind I drink. And it's got a label that looks familiar, white and black, but there's no rose on the front. It's not the *brand* I drink. It's close, but not the same.

Upstairs, the bottles in the recycling bin are also not my brand. I didn't buy this wine. I haven't bought wine in months.

Where is the money?

Did I give it to someone? Did I spend it? Did I lose it? What did I do with it?

What else can't I remember?

Everything spins and shakes.

I hold up the bottle in front of Harriett. "Where did this come from? Did you buy this?"

"Oh no, of course not," Harriett says with a small clap of her tiny, soft hands. "You know I don't drink alcohol, Diana."

I'm used to the judgement, silent or otherwise, but she's answered a question I didn't ask and did not answer the one I did. I open the new bottle and pour myself a glass, then top it with the cork and put it in the fridge. I take another long drink. The wine is not as good as Briar White, but it's crisp and cold, and I swallow almost convulsively in a gulp that threatens to come back as a gag because I've taken too much, too soon. I solve that with another, slower sip. Warmth spreads through me.

Harriett's fingers link together. She squeezes her hands. Releases. Her rabbity gaze is still focused too intently on me. I know she's aching for a smoke break, but I don't know why she doesn't simply slip out the back door to do it the way she always does. Why she tries to hide it from me.

What else is hidden from me?

"Thanks for dinner," I tell her. "You really didn't have to."

"It's no bother. I enjoy cooking for you." Harriett shrugs, but then gives me that coy, sideways smile I suddenly loathe. "Jonathan always loved the way I made his tomato soup. I use real milk. He loved it. He would never even touch it the way I made it for you."

"I know that. You've told me. Over and over." The words slip out before I can stop them, and it's too late to call them back.

Kicking a puppy would be less traumatic than watching Harriett's feelings get hurt. The wine helps me not to feel bad, making the world a warm and fuzzy place, and I haven't even finished one full glass. It was generously poured, true, but I've hardly drunk even half of it, and the first glass contained even less. Both together, not even one full glass.

"I'm going to read. In my room," I add pointedly before Harriett can say anything. "I have a headache."

Her glance at the wine glass makes me want to down the whole thing, but the truth is, my guts are churning a little, and the wine is no longer appealing. I take the glass with me upstairs, though. No sense in wasting it. After all, like Harriett says, I might want it later.

CHAPTER THIRTY-SEVEN

Cole

Diana has texted me twice, and I answered her, but she hasn't replied. I've resisted tracking her location. She knows where I am and how to find me, if she wants to. And if she doesn't want to? What will I do then?

There's still the matter of all that money. She wouldn't know if I just kept it. Nobody would. If I give it back to her, I'll have to tell her the truth about why I agreed to take it in the first place, about what she paid me to do and how I failed.

Or I could just finish the job.

CHAPTER THIRTY-EIGHT

Val

9:14 AM: *Happy Valentine's day, baby.*

9:35 AM: *Don't be like this. Come on.*

11:45 AM: *Answer your phone.*

11:55 AM: *Let's not go through this again. Please just answer me. I have plans for you tonight. I'll be over at 6.*

                Don't come over, I text. I don't want to see you.

                1:15 PM: *I'll be there at 6.*

CHAPTER THIRTY-NINE

Diana

There is blood everywhere, and the sickening thump still vibrates in my stomach. The rain is cold, and the world turns and tips in the lights from the oncoming cars. My hair is wet. My head hurts.

The mud is full of rocks.

My fingers are bleeding, my nails ragged and broken, caked with dirt, and maybe that's blood on my hands, maybe my knees are scraped and raw and covered with blood, maybe it's my blood.

Maybe it's not my blood.

There is my mother. There is the tub. She's sliced one wrist. Bleeding. The water is red. She looks at me.

"I never should have adopted you," my mother says.

There is my mother, with lines around her eyes and mouth. She says, "I wasn't fit to be a mother then. I hope you give me a second chance to try, Diana. I hope you can forgive me."

There is my mother. There is a hotel room. There is the bottle of pills and vodka and her dead body, and I am on my hands and knees, and my hands are covered in blood, and there is blood, and I am dreaming, but I can't wake up.

My broken bones grind together. Someone pulls me out of the car. Into water. Cold mud. I scream when he tries to get me to my feet.

"Did we hit someone? Did we hit someone?"

There is a hole in the ground and trees are all around, and I stagger to my feet, and there is a thump and a scream.

It's my own voice. My own scream. I am screaming.

* * *

My breath whistles out of me in a hiss, and I have time to be grateful I didn't scream out loud before the rest of the nightmare slams into my head, and I fall back onto the pillows. My head presses the headboard. I didn't mean to fall asleep with my book in my hand and my neck at this weird, cramped angle. My stomach lurches as I sit upright—too fast. The world spins, so I close my eyes and breathe through it.

When I open them, the wineglass on my nightstand accuses me with its emptiness.

Everything feels topsy-turvy, fuzzy, and for a horrible moment, I can't be sure I'm actually awake. I close my eyes and open them again to make sure. I am awake. I am. I have to be.

With a shaky sigh of relief, I swing my legs over the side of the bed and put my feet on the floor. The hardwood is chilly. A slash of rain spatters the window, and I turn to stare at it just as a flash of lightning turns the sky outside an eye-searing white.

Thunder might have been what woke me, but I check my phone anyway because I have the faintest memory of the sound of a text notification. Jonathan has not answered me, but there is a red notification from someone else. My heart leaps, but it's not Cole. I curse myself for hoping.

Ran 2 store 4 a few things. Txt if u need something.

Harriett must've been out of smokes. I rub at my eyes. They feel gritty. My mouth, dry. Everything is still tipping and turning, and for a moment I'm convinced I'm going to have to run to the bathroom to vomit.

A few deep breaths help push back the nausea. I thumb my phone to look at the message I sent my husband five hours ago. Delivered, opened, read, but not answered. I want to think this isn't like him, but I know it is. I know why he's not answering. I know where he is and what he's doing, and with who.

In another time, another life, I'd be the distraught wife in her cold bed alone, weeping for the loss of her husband to another woman. The truth is, I stopped caring about Jonathan's affair a long time ago, but I need him here, now, in a way I didn't before, not for a long time.

I need him, and I hate myself for that.

"Fuck you, Jonathan."

The words hang in the air, and when a thump of thunder fills the room, I'm glad that noise covers up the sound of my voice. I'm still shaking away the nightmare, but it's clinging to me, claws sunk deep. I'm being hag-ridden by it. It's so bad I hold out my hands to make sure they're not covered in filth and blood.

I clench my fingers into fists but stop myself from punching my pillows. Will I ever get over what my mother did? Can I ever just . . . stop . . . feeling it?

I never should have adopted you.

The same words, said decades apart, with very different intentions and yet the exact same result. The answer, I think, is no. I will never get over what my mother said and did. I can get beyond it, maybe, but over it seems impossible.

I go downstairs in search of some cold water. I don't scream when the lights go out. I mean, what's a little darkness during a storm when I can't stop imagining myself burying a body in the back yard? The body of someone I murdered? Because even though the dream never shows me that, I know that's what I've done.

Another flash of lighting. Another crash of thunder. Rain pounds the roof and the deck outside. The emergency flashlights that are supposed to come on automatically when the power goes off are still dark, and when I shine my phone to find them, all I see are empty outlets where they should be plugged in.

I mutter a few curses meant for dear, sweet, helpful Harriett and her relentless need to unplug things she fears might be wasting electricity. Explaining to her that the entire point of those automatic flashlights is that they're always plugged in wouldn't have done any good, but I wish Jonathan had been man enough to tell his mother to stop unplugging everything.

Now I'm in the dark, and since out here in the wild woods we lose power the second a squirrel sneezes, I can't be sure it's going to come back on. My phone has about twenty percent charge left on it. I think about texting Jonathan again, but then I don't.

I might have forgotten an entire swath of my life, but I do remember how to set up and turn on the generator. Usually, I'd wait out the storm and see if the power's been restored, but the temperature in the house was already chilly when I woke, and it's only going to drop further. This time, not because of a problem with the thermostat program. Also, if Harriett makes it home and finds the power out, she won't be able to use the automatic garage door opener. She'll have to park in the driveway and run through the icy rain. Worse, if the power stays off, I won't be able to get my car out of the garage, and even if I can barely drive myself and have no plans to go anywhere, the idea that I might be trapped here, stuck, is enough to get me moving toward the back door.

I swipe my phone screen, but of course with the power out, the internet is also down, and the cell service in the house is bad enough without a storm making it worse. One bar. I swipe the screen, typing in a command to search for an outage, but all I get is a site that reassures me yes, indeed, I can report that the power is out.

I need the lights back on. At the back door, I grab a sweatshirt and pull it over my head. For a moment, everything is even darker. The scent of my husband's cologne sweeps over me, and I press the cloth against my face for a moment as a sob breaks out of me.

I fall onto my knees there on the hard tiles, blindfolded by that fabric. Muzzled by it. I cry out, the sound muted, and yank it all the way over my head. My injured collarbones thrum. The sweatshirt catches my messy bun so that my hair falls wildly about my face.

I did love him, once.

Breathe.

Count to ten.

I make it to five and start again, but the next time I get to ten and manage to push myself to my feet. Jonathan's oversized sweatshirt hangs nearly to my knees and drags past my fingertips until I take the time to roll it up. It has a single front pocket running across the front, and I tuck my phone inside it.

Weeping won't make a difference. I've known that for a long time. I didn't cry when I found out about Jonathan sleeping with my best friend, so to do it now would be even more ridiculous. The time to mourn the demise of my marriage has already ticked its way around the clock a few times. So why, now, do my eyes fill with burning tears?

Why can't I just get myself under control?

Getting the lights back on will help. I swipe my phone screen to bring up the flashlight. I open the back door.

Frigid air blasts me, and within seconds of stepping through the glass door, I'm lashed with icy needles of rain that feel like they're stripping the skin off my face. My teeth are chattering. Gooseflesh ripples along my arms, and I rub them. Again, I didn't drink enough wine to feel this unsteady. Another edge of panic is trying to force its way up and over me, but I push it back.

I can't remember the last time I ventured inside the shed, and that has nothing to do with the amnesia. The shed has always been Jonathan's domain. It was supposed to be a small hut, just big enough for a lawnmower and some garden tools, but as with most things my husband desires, it had to be the biggest and the best, not necessarily the most useful or appropriate. This shed ended up being the size of a one-car garage. We have a full workshop in the basement and a three-car attached garage, not to mention the additional three-bay garage his mother lives above, but clearly he still needs a place to stash the equipment for sports he no longer plays and gardening tools for the yard he pays someone else to maintain. He needs this shed for all the broken things he refuses to throw away.

I know that's where he keeps the generator, and although I don't want to run outside through the frigid sleet and darkness, it's the only way I'll get some light. In the dark and cold and rain, all I can think about is the nightmare.

All I can think about is that I have done something so wrong, so bad, that my mind has blanked it out. It's not the surgery and anesthesia. It's guilt and fear.

"I am *awake*," I say aloud. I repeat it, louder.

The neighbors on the hill behind us have a generator that kicks on automatically if the power is out for more than five minutes, so their lights are on. That won't do much for me except emphasize the darkness I have to get through to reach the shed. I'll have to drag the generator out, hook it into the outside outlet. I've never done it, but I think I remember how.

I'm soaked through by the time I get to the shed. Shuddering so hard my bones hurt. Wet strands of hair slap me in the eyes as I yank at the garage door. It won't go up. I stumble around the side to the main door and pull on that. The knob slips under my wet hands, but I finally wrench it open and force myself inside and out of the rain. I have to push some bins and boxes out of the way because they've been shoved up against the door, but I make it.

Panting, shivering, sick to my stomach, and hating myself for being unable to stop pursuing this compulsion, I lean against the door and close my eyes. My breathing is almost loud enough to drown out the sound of the rain battering the shed's roof. It's so dark in here it would be easy convince myself that my eyes are closed when they're open, and I have another few moments of panic while I press my fingertips to my eyelids hard enough to make bright spots appear.

I am awake, but the dream slides into my mind. Here in the pitch-black shed, it's too easy to let myself believe my eyes are closed and I am in bed, suffering the nightmare.

None of the mental exercises Dr. Levitt gave me are working. Something is wrong with me, and I can't shake it.

The plink of a cold raindrop hits the top of my head. My hair is already chilled and soaked, so it's not the temperature that startles me, but the force of the drop. Blinking rapidly, I look up but can see nothing. Another drop hits me in the eye, then the mouth, and I sputter a low curse.

It's good, though, because it forces me to straighten and start to get myself together. The woozy feeling in my head is still there, but the nausea is abating. I dig for my phone in the sweatshirt pocket and pull it out, hoping that even though the fabric is wet, the phone itself has managed to stay at least minimally dry.

I swipe the screen. Pull up the flashlight. I'm looking for the generator, but what I see instead forces out a harsh, rasping, guttural cry that shreds my throat.

It's my car.

CHAPTER FORTY

Valerie

I'd told him not to come, but he did. How many chances are you supposed to give someone who constantly lets you down? As many as it takes, I guess, because when Jonathan showed up at my door tonight, I didn't turn him away. I let him in. I let him convince me that this time it would all be different.

This time.

Someday, I might not love this man enough to ignore his snoring, but for right now the sound of his grumbly breathing curls me toward him so I can bury my face in the warm, smooth curve of his bare shoulder. With my hand on his chest, I can feel his heart thumping away beneath his skin and behind the cage of his ribs. For a second, my fingernails dig into his skin, but I ease my grip before he can feel any pain and wake. I want him to stay here as long as possible. I want to wake up with him in the morning, every day, for the rest of our lives.

His phone buzzes against the nightstand, and I tense, waiting to see if he'll wake up, but Jonathan doesn't stir. I lean across him carefully to glance at the phone. I'm expecting another message from Diana. If my husband was "working late" on Valentine's Day of all days, you'd better believe I'd be texting his ass all night long, but this time it's his mother's name on the screen. Well, that bitch can wait too.

Lightning flashes, with thunder following a minute or so after. Jonathan's phone lights and buzzes with another message, but it's the thunder that wakes him. His eyes open and sits up halfway.

"Hey," I say to keep his attention on me.

No matter what fears I have about our future, the way he kisses me before he does anything else tells me this man loves me as much as I love him. We're just in a bad place, that's all. We have some tough things to get through, but in the end, it's all going to work out.

"Kiss me," I say against his mouth.

His hand slips behind my head to cradle it, his strong fingers digging through my hair. "What time is it? How long was I asleep?"

"Not long." It's not exactly a lie is it? Not when the concept of time is irrelevant. It didn't seem long to me, anyway.

He pulls away before I'm finished kissing him and grabs for his phone. "Shit. Shit!"

I already know what it is, but I ask anyway. "What's wrong?"

"Something at home. Mom says the power's out. Damn it, I didn't hear the phone. You should have woken me."

"I didn't hear it either." I don't tell him that I turned off the ringer hours ago. "You were out like a light."

Jonathan mutters a couple of curses and puts the phone on the nightstand. "I have to go. Jesus, Val, it's after eleven."

"You told her you were working late." I bite out the words one at a time, trying to keep my voice steady and doing a bad job of it.

Jonathan gives me a look just this side of condescending. "She won't believe it would be this late."

"What do you care what she believes?" I demand and get out of bed. I know he's watching me walk, naked, to the window, and I also know how good I look. I turn in the light from outside to make sure he sees everything at all the best angles. "She knows the truth. I don't know why you keep trying to pretend—"

"Don't start," Jonathan interrupts.

Another crash of thunder makes me jump. I grab my robe and pull it on. My hair catches on the collar, and I struggle with it a bit before Jonathan leaves the bed and crosses to me so he can help. His gentle fingers pull the weight of it free and let it fall down my back. Jonathan bought me this robe, one of his first gifts to me, back when what we were doing felt illicit and terrible and exciting and, most of all, impermanent.

He puts his hands on my shoulders. I don't turn around. I want to put myself into his arms and let him kiss me, but I can't move. As soon as he kisses me, he's going to leave, and I will spend the rest of this long night alone.

"Why don't you just go." My voice is hard and sharp as a fork of lightning.

"Don't be like that."

I shrug out of his grip. When I'm far enough away that he can't touch me, I turn. "What will it take for you to finally end it?"

"I'm just trying to give her time to get back on her feet—"

"Not her," I interrupt. "Me. This. Us. What will it take for you to finally just stop breaking my heart over and over again?"

He hesitates without responding, then grabs his briefs from the chair near the bathroom door. I try not to admire his lean form as he bends to get dressed, but I'm greedy in this moment. For all I know, it could be the last time I ever get to see him like this.

When he again doesn't answer me, my voice softens. "Why do you keep coming back to me?"

I want him to say it's because he loves me, but he does not. Maybe that's the real truth here. Maybe the question is not what will it take for him to stop breaking my heart, but when will I stop letting him?

"What are you asking me?" Jonathan won't look at me. He puts on his trousers and slides his long arms into the sleeves of his button-down. He sits on the chair to put on his socks, but he only holds them in his hands as his shoulders slump and his head hangs. "Val, please. I thought we were done with this."

"Why? Because we kissed and made up? Because you came over here with dinner and flowers and candy, and you fucked me? You think that's enough? I should never have let you come back," I cry, my voice shaking. "I should have told you to fuck right off!"

"But you didn't," Jonathan says quietly without looking at me. "You didn't."

And I know I never will.

I could go to him right now. Get on my knees in front of him. I could make him look at me. Kiss me. Hell, I could unzip his pants and take him in my mouth the way I've done hundreds of times before.

But I don't move toward him. I stay in one place, not frozen, not incapable of motion.

Choosing to remain still.

"She knows, Jonathan. You can keep pretending she doesn't. Both of you can. But she knows about me. About us."

He shakes his head. "No. She can't possibly. She might suspect, but she doesn't know for sure."

"Yes, she does," I say sharply, so he looks up. "She absolutely knows, Jonathan, because I told her."

CHAPTER FORTY-ONE

Diana

"Oh my god."

My ears are still full of that buzzing hum that reminds me of the vibrating pain in my clavicle, but even if I heard only silence, I don't think I'd have recognized the sound of my own voice. It's gone so tiny, so small, it's only the shadow of a voice. Until I repeat myself, loud and fierce.

"Oh my fucking god."

In the phone's beam of light, my Camaro's cherry exterior gleams against the gray and black shadows. I'm three steps away from it, maybe five at the most, but the path is blocked with boxes and bins of junk that I have to kick and shove out of the way. By the time I clear a way through, I'm breathing hard again. I stumble on something I didn't see in front of me and come up hard against the car with one hand on the hood. It's the hand holding the phone, and I cringe at the loud crack.

The screen is lined with crackles, but the light hasn't gone out. I shine it over my car, my precious hunk of glass and metal and rubber that was never just a vehicle for me, but a symbol. A talisman.

What happened to the car? I remember asking Jonathan.

I had it towed to the junkyard. It was totaled.

"Liar. You goddamned liar." I want to spit the words, their sour taste coating my tongue.

Looking over the car now, I forcibly wince at the enormous dent in the hood and let out a low, mournful groan. It's only a car, and I know it's foolish to care this much about something material. The damage looks like it could have been repaired, though, and that's what I don't understand. Why would Jonathan have put it in the shed and lied to me about it? We could have fixed it.

Story of our marriage, I guess. We could have fixed it, but both of us threw it away before we could even try. A harsh, gagging gasp hisses out of me.

"He always hated you." I give the car a long stroke against the cold metal.

Speaking to my car like it's a person doesn't make me crazy, but would hugging it? I want to. I shine the light upward and let out another cry at the sight of the windshield's glass, cracked in a spiderweb pattern on the passenger side. The airbag looks like a crumpled bedsheet.

"*Common in clavicle breaks sustained during car accidents. The seatbelt, you know, where it crosses over. You were the passenger?*"

"No," I say aloud. "I was driving myself."

I'd been alone. Wasn't I? I touch my right shoulder. I touch the car's cold paint and let out a sob. Was someone else driving that night? What really happened?

I shine my light again.

A dry, rusty brown stain coats the bumper.

This time, I don't gasp or mutter. I bark out a sharp cry and recoil, backing up so fast I knock into a bunch of tottering boxes. Some fall over. One hits my shoulder hard enough to shove me forward. I drop my phone.

The light goes out.

On my hands and knees, I struggle for breath. My throat and nose are closing. Tears scald my face. I'm whispering horrified prayers I can barely decipher for myself.

"Please, no."

My hand sweeps in the direction I remember the phone landing. I find it. I swipe the cracked screen, wincing in anticipation of slicing of my thumb on the broken glass. The screen lights. I tap to bring up the flashlight, already knowing it won't work. The battery is now at eight percent.

The flashlight does come on. I'm still on my knees in front of the car, inches from the bumper. I shine the light.

The blood is old and no longer red. Clumps of stiff brownish hair and gristle cling to the cracks and dents of the bumper. The light turns into a strobe from the shaking of my hands.

I turn off the light and stand in the darkness. I breathe. I count. I breathe again.

This time, Dr. Levitt's tricks work. I am not panicking. My head aches, and I still feel unsteady, ready to fall over, but I know I'm awake. I know this all is real. I'm no longer even thinking about looking for the generator.

It was a deer.

The blood and hair and bone on the front of my car are not a dream. But what if it wasn't a deer? What if my dreams are memories? I need to find out. Outside, more thunder rolls. The rain is coming down—if it's possible, even harder than before.

A shovel leans against the wall next to my car. I grab it and go through the door before I can talk myself out of it. My phone is useless out here, and I shove it into the sweatshirt pocket. I round the shed and dig the shovel into the sodden earth of the hill behind it. I haul myself up it, three or four steps until I'm over the rise.

The split tree is bigger than the others around it, and in the faint light from the neighbor's back porch, I head for its looming shadow. The hill isn't as steep here, but I still slip in the wet leaves and dirt. Behind me, the floodlights of my own house come on, bathing me in just enough light for me to see the direction I need to head. The power's back on.

It takes me several minutes to get to the tree. I'm here, in the place of my nightmares, and although I have no clear idea of exactly where to start digging, I stab the ground with the shovel. I grind my teeth at the pain in my sole when I use my foot to get the tool deeper into the dirt. I might as well be barefoot for all the protection my soft flats provide. The shoes will be ruined, but I don't care.

I grunt and groan with pain as I throw aside a shovelful of dirt and leaves. I push it down again. The lightning and thunder have eased, and the rain seems to be slowing, although it's still frigid as ice. My numb fingers slide off the shovel's splintery wooden handle. A bright sting stabs the base of my thumb, but I ignore it. More agony, hot as fire, in both my shoulders. I toss aside another clump of dirt. This time, when the shovel sinks into the earth, it hits something solid.

I sink to my knees and use my hands. I claw at the ground, determined. Focused. I can't see what I'm doing, but I will not stop until I've dug up whatever it was I buried there.

CHAPTER FORTY-TWO

Valerie

"What do you mean, you told her?"

I've never heard Jonathan sound like this. Honestly, I've never even seen him so angry. My gaze drops to his clenching fists, and I tense. Rough sex is one thing, but I won't tolerate a man who uses his fists. He notices, relaxing his fingers with an obvious effort.

"I *told* her about us," I tell him. Why should he need more explanation than that? He's not that stupid, even if he's acting like it.

He drags his hands through his salt-and-pepper hair until it stands on end. "Why would you do that?"

"Because she was my best friend," I snap, "and she deserved to know."

"When?" he demands.

I draw my robe closer around my throat. "In August."

That was when I told her that things had changed. That was when she'd promised to let him leave her without a fight. I am telling Jonathan only half the truth, but that's all I will ever tell him. If he knew that she and I had set this up from the start, would he still love me? I'm not taking the chance.

Lies to start. Lies to end. Because that's what this is, isn't it? The end.

"Because of Punta Cana?" Understanding dawns in his eyes. He pivots on his heel, again dragging his hands through his hair and actually pressing fists to his forehead before whirling back around to look at me.

I'm losing a battle I've been ready to fight for a long time. "Yes. Because of that damned trip. You told me she was insisting that you take her, and you said you couldn't think of a way to tell her no. She did insist, didn't she?"

Jonathan lies, Diana had said. Well. Don't we all? One of them had lied to me, and which is worse, the betrayal of a friend or of a lover? In the end, I was still losing someone I loved.

"Of course she did." Jonathan doesn't meet my eyes. This is a weakness in him, and I hate seeing it. "Jesus, Valerie, I can't believe you're bringing that up again. I *didn't* even fucking take her. She changed her mind. Said she had some final thing come up with work, that she couldn't make it. She even apologized for it being so last minute. We didn't even go!"

"No, you didn't go," I reply from clenched jaws. "Because she wrecked her car, and you had to stay home. How convenient was that?"

Jonathan recoils from me. "You act like she did it on purpose."

If I say it aloud, I will sound like a crazy, jealous bitch. I know there's no way Diana could have forced herself to need emergency gallstone surgery, and I know, too, how unlikely it is that she caused her own car accident just so she could ruin Jonathan's and my relationship. Still, that's how it felt then and still feels now.

"She can't remember August," he says when I stay silent.

"So she says."

Jonathan shakes his head. "She's not pretending to have amnesia, Valerie. How many times do I have to tell you that? She's been diagnosed by more than one doctor. She's not faking it just to keep me with her."

"And yet you haven't left her," I say.

Jonathan lets out a low, scraping groan and sinks into the chair. He puts his head in his hands and says nothing else for a minute. He's angry at me, but I'm furious too. Even months later, the memory of how it felt when he told me he was going to take her instead of me on the sexy resort vacation we'd worked so hard to plan still pushed my blood pressure high enough to start a throb of pain behind my eyes.

"Even if she really doesn't remember," I tell him, "I reminded her in October." I spit the words, my lips twisting around them. I don't care if this makes me ugly. I feel ugly about all of this, the way I did that day at the Blue Dove when Diana tried to smile at me and pretend like nothing had ever happened. Like she wasn't going back on her word, trying to ruin my life.

Silence creeps into the space between us. I want to break it, but I don't trust myself not to scream at him. I concentrate on my breathing, keeping it slow and steady.

"It's not that easy—"

"Isn't it?" I am not sympathetic to his hitching breath or the way he cuts his gaze from mine so he doesn't have to look me in the eye.

I love Jonathan, but right now I am not impressed with him.

He looks up at me. "She needs me."

At last, I know the truth. I see it written all over his face. Jonathan lies, she'd told me, but he's not as good at as he thinks he is. Too bad both of us underestimated how smart he was, how good at playing the game we thought we'd set ourselves up to win.

"You never intended to take me on that trip," I whisper. "It was an excuse to end things."

He can't possibly begin to guess the depths of what my ex–best friend and I have been through. He never will, because I don't think Jonathan Richmond is capable of loving anyone enough to sacrifice for them.

That's the terrible thing about loving someone. You know their flaws. You love them anyway.

I can't tell him why this began.

All I can say to him is the truth of what this has become.

"I love you. I know this didn't start off in any way that anyone would say is right, but . . . we are right, together. We are good together. We are happy. But I can't wait forever for you to decide you want to be with me, Jonathan. I can't be with you and break my own heart, over and over. Loving you this way is going to kill me."

"What do you want me to do? Go home now, in the middle of the night, and tell my wife I'm leaving her? She's still recovering . . ."

"There will never be a good time—don't you get it? There's always going to be something." I turn my back to him. I don't have to struggle now to keep my voice steady. Everything inside me has gone stone cold. "Figure it out. Tell her you're leaving."

"Valerie . . ."

"Give her both the houses, half the money—I don't care whatever it is," I tell him without turning around. I can't bear to look at his face when I see him deciding he won't do it. "I don't care if you give her everything. I don't care what I have to do, so long as I can have you."

CHAPTER FORTY-THREE

Diana

It's a box.

An oversized cigar box of thin wood, with a tiny metal clasp, wrapped in layers of plastic. I can imagine the cedar scent of it, but all I can smell right now is dirt and rain and the thick, heavy odor of rotting leaves. With trembling hands, I pull it from the hole and shake it free of the clotted mud. The shovel put a split in the top. The box is heavy enough to contain something important . . . but not big enough for a body.

The first sob rips out of me like a bullet from a gun. I clutch the box to my chest, not caring that I'm getting my husband's sweatshirt filthy, possibly ruining it. I rock, trying to bite back the tears and unable to. All of Dr. Levitt's reassurances wash over me, but here is the proof that I can believe. Relief tastes like orange juice, sickly sweet but with a hint of sour on the back of my tongue. Twisted laughter ripples through my weeping. I am hysterical.

My car is wrecked, and it's obvious I hit something, yes. Something that once was alive. But my nightmares have not come true. It was not a person. I did *not* bury a body beneath this old split tree.

I've killed someone, yes, but I didn't bury her in my back yard.

This box, though. I shouldn't want to face what's inside it, except I do. It has to have answers, and even if I don't like them, I'm so damned sick of not knowing that I'm willing to risk any upsetting truths I might reveal.

I leave the shovel behind and take the box with me as I slide my way down the sloping hill, then the steeper part behind the shed. I'm covered in muck, and not even the rain still pounding down will clean me.

Back inside, with the box still clutched tight against me, I sidle my way to the fridge and pull out the soup and sandwich from earlier. My head has cleared, and I'm starving. I need a hot shower and warm clothes and food before I can think about opening this box. I'm going to need all my strength.

I tear into the sandwich, adding swigs of soup right from the plastic container. I don't even care that it's cold. I'm ravenous. I finish it all within minutes. Belly full, a warm glow rises inside me. A sense of calm.

Whatever's coming, I'll be able to face it.

Upstairs, I toss my phone, totally dead, onto my side of the bed and lock the bedroom door. I take the box with me into the bathroom. I lock that door too. I put the box on the counter next to the sink. I don't recognize it. I lift the box and hold it, testing the weight. Something heavy slides inside it again. My fingers feel numb enough that I could drop it, so I put it back on the counter and take a few steps back.

I see myself in the mirror. Straggling, soaked hair. Filth spattered on my face. My lips are blue. Circles beneath my eyes. I look worse even than I feel, and that's saying a lot, because a bone-deep exhaustion has sunk in, turning my limbs to lead. I want so much to simply drag myself into bed and pull the blankets over my head.

I want to sleep, even if I might have nightmares.

I strip out of my filthy, sopping clothes and leave them in a pile on the floor. Naked and chilled, I shiver as water slides down my spine. I scrub myself clean as fast as I can, then wrap my hair in a towel and slip into my robe, moving slowly because of course my old injuries are now singing a new song. I take the box with me into the bedroom and make sure the door is still locked.

I need to open this box, but my hands are shaking too much. I hadn't noticed how ripped up my fingers got when they were covered with mud, but now the scratches and gouges are clearly outlined in red. I've lost a nail nearly down to the quick. My body is looking for every excuse to stop me from discovering what is in this box, but I peel away the plastic so I can tear off the lid and toss it onto the bed.

Inside is a cellphone I don't recognize. It's not even the brand I prefer. The case is clear, with an imprinted photo of a white rose with a barbed wire stem. I don't know this case, but it feels like . . . me.

New phone. Another item from the list I found has been explained but has given no answers. Only more questions.

The phone's dead, but there's a charging cord in the box. I plug it in. First, nothing but a black screen. It will take another few seconds for the phone to power up enough to be able to turn it on, so I set it aside and sort through the rest of the box.

A pressed flower, a white rose to match the back of the phone case. A couple of movie ticket stubs for films I can't remember seeing. A brochure for a state park campground. A keychain with a unicorn on it. A USB drive. A small packet of papers, printed with small type and tight lines.

The prenup.

As I flip through the papers, the phone comes to life.

The background art is blank. There's the keypad for a passcode. I try mine, but it's wrong. I try an old passcode. Also wrong. I try a third, fourth, and fifth time, but I have the sense to stop and take a breath before I get locked out.

If this *is* my phone, I have to know the passcode. I think hard. I've tried every combination of my birthday, my husband's birthday, and our street address that I can think of. I close my eyes. Wrap both hands around the phone. The passcode is locked up as tight in my mind as this phone, but if it's mine, and I know instinctively it is, even if I can't figure out yet how or why, then I also have to know the passcode.

I look at the back of the case again. I look at the pressed flower. My fingers type, hesitantly, ready for the phone to flash that it's been locked for the first minimum of one minute. Four numbers, each corresponding to a letter.

7673

ROSE

The phone unlocks.

CHAPTER FORTY-FOUR

Valerie

LAST AUGUST

I'd started this affair not knowing what it would lead to, but there we were in late August. Ten weeks seemed like an eternity when I looked into Jonathan's eyes.

If I'd ever been in love before, it had never hit this hard or fast. I'd never felt it this deep. Logic told me we shouldn't count on this as real, but logic can fuck itself sideways, without lube. Love is never about logic.

It was the trip that did me in. Our sexy trip to Punta Cana, derailed by a jealous wife. I no longer cared what she and I had agreed to. I was going to end this one way or another.

When I pulled into Diana's driveway, the garage door was up. Her car was parked inside. It was brand-new when she'd bought it a year ago, and she kept it so pristine it might as well still be new. For a moment, I remembered how we'd joked about what she was going to spend that inheritance on. I'd been the one to suggest she might want to off her husband, the man who, at the time, I didn't love. Didn't even really know.

A year ago, everything was different.

Before I went into her house through the garage, I saw movement from the corner of my eye. I wondered how Diana felt about Jonathan's mother watching every coming and going, the way she peeked at me through the window blinds. No matter how close Diana and Harriett were, that had to be annoying.

Of course Diana knew it was me before I got inside the house. That camera system she had set up alerted her. That was why she had two glasses of Briar White all ready to go as soon as I went into the kitchen.

She lifted her glass toward me, but I wasn't there to make a toast. I took the glass but didn't do more than sip from it. I couldn't stomach it.

Diana drained half hers. She put her glass on the counter. Normally, we'd both be heading to the living room to curl up together on the couch, but she didn't invite me there, so I didn't go. I put my glass on the counter next to hers.

"Say what you came here to say," she told me finally. "Let's just . . . finish this. Okay?"

"He told me you decided to go with him to Punta Cana. I want you to tell him you changed your mind. That trip is for us, to be together. Not for you." My words come out clipped. Brusque.

She didn't say anything at first, but when she did, her voice was low and rough. "He told you *I* decided to go with him?"

"He said you're insisting on it. That he has to take you instead of me."

More silence while she drank her wine. There'd been times in our lives when I'd been the one with the alcohol problem, but not now. She'd be sick if she wasn't careful.

"How did this happen, Val?"

"I don't know. But it did." I didn't ask her how she'd found out about how things had changed. I stopped worrying about Jonathan being able to keep it a secret long ago, knowing he was going to fuck it up, let it slip. He was constantly leaving his phone unlocked. I'd seen her messages to him; she had to have seen his to me. "You wanted this, Diana. You asked me to do this. Don't you forget that."

Diana looked surprised. "I never asked you to fall in *love* with him, Val."

"Well," I told her, "I did."

Diana laughed, but there was a sound of pity in it. I didn't hate her before, but now loathing rose inside me, a sickness.

"Has he said he loves *you*?"

I couldn't say anything.

"Take him," she said. "If you can keep him, you're welcome to him."

When she burst into tears, what could I do but hug her? Our wine sloshed in our glasses, but neither of us paid attention. Diana and I clung to each other, gripping hard, like this embrace could keep us from falling apart.

She was the one who pulled away. Her sigh was heavy and grinding. She laughed without any humor. She finished her glass, filled it again, and gulped. She didn't look at me when she spoke. "You think you love him—"

"I do love him."

"You *think* you love him," she repeated, but gently this time, looking me in the face, "but you don't really know him. Maybe you hate me now—"

"Stop with the drama. I don't hate you."

"I don't hate you either."

We clinked our glasses together. We sipped. The wine was cold and sweet. It was the taste of our friendship.

"If I get the proof I need, it will ruin him financially. Is that what you want?" Diana asked.

"Of course it's not," I snapped. "And you don't have to do it. You could just leave him without ever even bringing up the prenup."

"I'd lose the beach house," she whispered. "But you don't care about that."

"You could work it out with him. I could talk him into being fair."

Her laugh this time was ragged but amused. "Do you really think Jonathan would ever be fair if he thinks he can get away with being anything but? And he can."

"If you just let me talk to him—"

"I didn't tell him to take me on that trip." Her words cut me off, sharp as a knife. Diana lifted her chin.

My insides turned to ice. "He said you did. He said—"

"If he's in love with you, why would he agree to bump you from a sexy romantic getaway in favor of me? Think about it, Val," Diana said. "If he loves you, why would he take me instead?"

Something about her words rang true. I didn't want to answer her question. I didn't want her to be right . . . but what if she was?

"He lies," Diana said. "He's not as good at it as he thinks."

"Why would he lie to me about that?" I demanded.

Her gaze met mine. "Because I told him I want to leave him. He's trying to cut his losses because he's afraid it's about you."

"Isn't it?"

"No." Diana shook her head. "It's because of what I found out about my mother . . . and Harriett."

CHAPTER FORTY-FIVE

Diana

This phone has only a few apps displayed on the home screen. The standard ones I recognize, of course. A few I don't. I tap one, and it brings up Taktok, a message app I've heard of but have never had an account with. At least, not that I remember.

It's passcode protected, and I don't recognize the username, Briarrose132, that's already displayed. It takes me three tries, but I figure out the password. It's the one I used to use for my online journal, the one nobody else would be able to guess.

The profile picture for Briarrose132 matches the one on the phone case. The contacts list has only one name in it, TaktokGuy, with a gray silhouette as the profile pic. No messages show up, but this app automatically deletes messages when you log out. I don't type a message, but instead close the app without logging out of it. I look through the rest of the phone.

There's a banking app for a local credit union, not mine, showing a minimal balance. The last deposit was made months ago. The payout. Then, a large withdrawal of cash. No other information than that.

This phone has an app all set up for my security camera system, and I don't have to fight with the passwords for it. This system only saves clips for two weeks, but I know where to find the ones that have been deleted. I scan them quickly. There's only one that matters.

Darkness, the deck and the trees beyond lit only by the backyard floodlights. One figure, carrying a shovel and what looks like the cigar box. It crosses the deck and disappears into the trees just beyond the shed. When it comes back, the box and shovel are both gone. It looks directly into the cameras with a frown, the face clear enough to make a solid, no-questions identification.

It's me.

I buried this box beneath that tree, but I have no idea why.

Another app has caught my eye. I know this one. It looks like a calculator, but it's for storing pictures and files you don't want anyone else to see. This app is also passcode protected, but I take a chance and use the one that worked on the phone itself. It works. The app opens.

The first photo I see is black and white. It shows a woman, her face obscured by a panel of sheer fabric. She's wearing a bra and panties, and her dark hair is down. It's a sexy picture, clearly taken by and meant for a lover. It's not until I spot the inked heart on her shoulder that I realize the woman is me.

The phone slips from my fingers but hits the bed without pulling free of the charging cord. I stare at it. I'm shaking. My stomach churns, and I taste acid rising in the back of my throat.

I force myself to pick up the phone again. I swipe. More photos. My naked body, twisted and shadowed and filtered.

Pictures of someone else.

"Oh . . . my . . . oh my god." I choke out the words and hold the phone in both hands to help me focus on it. My hands are shaking so much I have to close my eyes and take a deep breath to keep myself from passing out. The world is threatening to spin right out of control.

There are pictures of Cole. His arms around me, both of us staring up at the camera, grinning like fools. His face turned to mine, eyes closed, lips brushing my cheek.

I sit on the bed, phone in one hand, and touch that spot on my face with the other. I close my eyes again, trying to remember this. Any of it.

Cole and I were lovers, but no matter how hard I try, I can't recall a single second of anything with him before the day we met at the coffee shop.

Then I'm stumbling, phone dumped onto the bed, into the bathroom, to heave up the leftover sandwich and soup I gobbled up such a short time before. My stomach empties, I flush, and then again, until I'm only weeping over the toilet. The sour taste in my mouth makes me spit over and over. When I think I can stand, I get to the sink and run the water so I can rinse my mouth.

Quickly, I brush my teeth. I rake a comb through my hair, tearing at the snarls and cursing under my breath at the pain. Back in the bedroom, I pull open dresser drawers and stare without seeing into them. I need to get dressed, but I can't figure out what to wear.

Underwear first, but what? Serviceable cotton, like I've been wearing the past few months? Or here, in the far back, the sexy, lacy panties I don't recognize but that definitely belong to me. I pull out a pair made of wispy material, sheer and clinging to my every curve, dipping low below my hipbones. A matching bra, also lace and satin. I fasten it not on the biggest set of hooks, but the smallest. My breasts surge into the material, plump and full and tempting, and the reflection in the mirror over the dresser is even more disturbing than the one in the bathroom. Another woman who's a stranger.

I don't know myself anymore.

I yank my feet into a pair of leggings. Socks. A tunic top. The phone I found in the box is still on the bed, charging. I gather the rest of the box's contents and shove it all back inside. The phone is at forty percent or so, and I unplug it and put it back in the box too, before I close the tiny hinge and put the entire thing into my oversized shoulder bag.

I make it to my car. Keys in hand. Unburied box in my purse.

And I go.

CHAPTER FORTY-SIX

Cole

I haven't had a ping from my Taktok app in months. Not since before the night of the car accident. I leave it open all the time, just in case, but I stopped expecting anything awhile back. In the months after that night of screeching tires and cold rain, I got a few of those messages from the bots that troll the app, looking to lure lonely dudes into conversations and, as soon after that as possible, into making contributions to a bank account in order to access "private pictures" or "conversation." I never fell for the bots' come-ons, but every time one pinged me, I sure as shit picked up the phone. Hoping it was her.

When the distinctive sound chirps from my phone, I have to do a double take. The phone is on the counter next to the daily mail and the glass of red wine I'd poured myself while I figured out what the hell I wanted to do for the late dinner I wish I didn't have to cook. Pizza delivery sounded like a better option, but I was too hungry to wait for it, so I've been scrounging in my freezer like the worst kind of bachelor stereotype.

With a jar of peanut butter in one hand and a package of frozen waffles in the other—because, what the fuck, it's a meal—I stop dead cold as the phone chirps again. I can't convince myself it's a regular text because the Taktok app has its own sounds.

It's a spam message, one of those pornbots. Right? It has to be.

Briarrose132: *I found the phone.*

That's it. I'm not even exactly sure what the fuck that means, but I know who is saying it.

202

I do the lame thing and reply, *Ok*.

The message is marked with an "R" for "Read" within seconds. Briarrose132 is typing. I wait, uncertain what the hell is going on, not sure what I ought to do. I'm still holding the box of frozen waffles, and the cardboard is going warm and soggy in my fist, so I put it back in the freezer. Suddenly, I'm not so hungry.

Comgin vr

A second after that: *Coming over.*

I could have listed a hundred or more reasons why I fell in love with Diana Sparrow, but one of them had always been her insistence that, even when using text messages, she was always careful to spell out entire sentences and use proper grammar. *"No shortcuts,"* she'd always said. Language and communication could evolve, but that didn't mean it had to be disrespectful. If a conversation was worth having, she'd said, it was worth typing correctly.

I put my jar of peanut butter on the counter and contemplate my life choices because, fuck, it seems like everything is on the verge of going to shit, and even though I know it's not all my fault, at least part of it is.

TaktokGuy: *I'm home.*

Radio silence. She's not even typing. I drain the rest of my glass and wait. Then.

Briarrose132: *I'll be there in half an hour.*

TaktokGuy: *I'm ready.*

I'm not. I have no idea what's coming. I toss the dirty clothes in the basket and have another wine glass ready. She likes white. I like red. I only have one bottle of white, but since I have no idea how much she'll want to drink, that seems like enough. It's cold, at least.

She's coming over, and I am, no joke, pacing the floor until the headlights of a car sweep across my front window. Then everything goes into a kind of slow motion. I wait a minute or two, then open the door when I figure she's on the porch.

She looks like death, not going to lie. Wet hair. Smeared makeup. Whatever is going on, she isn't dressed for seduction. She still looks as beautiful to me as she always has. The look in her eyes, though. That's ugly.

I step aside so she can get through the door, and I close it behind her against the storm still battering my trailer's metal walls and roof. "You look like you could use a drink."

Diana barks out a sharp, humorless laugh. "Sure. Right. That's exactly what I need. I'm a real boozehound, right? Didn't you know?"

She had occasionally sipped from a glass of wine with me, the precious and rare moments we'd had the time to indulge. And once, that one time, she'd been tipsy enough to promise . . . I shake off that memory, not wanting to dwell on it right now. Stuff that happened before the accident has to stay in the past.

"I wouldn't describe you that way," I say.

Diana hangs her head. Water from her dripping hair plinks onto my floor. Her shoes squish when she shifts from foot to foot. My teeth want to chatter just looking at her.

"How about some hot tea. Or cocoa," I offer. "I have marshmallow fluff."

I can't see her face behind the wet curtain of her hair, even when she half-twists toward me. I catch a glimpse of her mouth, lips pressed together. She crosses her arms tightly over her belly.

"I love fluff. How did you know?"

"I just . . . who doesn't love fluff?" I step toward her, but it's too fast. I can see that in her face, how she tenses, so I stop. I try again. "Diana, come into the kitchen—"

She shakes her head hard enough to fling cold water toward me and retreats a few steps. She lifts her head. Her lips are blue with cold, matched by shadows beneath her bright blue eyes.

"How did you know, Cole? About the fluff? About the color of my car, way back when we first met?"

I've been waiting for months, hoping Diana would remember us. Now, faced with the possibility that she might have started to regain her memories, I'm not sure what I'm going to do about it. I'd imagined her showing up at my door and flinging herself into my arms to kiss me. Stupid adolescent dreams that bordered on wank fantasies. I'd also resigned myself to the fact she might never know me the way she once had. In this moment, I'm stuck between the two possibilities, and I'm not sure I'm ready to face either one.

"Come into the kitchen with me," I say again quietly, my hand still out to take hers.

When she learns the truth she might already be remembering, she can hate me if she wants to, but Diana is clearly in pain and distress, and I can't stand to see her like that. She can hate me, I think, but she still deserves to know the truth.

She won't take my hand, but she looks toward the kitchen and lifts her chin to indicate that she'll follow me. I pull out a chair for her and busy myself at the counter, heating water in the electric kettle and pulling out powdered cocoa, sugar, and the fluff. "I don't have any milk. Sorry."

She warms her hands on the mug I hand her but doesn't say anything. I mix myself a mug of cocoa and debate adding some Bailey's to it, but whatever's coming, I want to be sober for it. I take the chair across from her at my Formica table.

"My grandma had a table like this." Diana traces the Formica's swirling pattern.

"Mine too. I picked this up at the Blue Mountain thrift shop." I sip my cocoa, keeping my voice neutral.

I can't tell her, not right now, that she was with me when we bought it. That she was the one who told me I should get it because *"You can't eat standing up at the counter or on the couch forever, Cole. You need a table where I can sit with you."*

Diana looks up at me. The tip of her tongue dents her top lip as she licks it free of a sticky wisp of marshmallow fluff and chocolate. My heart skips a beat at that simple, sensual gesture. I know she's not doing it to turn me on, but that doesn't matter. I can't forget how it felt to lean across this table and kiss her. Maybe I'll never have the chance again.

"I'm not here to go to bed with you." She says this matter-of-factly, and although I'm glad to hear that her voice isn't shaking or shuddering, I wish she was a little less . . . robotic.

"I didn't think you were."

There it is, a quirk of a smile that sets me back in my chair with a rising bubble of hope in my chest. Diana sips from her mug again. She lets out a long, deep sigh and pushes the mug away from her to put her head in her hands for a moment, her fingers scraping back the mass of her wet hair. She looks at me.

"Can I have a towel?"

"Yes. Sure. Of course. I'm sorry, I should have—" I'm already up and moving to the hall to grab a towel out of the small closet. I take the first one my hand touches and bring it to her.

She shakes it out, staring at the faded pink pattern, the green leaves and darker pink roses. Whatever she meant to say is kept silent as she squeezes water from her hair. She pauses to groan, and it's clear she's in pain, but when I lean to take over, she gives me a look so cold I stop. She toes off her shoes as I watch. She pushes them carefully to the side and settles back into her chair with the towel draped around her shoulders.

"I texted you," she says. An accusation. "You didn't answer."

"I answered you. You didn't reply."

She pulls her phone from her jacket pocket and swipes in the code, then brings up the text thread between us. After a moment, I do the same. She stares at it, then at me. Then at her phone. The screen is cracked.

"I didn't get those messages." She taps the screen, pulling up her settings. Scrolls. She closes her eyes and tosses the phone onto the table. "You're blocked. So is Val. I didn't block either one of you."

Before I can answer, Diana reaches into her jacket's inside pocket and pulls out a different phone. She slides it across the table toward me. We both look at it. Then at each other.

"I found this," she says, "buried in a box in my back yard."

I don't understand. "You put it there?"

"If I didn't, who did?" Her voice grates. "I don't remember doing it, but I have video footage that proves I did. Can you imagine what that's like, Cole? To see yourself doing something you not only can't remember doing but can't imagine why you'd do it in the first place?"

I don't have an answer for her. The night of the accident, she'd been acting erratically. She'd told me a lot of things that were going on, but burying a bunch of stuff in the back yard wasn't one of them. I shrug.

"Do you recognize this phone, Cole?"

Of course I do, but I hesitate. There were times I stopped myself from telling Diana the truth because I thought it was the right thing to do. For her. There were times when I knew it was just for me. I'm not sure what the right choice is now.

I go with truth.

"Yeah, I do. It's your phone. You got it because you were worried Jonathan was snooping through yours."

"Why was it buried in my back yard?"

I shake my head. I don't have to lie. "I swear to you, I don't know."

Diana gets up from the table to shrug out of her jacket and put it on the back of her chair. Wincing and groaning, she pulls an elastic band from around her wrist and ties her hair on top of her head in a messy tangle that I know she would think looks like shit, but breaks my heart with how casually sexy and beautiful it is. She leans on the back of the chair, her fingers gripping the sparkly blue vinyl.

"There are pictures of us on that phone. Together. I don't remember taking them. I don't remember anything about that. But you do," she says, "don't you?"

"Yes."

Diana mutters a string of curses under her breath, nothing I can totally catch. When she looks back at me, her eyes have gone narrow and furious. I can't blame her.

"Why?" she demands. "How? Why wouldn't you tell me? All this time? Months! Were you stalking me?"

"It wasn't like that."

We need something stronger than hot cocoa. I get up from my chair and cross to the fridge to pull out the bottle of white wine and pour her a glass, without asking if she wants it. I hand it to her, and I think she takes it because she's surprised, not because she does want it. But she takes it, and I lift my glass of red from where I left it on the counter and tip it toward her before taking a long, deep swallow. I find my voice. Steadier now. I give Diana a hard, intense look.

"The day you walked into the coffee shop was the first time I'd seen you in weeks. My heart stopped. I hoped you were there because you were looking for me. But your eyes slid right across me like we'd never met. It was so clear that you had no idea who I was or what we'd . . . what had happened . . . with us."

"What *did* happen with us?" Diana's voice breaks. The wine splashes from her glass. She doesn't drink any.

"We fell in love, Diana."

I drain my glass and set it on the counter. I don't make the mistake of approaching her. I give her space. "It happened crazy fast. You used to say to me it was like lightning had struck both of us, and that's exactly how I felt about it too. It wasn't something either of us expected."

"I don't understand." She shakes her head again. "How?"

That's the truth, although not all of it, and as I watch her try to process it, I vow inside I will never, ever lie to Diana again. So I take a deep breath and man the fuck up. And I tell her the rest of it.

"You hired me to prove your husband was fucking your best friend."

CHAPTER FORTY-SEVEN

Diana

For a long minute, I can only stare at him. My head tilts, like that little dog who used to listen to the Victrola. A strangled, confused sound slips out of me, and I start to laugh. A small chuckle at first, but it becomes a choking guffaw seconds after that. I laugh so hard I sound like I'm screaming, and when I clap my hands over my mouth to stifle it, the sound becomes a groan, only half of physical pain. More laughter. I'm shaking with it.

Cole takes me in his arms, and although I've thought about him doing that over and over again all these days without hearing from him, I squirm out of his grip and take a couple unsteady steps away from him. I hold up the hand not covering my mouth. He frowns but stays put.

"I hired you," I say finally, through clenched jaws, trying to hold back another flood of hysterical giggles, "to collect proof of my husband's affair. And then *we* had one, the two of us."

Cole's dark golden brows knit. The brackets around his mouth deepen. He nods.

I'm still laughing, but now I'm also crying and gasping and everything around me is spinning, and this time when I end up in Cole's arms, I cling to him like I'm drowning and he's the life raft. I press my face to his chest. He smells good. Like laundry detergent and a little bit of sweat, and it's familiar. I know this scent. I know this man. I've known him for a long time, I think, even when I didn't understand how or why.

It all hurts so much, and again, it's more than just a physical pain. All of this hurts me, inside and out. Up and down.

"The night I came back here with you, the night we . . ." I begin, but I can't say anything else.

Cole strokes my hair. "I wanted to tell you everything the first time I saw you at the coffee shop, Diana. And every time after that, all those weeks. But I couldn't."

"How long?" I can see I haven't been clear enough, so I continue before he can fumble an answer. "How long were we fucking?"

"You found me in June. We agreed to meet up for regular reports once a week."

"How many weeks?"

Cole hesitates, clearing his throat. "Uh . . . it was the third time we met up."

More laughter spits out of me in hacking spasms. I choke on it. Cole hugs me tighter, then eases up, clearly making sure to be careful of my injuries. He presses his lips to the top of my head. I want to bury myself in this embrace, close my eyes, and let Cole comfort me until I wake up from this. Because surely this has to be a nightmare. Right? I dreamed about digging up the box in the back yard, and I just kept dreaming. None of this can be real. It's too much.

"Maybe we should sit down," he says. "C'mere to the couch. You're shivering. Let me get you something warm to put on."

I withdraw. I don't feel calmer, but my voice is steady. "Sure. Right. You want me to what, strip out of these wet things? That's not suspicious at all."

"If all I wanted was to fuck you, Diana, I'd have done it and been finished with you." Cole snaps these words at me. He looks immediately ashamed. "I'm sorry."

We stare at each other. I am shivering. My teeth are trying to chatter, and I clench my jaw to stop them. I'm making fists too, but I relax my fingers. The vibrating, humming pain in my collarbones eases.

"Come sit with me," he says finally. "I'll get you a blanket at least."

On the couch, Cole pulls a thick, knitted afghan from the back of the recliner and hands it to me. I wrap it around my shoulders and tuck my hands beneath it. I'm still shivering, but I'm not sure it's still from being cold.

"Tell me everything," I say.

CHAPTER FORTY-EIGHT

Cole

BEFORE

The woman sitting across from me was in her mid-forties. Dark hair with some sexy streaks of silver at her forehead. Blue eyes with lines in the corners. Her lips smiled, but her eyes didn't.

"I'll want pictures. Screenshots, whatever it takes." she told me. "Video, if you can get it."

"I can do that."

"How much?" Her expression was neutral, but the wobble in her voice gave her away.

We talked price. Of all the things I'd ever been paid to do, surveillance work paid the worst and was the biggest pain in the ass. That's why I usually tacked on a "convenience" fee and always, always got paid up front. I outlined it for her. Cash in an unmarked envelope. Small, spendable bills.

This didn't seem to faze her. "I'll need a day or so to get that much in cash."

People usually did. I nodded and pulled the platter of fries toward me. She'd ordered a club sandwich but hadn't taken a single bite. The diner where she'd agreed to meet was an hour from the town where we both lived, but she still looked around every time someone new walked in the door.

"I need it to be indisputable," she said as I dragged a fry through the ketchup and stuffed it in my mouth. Her gaze lifted to meet mine.

"Pictures and video are usually pretty damning."

She shook her head. "It has to be proof of an affair, not just a fling. It has to be proof that it's been going on at least a few months. There has to be actual talk of an emotional connection. Love. Like, he actually has to say it."

Some people have a real boner for getting kicked in the teeth. When I pointed out that putting herself through that level of torture isn't necessary; that unless her husband hired a shark of a lawyer, pictures and video would be enough; and that Pennsylvania is a no-fault divorce state anyway, she looked faintly surprised. Then frowned. Her fine dark brows knitted.

"Are you a lawyer?"

"No," I admitted. "I just deal with a lot of people who want to get divorced."

"Pennsylvania is an equitable distribution state," she said. "That does not mean fifty–fifty. And my dumb ass signed a very, very detailed prenup."

I shouldn't have laughed at that, but I did. She joined me after a moment. Her head tilted as she looked me over, up and down. I wished I'd shaved. Or something. Under her sharp assessment, I wanted suddenly to impress her.

"We should meet in person. Once a week. I can give you whatever I've collected in hard copy and a USB drive. It's safer that way. Less worry of corrupting the materials." None of this was exactly a lie, but I really didn't need to meet her once a week in person. I just wanted to.

"Once a week, then," she agreed and stood to offer me her hand across the table. "Until then."

CHAPTER FORTY-NINE

Diana

Cole runs a hand through his hair, then sits on the edge of the recliner so he can put his elbows on his knees. He put his head in his hands for about half a minute. I'm okay with the silence. I need some time to process all of this.

I can't remember meeting Cole before the coffee shop. I can't remember kissing him or touching him or having him inside me, except the two times we've been together since then. The pictures on the phone don't lie, though. I have to believe him.

"My skin is crawling," I say. "I can't remember any of this. I feel so violated."

He's on his feet in a second. "No, please, Diana. Don't say that. Then or now, nothing that ever happened between us was forced. It was all consensual. I swear to you."

"You knew I didn't remember any of it, but you . . . you did it again, knowing everything about before and knowing I did not. So how can you really say that it was consensual?"

"You're the one who came here," he says, but his voice is gritty and broken.

"You could have . . . *should* have turned me away. As far as I was concerned, we met in that coffee shop at the rec center a couple months after my car accident." I stagger but keep my feet. "But you already knew about that too."

Cole turns away from me to pace. He drags his hands through his hair and whirls to face me. His face twists, expression fierce and frightening, but the light in his eyes is also somehow comforting because it means all of this is important to him. It means *I* am important to him, and my heart wants to embrace this and make it something important, but my mind can't quite wrap around any of this.

"Give me a minute." I take a deep breath, then another, doing everything Dr. Levitt recommended.

Maybe quitting my sessions with her wasn't such a bright idea.

Cole watches without trying to touch me, and even though I imagine, maybe a little desperately, throwing myself into his arms, I keep my distance. When I'm calmer and can focus, I sit back on the couch. I wrap the blanket around me. I clear my throat, keep my voice steady, and look up at him.

"How much did I pay you?"

He doesn't answer.

I think of the envelope in his bathroom. I think of the withdrawal from the bank account I didn't remember. "How much, Cole?"

"We started with five grand."

I'm missing four times that amount. "And then what?"

Again, Cole hesitates. "Diana . . . look. After we got involved—"

"Did I pay you to have sex with me?" The idea of it is sour, a physical taste on my tongue, like bile. "Please tell me that you are not a gigolo. Oh my God, Cole, is that why?"

"Are you insane? No man on earth would need a paycheck to go to bed with you." Cole says this with shocked conviction, and I want to be flattered, but I just can't.

"The first night I was here . . ." I trail off with a withered, bitter laugh. "I guess it wasn't the first time. The first night I *remember* being here, I found an envelope full of money in your closet. It was an accident. But it was a lot of money. Was it from me?"

"Yes."

"There was more than five grand in there," I say.

"You gave me twenty altogether. To keep for you. You said that if you didn't have it, he couldn't make a claim to it."

"If I had proof he was cheating on me," I say, "I wouldn't have needed to hide it. He wouldn't be entitled to any of it anyway. It was my payout from Gen-Tech, and it came in after he and Val started sleeping together."

"I'm only telling you what you told me," Cole says.

My lips press together and I look down. "How can I possibly believe you're telling me the truth?"

"Because I am. That's all. You know me," Cole says.

I shake my head. "No. I don't."

"You know me," he whispers and moves close enough to touch my knee with his shin.

My instinct is to pull away, but I don't. I close my eyes for a second or so, thinking that when I open them, I'm going to be in my own bed, that this is a dream, but I know it isn't. This is all real, and it's happening, and I need to keep pushing for the truth.

"You were taking that painting class, and after you hired me, the first couple times we met at the coffee shop after it so I could drop off the stuff for you," he began. "For our third meeting, I finally managed to get you video of them together, doing more than talking. I figured you'd want to meet at the coffee shop again, but you asked me if it was possible to meet you at my place instead."

"Are you in the habit of allowing your clients to see where you live?" I toss out the words like a challenge.

Cole shakes his head. "No. Never."

"But you let me."

"Yeah," he says. "I let you."

There's no use in me trying to recall any of this or to make sense of it. I might as well have put all of this into a box like the one I buried. I might as well just keep listening.

"I invited you in and gave you the envelope with the USB drive in it. You looked me in the eyes and said, 'Cole, you seem like the sort of guy who appreciates a woman who knows what she wants, and right now, I want you.'"

"So . . . I seduced . . . you?" I shift on the couch. I'm still wet, but not as cold.

"I kissed you, hard as you wanted, and you wanted it hard. And then we went into the bedroom and had the most amazing sex I have ever had, and when it was done, you sat up and shook my hand and thanked me for my time."

A bubble of confused, startled laughter slips out of me. "What?"

Cole takes the chance to move closer. "I knew that if I let you walk out that door, I was going to regret it for the rest of my life. So I kissed you again, and you stayed for a while longer, and after we were done, we talked. For hours. You finally went home about three in the morning. I never asked you what had prompted any of it. Honestly, I didn't care what had started it, I just knew I wanted to keep it going. I didn't see you for three days, and I was sweating it. I was sure you'd never show up to meet me again, that you'd just give me a drop-off point or something. Then you told me to meet you after your class, at the coffee shop. You bought us both coffees and told me to get the Taktok app. And that was it. That's how it started."

There's silence now while I think about this. "When did this happen?"

"The end of July."

"The accident happened October first. We were together for what—two months?"

"About that. Yes."

I shake my head. "That's not a very long time to have met someone and fallen in love."

"Not if you've both been waiting for it for so long that, when you find each other, it's like you were in a dark room and finally learned how to turn on the light."

Something inside me recognizes those words. I force myself to answer him lightly, but my voice shakes. "Did you read that in a book?"

"You're the one who told me that." He reaches for me gently and takes my hands in his. I move a little closer. "You said we fell in love like the flash of lightning and the crash of thunder, everything all at once."

"I said that too?"

"Yes. The night you told me you were going to leave him," Cole says.

"Why would I bury my phone in the yard?"

"To make sure he didn't find it? I don't know, Diana. I really don't. You never told me you did that. I know you were kind of flipping out a little bit that he was going to find out."

"There must have been something else," I say in a low, tight voice. "Something I didn't tell you, maybe?"

We're both silent for a moment. Cole looks sincere in his confusion. I press a hand to the space below my right ribs, the spot that still aches sometimes. Like my body can remember what my mind can't.

"How did it end?" This feels more important to me than how it started.

Cole stands to pace. He runs his hands through his hair, pushing it off his forehead. When he faces me, his expression is grim. His hands are on his hips. He shakes his head a bit, then at last answers.

"It ended in a ditch on the side of the road."

CHAPTER FIFTY

Cole

"Were you with me that night?" Diana demands. "Were you in the car with me?"

"No."

"Do you know who was?"

"No. I don't. I thought you were alone," I tell her.

Diana frowns. "Yeah. So did I."

"You came to my house in the late afternoon. Three or so. You told me you didn't need any proof about his affair. You had something else that could easily end things, and you were going to leave him whether or not I wanted you."

"What was it?" She blinks hard, each word sharp. "What did I have?"

"I don't know." I go to my knees in front of her to take her hands. "But I told you I loved you. I told you that I wanted you."

"Did we fuck?" she demands.

I don't flinch, even though I'm pretty sure that's what she's trying to make me do. "We made love."

"We fucked," Diana says coldly.

I shake my head. My fingers squeeze hers. I don't correct her with my words, but I hope she feels that I meant the distinction.

"You were happy, Diana. I mean, just look at the pictures on that phone. Look how happy we are."

"Were," she corrects. "And it might has well have been someone else."

I try again. "You said that you were going to make sure it all worked out. We had a meal together. Steak. That wine you love. A celebration." I can still smell her perfume from that night. Taste the wine on her mouth.

"And then?"

"You left to go home. I thought you were going to tell him it was over. When I didn't hear from you for a few days, I got worried. You weren't answering messages. So, I searched the local news and found out about the accident. I came to the hospital to see you. At that point, I didn't care who found out. I lied, said I was your brother. But you didn't know me. The nurse on duty told me you had amnesia. I left."

"And that was the last time you saw me until that day at the coffee shop?"

I nod. It's the truth. She gets to her feet and lets the blanket drop from around her shoulders.

"How could you leave me alone so long? If you loved me, Cole, how could you do that?"

"You had no idea who I was. I thought you'd remember, in time. But so long as you didn't, what was I supposed to do? Wreck your life? No," I tell her. I sound bitter and angry, and I guess it's because I am. "No, Diana, when you love someone, you let them go if that's what's best for them."

"When you love someone, you don't lie to them," Diana spits out. "If you loved me for real, you'd have stepped up, and you sure as hell wouldn't have lied to me when we did meet up again. You wouldn't have kept the truth hidden from me. If what we had was truly love, you would not have just let it go!"

"Letting something die is not the same as killing it!" I shout.

Diana recoils with a gasp, and the color drains from her face. "Where did you hear that?"

"From you." My voice softens. I know better than to try to pull her into an embrace, but I do my best to touch her with my voice. "When you told me about killing Val's mother."

CHAPTER FIFTY-ONE

Diana

I told him about Val's mother? I've never told anyone. Not even Jonathan. "Why . . . why would I do that?"

"Because you loved me," Cole says, "and you wanted me to know everything about you."

Loved.

Such a difference that one letter makes, turning the word from present tense to past.

"I should go."

"Stay," he says. "Just for a few hours. Until you calm down."

If I do that, I'm going to end up in his bed, and tonight is not the time for that. It might never be the time for that again. I can't decide. His arms around me, his mouth on mine, the sound of his voice . . . all of that is delicious and a comfort, and I want it. I want him. But right now, I have to go home.

I let him kiss me first, though. I'm supposed to love this man. I can't remember how we got to this point, but here we are, and I can't deny it feels good to have him hold me. The press of his lips on my forehead is a consolation I want to sink into, but already there's a heat building low in my belly again. Like the pain below my ribs, that ache that comes and goes, my body remembers.

"I have to go," I tell him.

Cole frowns. "Call me when you get home. Or text. Or Taktok. Whatever works."

He doesn't ask me if I'm going to tell my husband about him. Us. To be honest, I'm not sure what I would say if Cole asked me that, because I'm not sure I know what I'm going to do once I'm face-to-face with Jonathan.

I leave without promising Cole anything.

I hate this car. This bland, neutral, "safe" car. It's supposed to be a sign of how much my husband loves and cares for me. I'm supposed to be grateful. The very thought of it makes my stomach churn.

The storm has stopped by this point, which is good, because suddenly I'm so exhausted that I have to roll down all the windows and slap myself across the face to keep awake, even on the short drive home. I'm light-headed. Nauseated. By the time I pull into the driveway, I feel like I'm ready to pass out, so much so that I sit in the driver's seat for a few minutes before I can manage to get myself out of the car.

At least I think it's a few minutes. I come to with the car dinging to remind me that the door is open. The garage door is also open, although fortunately I didn't try to pull my car inside, because at this angle I would have crunched into the wall.

My husband is still not home.

I get to my feet. Slam the door. I'm so tired that I weave my way to the door into the kitchen, which is locked. It's never locked, which means someone must be inside. I guess Harriett's not giving me the silent treatment anymore. I can't find my keys. Shit, my purse is in the car.

I bang on the door. Again. Again. My fist hammers down until finally the door is yanked open.

"Diana! Where were you?"

"Out."

I push past her. She follows me into the kitchen, where I grab a jug of orange juice from the fridge and start to drink. I'm thirstier than I can ever remember being. I turn to see her staring.

"You want to know where your precious son is? Out so late? Missing his dinner with us again?"

"He's working."

A sigh shudders out of me. I drink more juice. The thirst isn't being quenched, and my stomach is churning, and now a wave of dizziness threatens.

After a few more gulps, my stomach revolts, and I bend over the sink, expecting to vomit. I keep my stomach's contents inside, but barely.

"Jonathan is having an affair. It's been going on for months."

I expect her to deny it, but Harriett only shakes her head. "Like father, like son."

"What?"

"Jonathan's father also had a wandering eye and stepped out on his marriage." She shrugs. "Why do you think I insisted you sign a prenup before you ever married him?"

"Is that supposed to be an excuse?" I drain the jug and toss it into the sink.

She crosses her arms. "You're drunk."

"I'm not. Just tired." One glass of wine. Half a glass—no more than that. That's all I drank. Hours ago. Nothing at Cole's. He poured me some, but I didn't drink it. Nothing since this afternoon.

That's all I remember drinking, anyway.

I shake my head, but that sends a fresh wave of dizziness through me. I breathe in through my nose. Out through my mouth. I close my eyes, trying to steady myself. It's not really working.

"You were drinking and driving," she accuses. "It's a wonder you didn't crash *another* car."

I lean against the counter and focus on my breathing, pausing only to say, "Yes, Harriett. Let's talk about that, why not? Let's talk about my red car. My amazing, sexy as fuck, bright red car. That I loved."

"A showy, vulgar car. Jonathan should never have indulged you in it. It was trashy. A waste of his money!"

"Oh. My. God." I manage a laugh. "It wasn't *his* money. We're married. It's all *our* money, Harriett, but aside from that, it was literally bought with money I inherited from my own disaster of a mother."

I turn to face her. With the counter sturdy and supportive behind me, I'm able to stand upright. I'm still so thirsty, my mouth a desert; every swallow cuts me from the inside like razor blades.

"Oh yes, I remember now. How she came back around, trying to weasel her way back into your life. Trying to buy your love. The world was eased of a tremendous burden when she left it."

It's an awful thing to say. True, but terrible. A sob slips out of me.

"Oh dear. Don't cry, Diana. Why don't I put on some tea for us, and we can get caught up on *Runner*? It's been forever since we were able to settle in on the couch and just hang out together." Harriett puts an arm around my shoulder, squeezing.

She stands so close I could count the hairs on her eyebrows, if I want to. The crinkles in the corners of her eyes are filled with dusty makeup. For a second there seem to be two of her, and damn it, one is more than plenty. I straighten and grip the counter behind me, trying to keep my balance.

"Did you put him up to it?"

"What? Who?"

"The car, Harriett. The car!" My words slur.

She looks confused for a second. "What about the car?"

"I think you know exactly what I'm talking about." I wave a hand at her, but the gesture sends another round of weariness through me. "My car. My red car. It's in the shed."

"What on earth is it doing there?"

The world spins and turns, but I'm not drunk. Just like all those other times the bottles were emptied when I was not drunk. I don't know what the hell is happening, but I do know that something else is going on. Something very wrong.

I think I make some excuses to her, but my words are mumble-jumbled, my mouth full of mush. Not sure how, but I'm upstairs. In my bedroom, I pull up Dr. Levitt's phone number and call her. I hold my breath, waiting for her to answer, but it goes to voicemail.

"Dr. Levitt, this is Diana Sparrow. I just wanted to tell you that I'm pretty angry with you about talking to my husband about me and my mother without my permission. He said you asked him about it, and that's just wrong. But I still need to talk with you." That seems like the right thing to say, but I'm not sure I have any more words. "I'm tired now. You know what? Sometimes I'm so damned tired, I want to go to sleep and never wake up. Just so long as I don't dream. I'd sleep forever if I didn't have to dream."

The phone slips from my hand and lands on the bed with a thump. I stare at it, stupid and clumsy and tired. I can barely keep my eyes open, and I strip out of my clothes to leave them in a pile on the floor. In the shower, on my hands and knees, I let the water pound down all around me. My forehead is pressed to the tiles. The water is a little too hot, but I can't get myself up to adjust it. I curl onto my side and cover my face with a washcloth so water doesn't get in my ears or nose. I'm comforted by this cascade of warmth, the sound of it, the steady thump of it on my skin. After being chilled to the bone by the rain, this is heaven.

Lights in my eyes. Figures. Men in my bathroom—no, a man and also a woman. They're wearing blue uniforms. A light in my face, passing over my naked body, a gust of cold air when they open the shower door.

"Ma'am, I need to ask you to get up now."

I don't understand, and I can't get up, I'm naked and wet, and there are strangers in my bathroom. The light again, hurting my eyes, so I cover them and the shower water disappears, leaving me cold and wet and still naked, and there are hands on me. Gentle but firm, pulling me upright. I grab for a towel, and one is pressed into my numb fingers. I cry out in pain. I almost drop it.

"Ma'am, I'm Officer Gaines, this is Officer Terry. We're responding to a request for a wellness check. Can you tell me your name, please?"

"How can you be in my house to check on me and not know my name? What the hell is going on here?" I hold the towel in front of me. I'm a little more clear-headed but still so tired.

Officer Gaines is the woman, and she looks past me to see my robe, which she grabs and hands me. "Ma'am, your psychiatrist called us because she was concerned you might be trying to harm yourself."

Over Officer Terry's shoulder, I see Harriett, standing in the bathroom doorway. "She was drinking earlier, officers. A lot. That's not unusual for her, but this time she said several times that she wished she could go to sleep and never wake up."

"You were eavesdropping on me?"

Again, the light in my face. Officer Gaines steps between me and Harriett. The cop is looking deep into my eyes.

"Mrs. Sparrow, have you taken anything tonight? Any prescription medicines?"

"No, I—" I can't stop myself from looking beyond them to the bathroom counter.

Pill bottles. At least six. They're all open. Some on their sides, the caps missing. A few pills are scattered on the countertop. Officer Terry sees me looking and moves toward the counter.

"I didn't take anything! She's lying! I never said I wanted to hurt myself!" I lunge toward the bottles.

Officer Gaines restrains me. I'm slippery, but she's able to grab the robe. It pulls off me, but I don't even care. I lunge again, but it's too late. Terry's got one of the bottles in his hand.

"How many pills did you take, Mrs. Sparrow?"

"She's not *Mrs.* anything," Harriett says condescendingly. "She didn't take my son's name when they got married, though she really should have."

I. Lose. My. Shit.

I don't know what I'm screaming, but it's loud and fierce, and I am blinded by the sheer violent force of my fury. I might not even be making words, only incoherent war cries. My right hand cracks Harriett across the face, knocking her back. And then the two police officers grab me, wet, naked, fighting like a pit bull, and they put me down, and everything goes black.

CHAPTER FIFTY-TWO

Valerie

I hate the smell of hospitals.

When my mother was dying, I spent hours by her side. I didn't want to. I was fifteen. I wanted to be watching TV or talking with my friends, or really, doing anything else. But at fifteen, I had no car and was at my father's mercy, and he wanted me there. I'm sure he told himself that it was for my sake. But even then, I knew it was never because he thought I would regret it if she passed without me there. I knew it was so he could have a break from her.

My mother did not pass alone. I was there, and Diana was there. I turned my back, at the end, and Diana finished it. It didn't take much. My mother was already so far gone. Later, my father would say that all we'd had to do was call for the nurse and she'd have been saved, but she would not have been saved. She'd have been extended, that's all.

I didn't think a psych facility would have the same kind of stink as a palliative care unit, but it's similar enough to force me to cough into my scarf as I approach the admission desk. The young guy sitting behind it wears a neat navy polo embroidered with the Solace Point logo, and a hipster haircut, but he looks friendly enough when I put a hand on the desk to get his attention away from the computer screen.

"Hi. Can I help you?"

"I'm here to see a patient. Diana Sparrow."

He smiles at me. I smile back, although mine feels fake. He turns in his chair to face the screen again, tap-tapping away at the keyboard and then frowning. He doesn't look up at me.

"Your name?"

"Valerie Delagatti."

"Does she know you're coming?"

I sigh. "No. I'm sure she doesn't. But I called ahead to make sure it was okay if I came during visiting hours. Is there a problem?"

"I . . . don't think so. Hold on, please let me just check something." He taps some more.

The last thing I want is for them to turn me away. I won't come back if they do that.

And I have to see her.

"Third floor, you'll see a nurse's station. You have to show them this." He hands me a laminated badge on a lanyard, "and sign in there. I'll need to see your driver's license."

By the time I get to the third floor, I'm too warm and have to take off my jacket. I leave the scarf around my throat, even if it would look weird and too obvious if I put it over my mouth and nose against the residual stink. At the nurse's station, I show my lanyard and say I'm here to see Diana.

"She'll be in the lounge. Down there, third door on the left. You can't miss it," the nurse says as she points.

I definitely don't. The big double doors have large windows in them, each pane of glass crisscrossed with hexagons of metal wire inside. The outside of the doors is decorated with large flowers, the sort you make from tissue paper and pipe cleaners. Like a kindergarten classroom.

The doors open easily enough, although my fingers feel a little numb. Beyond the doors, the lounge is a large space painted in a welcoming, creamy white. Large windows overlook the hospital grounds, although from here all I can see is the tops of the pine trees. There's a fireplace covered by a metal screen, the bricks painted that same white, but it doesn't look functional. The flat-screen TV mounted above it is tuned to a daytime talk show, the volume low enough not to be distracting. Some of the patients work on puzzles or color in those elaborate adult coloring books. A few are scribbling in journals. Nobody has a tablet or cellphone.

Diana is standing along the far wall, her arms crossed over her belly. Her face, turned to the glass, is half-lit in golden light. Her dark, thick hair falls halfway down her back but is pulled back from her face with a wide, thick band. She wears a pair of charcoal-gray yoga pants, a matching, slim-fitted T-shirt, and a navy hoodie, zipped halfway.

She's thinner now than she's ever been. Her cheekbones look sharp, her face shadowed and hollowed. She ought to look like a hag, but when Diana turns to look at me, all I see is a statue, a portrait hung in a museum. She looks like the angel on a mausoleum, but I can't tell if she's the weeping or the avenging sort.

I am instantly, ragingly jealous.

She was always not just the pretty one, but the beautiful one. Perfect hair, perfect teeth, perfect skin. Never a blemish, never frizzy, and as we got older, the silver that came in at her temples made her look glamorous, not just . . . old.

"Hi." Her flat voice matches her total lack of expression.

I look around the room and keep my reply pitched low. "Are you allowed to go somewhere else? More private?"

"No. There is no place to go. They don't like us having privacy."

"Can we sit?" I point at the small, two-person table in the corner farthest away from anyone else in the room.

She shrugs and moves toward it without saying anything. She takes the seat with her face to the window. I take the one across from her. Diana folds her hands on the table, her fingers linked. She stares out the window over my shoulder, not at me. I wonder what sorts of pills they're making her take. I wonder if it's rude to ask.

"Didn't expect to see you here," she says, finally looking at me.

"I'm sorry."

Diana's brows lift, and I'm petty and jealous enough to notice that she hasn't had them groomed in a while. Long enough to be a little shaggy. It's an imperfection I can cling to, even though I'm ashamed I want to.

"For what?" she asks in a low, pleasant voice tinged with the first hint of emotion she's shown since I got here. "Fucking my husband?"

"For showing up here without letting you know in advance" is my answer, spoken through grimly pressed lips and clenched teeth. "I'm not sorry about Jonathan."

Diana laughs under her breath and mutters something I don't catch.

"What?"

"I said," she repeats slowly, her eyes meeting mine without so much as a blink, "you can have him."

I sit back a little in my chair. "You already told me that. We've had this conversation before."

"If we did, I don't remember it."

"I believe that now," I tell her. "I'm sorry I didn't before."

"Did Jonathan tell you I was here?" Diana's low laugh sounds sharp and ragged, like rusty barbed wire.

"Yes. Of course he did. He feels terrible," I say.

Diana recoils. Her lips skin back over her teeth. For a moment, a brief and flashing second, she looks skeletal and scary. "I'm sure he does. Not terrible enough to visit me, though. But I'm sure he's very, very busy at work."

He could be. Aside from him calling to tell me what happened to her, I haven't heard from Jonathan myself. "How long do you have to be in here?"

"Minimum twenty-four more hours. It was a seventy-two-hour involuntary hold. That's standard, they said. But they have the right to keep me longer if they determine I'm still a danger to myself. Or others," Diana adds with a significant look at me and a shuddery chuckle that reminds so much of how we used to laugh that it makes me want to cry.

"Are you? I never thought of you as the suicidal type."

She shakes her head. The laughter fades. She draws in a long, deep breath. "I'm not. My doctor took what I said the wrong way. Now that I've been in here, she thinks I've got issues from my meds. Wrong dosages, interactions. They're saying that I'm paranoid. Suffering some kind of breakdown. Anesthesia-induced psychosis in addition to the amnesia, or maybe it's all the same thing. Did you know that was a thing? I didn't know that was a thing."

"No. I didn't either." I give her a second, but she doesn't add anything. So I do. "Do you think they'll keep you longer?"

"Why do you want to know? So you and my husband can canoodle without fear of getting caught?"

Now she looks ugly. I wish I could take some pleasure in it, but I really can't. "He's not going to leave you while you're in here. I can guarantee it. So, thanks for that."

"You think I'm doing this to keep him from leaving me? Oh, Val. Did it ever occur to you that if Jonathan wasn't leaving me, it was because he didn't want to? I mean, I couldn't have kept him if he didn't want to stay with me. Just like you couldn't have made him leave me for you if he didn't want to. People don't work that way. At least, *he* doesn't. You sad, silly bitch."

For a moment, she rests her face in her hands. Is she crying? I don't want her to be crying. I won't be able to stand it if she is. But when she raises her head again, her eyes are dry. Red-rimmed, but no tears.

"Do you remember that palm reader we went to in New Orleans?" she asks suddenly.

I can't forget it. "Yes."

"She said we'd be friends forever," Diana says with a hitch in her voice. "Maybe I should get my money back."

For the first time since I got here, I move close enough to touch her. I close my hand over hers. She looks up.

"She said we'd be connected forever," I tell her, "not that we'd be friends forever."

She takes her hand from mine.

"Well, in that case, then, I guess she was right."

CHAPTER FIFTY-THREE

Diana

"I love him," Val says, as though that's a good enough reason for what she's done.

Hell. Maybe it is. It's not like she did it all on her own. My husband did more than his share of it, I'm sure. And, even though I can't remember it, I guess I did too.

"I wish you didn't," I say.

I shouldn't have been surprised that she showed up, I know, but sitting across from Val right now, I can still hardly believe she's here. It's not about having the nerve either. I can tell by the way she's twisting her hands in her lap, by her shaking voice, and how she can hardly meet my gaze. She had to steel herself to come here to see me. She had to make herself brave, and that's not something my dear friend Valerie was ever very good at.

"I never did this to hurt you, Diana."

Another slow curl of surprise twists through me. "I never thought you did."

Her tears make me uncomfortable, which is stupid because here at Solace Point, you get used to people randomly crying. Sometimes, it's yourself. Still, watching as she buries her face in her hands and her shoulders shake, I don't know how to feel or what to do. Once upon a time, I'd have hugged her without a second thought. Now . . . now all that's changed. She did that. Not me. Why, then, am I the one feeling so sad?

"What do you want me to say, Val? That it's all okay? That I forgive you?"

"No. I don't expect that." She raises a tear-streaked face. "How could you?"

We've forgiven each other a lot over the years, my best friend and I. Gone through a lot together. This is just one more thing, isn't it? I want to tell her this, but my mouth is dry, my tongue is thick, and my eyes are heavy. I barely have the energy to talk to her right now.

"Why are you here, then?" I ask.

"I wanted to make sure you were—well, I guess to make sure you were going to be all right."

I shift in the chair. Everything here in Solace Point is top quality, the finest of everything, but these chairs are hard as rock. Half an hour in one, and your butt starts to go numb. I put my hands flat on the table and lean toward her.

"I'm in a psych ward, two days in on an involuntary admission. I'm detoxing from drugs that I swear to you and God and anyone else who will listen that I have not been taking, and because it takes a week or some absurdly long time, they don't have any kind of blood test results back to prove I'm right. They don't believe me. Why should they? My memory is gone. I've given my husband, his mother, and my doctor every reason to believe I am not competent to decide things for myself. Oh, and the nightmares I've been having about burying a body in my back yard turned out to be sort of true. I dug up a box full of a bunch of crap I don't remember, but there it was in full color." I'm speaking with the voice of a stranger, like that kid in *The Exorcist*. I can't recall her name. That's how I feel, though. Possessed. Ready to spew green puke.

Val flinches. "What the hell do you mean, you're detoxing from drugs you weren't taking? What the hell is going on?"

"You wouldn't believe me if I could even manage to put it into words. Anyway, what makes you think I'd want to tell you?"

"I guess that's fair." She looks stung, though. She cuts her gaze from mine again. "That night you were with Trina at the Blue Dove, I was so sure you were just trying to mess with me. You already knew about us, because I'd told you everything. I knew you'd had the car crash and the surgery, but I thought you were just trying to use that for sympathy, so Jonathan wouldn't leave you. I couldn't believe you'd actually lost your memory. It was like something out of one of those bad movies we used to watch on cable."

"It's not a movie. It's my life."

"I know. I'm sorry. God, Diana, I am so, so sorry." She does have the grace to look shamefaced.

I look around the lounge. Nobody's paying attention to us, not that I can notice. Solace Point is swanky enough that the people who become patients here are not the sort to eavesdrop on embarrassing conversations. I look back at Val. "I know how hard it must have been for you to come here. Thanks, I guess."

She doesn't reply but she looks stricken. More tears well in her eyes, and she swipes them away with a fierce gesture. Her mouth works, but I can tell she's trying so hard to keep from crying that she's not going to be able to answer me. I don't really want her to.

"Remember when your mom was sick," I ask my friend gently, "and you'd come over to my house after your dad brought you home from the hospital?"

Val nods. She takes her hands out of her lap and puts them on the table. I take one, both of us leaning in toward each other. Her fingers are cold, or maybe it's mine that are freezing.

"And we would make microwave popcorn and fold out the sofa bed in the den. We'd watch those terrible movies on cable all night long and talk about boys. When Joey Lentini stood me up for the prom, who went with me, instead?" I ask, gripping her harder, not to hurt her, but because suddenly I feel as though if I don't hold on tight to something, anything, my body is simply going to fly away like an unknotted balloon.

"I did. We already had—" Val chokes to silence, then forces herself to finish. "We already had the matching dresses."

"That time in college, I held the cowboy hat for you to puke in when you thought it would be a good idea to see how many shots of tequila it would take before you stopped thinking about the awful things your dad said to you and how he acted when you didn't quit school to help him do all the things your mom had always done or Peggy had done after her."

At the mention of her stepmother, who'd divorced her dad during Val's freshman year of college, my friend manages a watery, wavy smile. "You said,

'Your dad's an adult, and if he can't figure out how to be one, that's not your fault.'"

"All those years, all that stuff. So many secrets we kept for each other. So many truths we shared. We never lied to each other in all that time. So why did you think I would lie to you about anything ever? You thought I was making it all up. To what? Keep *him*?"

"Yes." Her shame comes out in the tremble of her voice.

"You've been my sister-friend since we were in the fourth grade," I say after what feels like forever. "Damn it, Val. Between the two of you, who do you think I'd rather have kept?"

CHAPTER FIFTY-FOUR

Valerie

I know Diana and I won't ever be friends again. I think I knew that the first time I let Jonathan kiss me. I know, too, that it's selfish of me to mourn for that lost friendship since I'm the one who willingly broke it. But damn it, something has to be said about love, doesn't it? Something has to be said about sacrifice in the name of it.

"I knew you were unhappy," I tell her over cans of soda we got from the vending machine, using the coins I dug up from the bottom of my purse. I also bought a package of snack crackers for me, a candy bar for her. For the first time, I don't envy her body. As it turns out, there is such a thing as "too thin."

Diana opens the package but doesn't nibble the candy. She sips the cola slowly, with a grimace. "So much fizz. I gave up soda a while ago."

"You did?" This sets me back for a second or so. Diana used to drink a six-pack of diet soda every day, easily. "When?"

"A while ago. After you stopped returning my messages." Her hard grin isn't cruel so much as it is resigned. "A lot of things happened after that."

"You were miserable with him. You bitched about him all the time," I remind her. I hate feeling like I have to justify myself.

Diana nods. Her long, dark lashes cast shadows on her cheeks as she looks down at the chocolate bar on the table. "Yes. I did. I'm sure he did the same about me."

"He's never said a word against you." This is the truth, even if I wish it weren't.

She looks surprised. "No?"

"No. Never."

"I know I wasn't happy with him, but divorce . . ." She shivers. "I don't remember talking about that at all. I really can't remember anything beyond the drive down to the beach with you. I probably won't ever be able to. I need you to tell me what happened, Val. I need to hear it from you."

So, I tell her. About the Christmas kiss that led to the conversation at the beach house, which turned into her proposition. "If it makes you feel any better, I heard you complain about him a lot, but it was the first time I ever heard you talk about divorcing him. You're not remembering wrong."

Diana voice is low and disbelieving, but when she looks at me, I can tell she knows I'm telling her the truth. "It was supposed to be so simple, right? Dump the dick, keep the beach house and my bestie. Plenty of money. No worries. That was it?"

"That was it," I say.

"And then you fell in love with him."

"I know he's not perfect. Believe me, I do. But with him, I feel more like myself than I ever have in all my life. Can you understand that?" I hate to sound like I'm pleading, but how else can I sound?

"Is that why we fought in August? I don't remember it," she says, like she needs reminding. "But I found an email from you telling me to never contact you again."

"You gave him to me, and then it seemed like you were trying to take him back. He and I were supposed to go on a trip—"

"Punta Cana." She rubs the spot between her eyes. "You mentioned it at the Blue Dove. I had no idea what you were talking about."

"Yes. Punta Cana. But he told me you were insisting he take you instead. I thought you were just being an asshole, like you'd changed your mind or you were mad. I know," I add at the look on her face, "I should have known better. Especially when you told me that you hadn't insisted on anything. You told me, 'Jonathan lies.' I know he does, but I didn't want to believe it, then."

"I'm not having a breakdown, Val. You have to believe me. Whatever's going on, it's not any kind of psychosis, anesthesia related or otherwise."

"I believe you." I squeeze her hand. She pulls it away after a few seconds. "Do you remember what you were going to tell me about your mother and Harriett?"

She looks up, eyes narrowing. "What do you mean?"

"In August, when I confronted you about the trip, you said that you didn't need to have any kind of proof anymore. You had something else that would nullify the prenup. Something about your mother and Harriett." I pause to clear my throat and lower my voice, thinking of that night in the motel. What I heard. What I'd suspected. "Did you do something to your mother, Diana?"

She sits up straight, her shoulders square. Her lips part, but only a hiss escapes. No words, not at first. When she does speak, her voice ripples.

"What do you think I did to her?"

"She was found dead in her motel room. I never told you, but I saw her that night. It was right around the time my dad had just started getting sick. I was staying in the same motel. But you didn't find out for another couple of weeks."

"Why do you think I had anything to do with it?"

I tell her quickly of the shouting and the voices. The car that might have been hers. Diana shakes her head over and over until I stop speaking.

"That was an entire year before the summer I can't recall," she says. "I haven't forgotten anything about it. I swear to you, I wasn't there that night. But you think . . . maybe someone was? That maybe she didn't die by accident?"

"I can't really say for sure."

"She was an addict. Nobody blinked twice when it looked like an overdose. But Val . . . it wasn't me. When she stopped answering my texts, I assumed she'd left me again. Even though she'd promised she wouldn't, that she wanted to see if we could repair things." Diana shivers, pulling her hoodie closed around her throat. The shadows under her eyes look like they've gotten deeper since I arrived.

"All I can tell you is that last August, you told me you didn't need any kind of proof to use for the prenup and that you'd found out something else. You didn't tell me what it was."

"Did I tell you about burying a box in the back yard?"

I almost laugh, but I see that she's not joking. "No."

"Did I tell you I was sleeping with someone, who apparently I was also in love with, who I was going to leave Jonathan for?"

"What? No!"

"I thought I just forgot telling you." She giggles, low, but it sounds more like her old self.

I join her, and for a minute or so, it's nice. Not like old times, but it's nice. When it fades away, she shifts in her chair.

"What are we going to do about all of this?" I ask her finally, when a minute's passed and neither of us have said anything.

Diana looks at me, and then she shrugs. "I don't know."

CHAPTER FIFTY-FIVE

Diana

The house is very quiet and feels very empty, even though Jonathan and I have both been sitting at the kitchen table for over an hour. We've each drunk about a pot of coffee apiece, but the cinnamon crumb cake he pulled from the fridge has gone untouched. I think we've both lost our appetites.

"You're lucky. They could have kept you a lot longer," he says.

"Sure. Right. Lucky."

Dr. Levitt signed me out, so long as I agreed to continue treatment with her, or someone else if I didn't trust her. Someone had to oversee my meds, but, she said, she no longer believed I was a danger to myself.

"By the way," she'd said, "I want to assure you that while I did have a discussion with your husband about the time period of your amnesia, he was the one who called me. I would never have reached out to him without your permission, and I told him that I wouldn't continue to discuss you with him unless you knew about it."

Now, home, facing him, I can't deal with any more lies. I tell him everything I know, including that I've found my car. It's far from enough, but at least it's something. It's the first time in years—maybe the entirety of our marriage in fact—that I've felt like Jonathan not only listened to me but actually heard what I was saying. No nodding along only to completely ignore everything I'd told him. No gaslighting or backpedaling to excuse himself. I wouldn't say he's owned everything that happened between us, but it's a start.

His guilt helps.

What surprises me are his tears. He listened stone-faced when I confessed that Val and I had conspired against him to start their affair, and why we'd done it. But when I tell him everything about Cole, the length and depth and breadth of the relationship that I still can't completely believe existed, Jonathan buries his face in his hands and weeps. Heart-wrenching, body-wracking sobs. The sound of it is horrifying, worse than listening to someone vomit. It's the sound of agony. Of something dying.

"You can't possibly *love* him," my husband says finally through the rasp of his tear-torn throat. He looks at me through swollen eyes. His nose drips.

It's disgusting, but that's not what makes me turn away. I've never seen him cry, so this is unsettling enough for me to get up from the table and lean against the kitchen counter. He swivels in his chair to follow me with his gaze. I should comfort him, shouldn't I? But I can't, and more than that, I don't really want to.

"I don't know what I feel about Cole. But what about you? Do you love Val? Because she loves you."

Jonathan doesn't say anything, which is not fair, but totally typical. Hours of conversation about what we are going to do and how we mean to do it, and yet in the end he's still got to control every goddamned thing, even his own truth.

"You can admit to me you had sex with her," I say, "but you can't look me in the face and say you love her? You can't say it even without looking me in the face."

"So this is the end of us," Jonathan says. "For real."

His words rock me harder than I expect them to. I close my eyes. Having known it forever doesn't make it any easier to accept now.

"Yes, Jonathan. This is the end of us. For real."

"I never thought you'd remember. When they told me you had amnesia, I thought, man, what a lucky break, she won't ever remember," he says in a small voice that sounds like someone kicked him in the nuts.

Again with the *luck* for something that was anything but. "I wouldn't ever remember what?"

"That you were going to leave me. You told me the night of the accident that you knew all about me and . . ." He stutters on her name. Coughs. "Valerie." I listen for the sound of love in his voice when he says it, but I don't hear it. "You told me that you knew I was planning to take her to Punta Cana. All of it. But you were willing not to bring any of that to court if I just agreed to your terms."

"Did you agree to them?"

His laugh is derisive. "Hell, no. You were being ridiculous. Totally out of line. Just . . . honestly, Diana, I thought you were having a breakdown. Wanting to divorce me? Okay, fine, but trying to screw my mother over?"

A chill spikes through me. "What do you mean?"

"You wanted to draw up legal documents kicking her out of the apartment and banning her from any of our jointly owned property, ad infinitum, no matter which one of us ended up being awarded it. You wanted me to agree, as part of our divorce agreement, never to financially support her in any way for the rest of her life, and you even wanted me to take back any gifts we'd given her. Which you know, Diana, you can't do. It was insane." Jonathan lets out another laugh, this one more confused and sadder. "Insane. There was no way I was going to settle on all that, no matter if you did take me to court about the prenup. I mean . . . she's my mother."

"Why would I have done that?" My memories are shredded lace, slipping through my fingers. "I love your mother."

I *used* to love his mother.

"Like I said. Batshit crazy. I have no idea why you wanted any of that, and you wouldn't tell me." Jonathan gets up to pour another mug of coffee, the last in the pot.

All of this is making me so tired. I don't feel the way I did before going into Solace Point. No fuzzy head, nothing like that. But I'm not a machine. I really want a nap.

"Speaking of your mother, where is she?" I'd been expecting her to welcome me home.

"At her place, I assume. I told her to wait until one of us texted her before she came over. I thought you could use some time. That . . . we . . . might need some time. To talk."

It's rare moments like these, when he shows even the tiniest scrap of aware-ness beyond himself, that I can tell myself I wasn't an idiot for marrying him in the first place. Our marriage is over, but at least maybe I wasn't a total fool at the start of it. Only, as it turns out, at the end.

"I'll text her. I'm sure she's rabid to get over here and cook us some dinner or something." I sigh, the weight of this task suddenly daunting. "Where's my phone?"

CHAPTER FIFTY-SIX

Cole

I haven't heard from Diana in four days. I tried the Taktok app, but my message to her remained not only unread, but undelivered. She might have deleted the app. I resorted to the tracking app. That little blue dot hasn't moved in four days.

She's at home.

Still, something bad's happened to her. I know it. I feel it. So, although I've done a lot of stupid things in my life, I go ahead and do one more.

I know the big house, of course, since I've dropped her off there in the past. But the app is showing her location in the smaller structure next door. Where her mother-in-law lives, I remember that, and the thought that maybe Diana's taken refuge there is a relief I'm not quite ready to allow myself. If she's separated herself from him, why hasn't she tried to get in touch with me?

I pull into the lower driveway and park. I have the chance to back up and leave without taking this next step, but damn it, I left her once when I could have changed things. I'm not doing it again. She might not want to be with me—and that's a chance I have to take—but I do have to make sure she's all right.

I'm expecting Diana's wanker of a husband to answer the door, and I'm more than half-hoping he does, so I have an excuse to punch him in the face. Instead, an older woman with short platinum hair opens it. Her lip curls at the sight of me.

"Yes?"

I don't bother with niceties. If shit's going to hit the fan, it might as well start blowing now. "Hi, I'm looking for Diana. Is she here?"

"Who are you?"

"I'm a friend of hers. We were supposed to be in touch, but she hasn't been answering my messages."

"Maybe that's because she doesn't want to talk to you," the woman says.

I hold out my hands to show her I mean no harm and give her my best old-lady-charmer grin. "I'd sure like to be able to ask her that myself."

The woman's eyes narrow. "What did you say your name was?"

"I'm Cole. Is she here?" I'm tall enough to look over and beyond her, but she's got the door closed enough to keep me from seeing too much.

"Cole?" The woman blinks rapidly, then smiles. "Oh my. Diana *has* mentioned *you*."

"She . . . has?" Taken aback, I don't know what to say next.

The woman stands aside, door wide open. "Would you like to come in? Diana will be right back."

I follow her inside the small, well-furnished apartment. She waves me toward a table set with a mug of coffee and a puzzle book. I don't see any signs of Diana here, but I stop myself from calling out her name.

"Would you like something to drink? A cup of coffee? I have some fresh, right here," Diana's mother-in-law says. "Let me get you some while you wait. It won't be more than a few minutes, I'm sure."

"All right," I tell her. "A cup of coffee sounds great."

CHAPTER FIFTY-SEVEN

Diana

"Have you seen my phone?" I sort through my oversized purse, which was hanging on the back of the chair and look up at Jonathan. "I haven't had it since before they took me away."

He grimaces, like my description of what happened has offended his delicate sensibilities. I can't care very much about that. What happened sure as hell offended mine.

"Text it, please," I ask him.

He does but neither of us can hear anything. Now I've lost my phone again. At least it's *probably* not buried in a box in the back yard. Probably.

"Tell me the rest of what happened that night," I ask him and get up to make us both more coffee. When I pull the filters out of the cupboard, I knock against a few of the prescription bottles. Empty. I toss them into the trash. I have new prescriptions now anyway—ones that are not supposed to make me into a lunatic.

"We were fighting. About my mom, about everything. You started complaining that you felt sick. Then you got a really bad pain in your side. Like, you were doubled over with it. In agony. We decided it was quicker to drive you to the hospital." Here he hesitates. I can see him struggling. Finally, he admits, "I'd been drinking. I thought I was okay to drive, but the roads were wet, and those damned deer—you know how bad they are. One ran out right in front of us. We hit it."

"You were driving. *You* hit the deer."

"The road was pretty empty. We both managed to get out of the car before anyone came. I called for help. You told me to just get out of the way, and we'd say you were driving."

He's lying again, of course. That's what he does. I don't bother to call him out. "There was no tractor trailer driver."

"No."

The voice in my dreams, the one telling me I'd be okay. That was a real voice, but it hadn't belonged to a stranger. It was Jonathan's.

"Nobody questioned it? The police? Nobody?" I ask.

"It's not like you were unconscious," Jonathan snapped. "You were in pain, but it wasn't like you were in a fucking coma, Diana. You told the cops you were driving and I was the passenger, and they didn't care about anything other than making sure you got to the hospital. And then, when you woke up—"

"I had no memory of any of it."

"Yeah." He sighs. "And you were in pain, on drugs . . . I just didn't tell you anything because . . . why? I mean, why, really?"

"Because it was the truth?" I ask, but I don't really expect him to agree with me. I mean, if my husband was the sort of guy to make the right choices, would we even be here? *For that matter,* I think, *if I was that sort of woman?*

"It was easier. And I didn't really want us to get divorced," Jonathan says. "I still don't."

We stare at each other then. Silent. Both of us weighing what has come between us; maybe both of us wondering if there's a way, now, to salvage anything we once had.

"Why's my car in the shed?" It's the final question I need to ask. "You told me it was totaled."

"The airbag deployed, so the insurance company totaled it."

"Then why is it in the shed?" I'm not going to let him get away with more lies. Not about my car.

"I was going to get it fixed, but it would have cost thousands of dollars. I thought I'd sell it, surprise you with something else, but your name's the only one on the title. So I put in the shed until I could figure out what to do with it.

I knew how upset you'd be if you saw it like that," he says, defensive. "I did it for you. I do everything for you. Anyway, that car was . . . unnecessary."

There, then. That's it. The final nail. If there was the slightest, most minuscule chance we might reconcile, there it went.

Both of us turn toward the sound of the front door opening. In the next minute, Harriett's in the kitchen. She hands me my phone.

"I knew you'd want this," she says. "I was keeping it safe for you. It's been going off for days."

When I open my phone to find twelve texts from Cole and a few missed calls and voicemails, including one from Dr. Levitt, I wonder if she saw any of the notices. Because there's something I knew but hadn't thought about for all these months. Harriett knows my passcode. What has she seen?

More importantly, what has she done?

"Thanks," I tell her.

Harriett hugs me. "It's so good to have you home, honey. All the family back together, just how it should be. Are you hungry? I was thinking of making a nice garlic and oil pasta and a big salad. How's that sound?"

"Delish," I lie and hold the phone to my ear to listen to the message from Dr. Levitt.

Hi, Diana. I wanted to let you know something important. I got your toxicology report back, and . . . listen, I have some real concerns about the meds that were found in your system. They were definitely causing bad interactions, and frankly, I need to talk with you about where you were getting them without a prescription. I am legally bound to report instances of illegal use, but I want to talk with you first. Call me back.

Harriett is staring as I disconnect the call. "Everything okay?"

"Yeah. Sure." I take one of the pill bottles out of the trash and study it. "When's the last time you filled these?"

"Oh my. I don't know." She's puttering with something in the fridge. "Jonathan, set the table. This is only going to take a few minutes."

"Actually, Harriett," I say, "I don't think dinner is a good idea."

She pauses with her back to me. Straightens. She turns her head halfway but keeps her body still. "Why not? I'd think you were starving for a good home-cooked meal after having to put up with whatever slop they served you in that place."

"Harriett, Jonathan and I have something really important to tell you. Can you turn around, please?"

One of the reasons I stayed so long in this marriage that wore me down to nothing was because of the woman in front of me. Telling her I'm divorcing her son, or he's divorcing me—whichever way it goes—is harder than telling Jonathan. I wait for her to face me, but she won't.

"Harriett."

"Ma, Diana wants a divorce." Jonathan snaps this out like he's cracking a whip. "We're splitting up. She doesn't want to eat dinner together right now. You need to go home."

Harriett does not turn around.

A sound begins, something low and dark and growling. It takes me a few seconds to realize it's her voice. Words—actually, one word—over and over again.

"No. No, no, *nononononono!*"

Harriett slams both her hands against the counter, hard enough to rattle the dishes in the cupboard. I back up a step. I have never heard my mother-in-law raise her voice, much less shriek this way. It is the sound of fury. It is the sound of ferocity. It is the sound a woman makes when she has lost her mind.

She whirls, her fingers curled into claws. She shakes. For a second, a single, gleaming strand of drool slips from the corner of her lips. I watch in horror as she doesn't even try to wipe it away.

"After all I've done," Harriett says in that same awful voice. "After all. I've. Fucking. *Done.*"

I have never heard her swear.

"Ma—"

"You. Shut up. You've done enough," Harriett spits at him. "You and your little man doing all the thinking for you. And *you.*"

She turns to me. Her finger stabs. I take another step back, getting out of range. My heart pounds, my palms are clammy, and a red haze is creeping in around the edges of my vision. When they become blinking black spots, I realize . . . I'm going to pass out.

"You, you, you . . . you stupid little girl. You've ruined it all. I just had my family all together, all of us, happy and content and together. And you had to go and ruin it, didn't you?" Froth curdles in the corners of her mouth.

I manage to find my voice and keep my consciousness. "What the hell are you talking about?"

"I tried, Diana. Oh, I've tried. I accepted my mistake in giving you up, but you can hardly blame me for that, can you? After all, I've done everything I could since then to be a mother to you. A *real* mother. Not like that addict whore who adopted you."

She's pacing now. Back and forth. Her rubber-soled shoes squeak on the tiles. Her fists clench. Release. Clench.

Then she's grabbing at Jonathan with both hands, and he's fending her off as he tries to get up and out of his chair, but she's blocking the way, and so all he can do is shake the table.

I wait for the flicker of a memory to hit me. Something. Anything. I wait for the doors to fling open to all my dark rooms and let in the light.

Nothing.

"What do you mean? Giving me up?"

My body remembers, though. I can't catch a breath. I'm shaking.

"Ma. What's going on? Nothing you're saying makes any sense," Jonathan says.

"It was a miracle, your accident," she says to me. "It took away all the bad things, and it let us be a family the way I knew we were meant to be, but no, *no*. You both had to go and mess it all up!" Harriett turns to me. "You blamed me for it all, Diana, but anything I ever did was for you."

Now I know where her son gets it.

"What do you mean, I blamed you?" I say.

She's ranting. Making no sense. Her voice is raw. Hoarse.

"I was young. Naive. When the man you love says he's going to leave his wife for you, well, you believe it, don't you? I did. Until he changed his mind. Said he was going to stay with his swine of a wife."

Like father, like son.

"You said Jonathan's father cheated on you . . ." I manage to say.

Jonathan recoils. He's still stuck between Harriett and the kitchen gable. "What? Dad did what?"

"I said he stepped out on his marriage," Harriett tells me in a voice as calm and deep as a well.

"You were the other woman."

"He loved me!" she cries. "He felt obligated to her, that was all! So he stayed with her and left me to raise our baby all on my own. I thought I was being smart, but at the time I was young. I was heartbroken. Giving you up for adoption was the only choice I had, and I regretted it every single day, Diana. It took me years before I was able to find a way back into your life, to be the mother to you that I'd always wanted to be."

"You're my biological mother?" Each breath comes shuddery and shivery, but I no longer feel like I'm going to faint.

I'm not sure what I'm going to do. In all the years of dreaming of who my biological parents might be, never once had I thought it might be . . . Harriett. Because that means . . . Oh. God.

Oh my fucking god.

Jonathan makes a guttural noise. "No. What the fuck?"

"I am your only mother," Harriett says. "I am the only mother you ever really had, and I am the only mother you will ever really need."

CHAPTER FIFTY-EIGHT

Val

I got the text from Diana a few hours ago but didn't see it until a few minutes ago. She's home. She wants us to talk things out. Her, me, and Jonathan.

Want u 2 come ovr, she texted. *We need 2 talk.*

I should feel more nervous when I pull into the driveway. This confrontation has been a long time coming, and I wish I felt more confident that it is going to work out in my favor. What will I do if the two of them tell me, together, that they're not splitting up?

Nobody answers the front door when I knock, so I let myself in. I hear voices from the kitchen. Jonathan's raised in a half shout. I'm expecting to see him and Diana arguing, but he's facing Harriett.

What the hell is going on?

Jonathan catches sight of me. The look on his face is not one of love or relief, and I instantly regret coming here. He takes a step toward me.

"Valerie, get out of here."

Harriett twists. She's a tiny woman, small and frail looking. She wears too much makeup. She's got a wide grin. Crazy eyes.

"What's going on?" I stay in the doorway, wary, and shoot a glance at Diana.

She is pale and looks sick, one hand over her mouth like maybe she's trying not to throw up or something. She looks at me over her fingers, and her eyes are wide, the pupils huge, her gaze slightly unfocused.

MINA HARDY

"So, this is Val. Diana's friend Val, the one I've heard so much about. Like a sister to her—she's said that more than once." Harriett's voice drips with contempt. She never remembers who I am, no matter how often we meet, and I see now it's always been deliberate. "This is the woman you couldn't keep your dick out of, Jonathan? Did she ever tell you it was all Diana's idea, that the two of them—"

"Yes. Diana told me." I've never heard Jonathan sound this way. Defeated. Exhausted. Demoralized.

"She told me too. Months ago, she told me. Confessed it right to me, told me she couldn't be married to you anymore. You were sleeping with Val. She was messing around with that Cole. Both of you, so stupid and selfish. You make me so ashamed!"

"I told you about Cole?" Diana takes the hand away from her mouth.

Something big has gone down here, but I have no clue what it might be. Only that the man I've loved for so short a time looks as though someone died, and the woman I've loved for a lot longer than that looks like she wants to kill someone.

Harriett sneers. "You told me *everything*. And I told you everything too. All of it. That addict bitch was going to tell you the truth, but I couldn't have that, could I? I had to take care of it. Make sure she wouldn't fill your head with nonsense. And I thought when I told you all of it, everything, surely you'd understand, but no, no—you blamed me for it and everything that happened."

"There's the reason I wanted you banned," Diana says, but I have no idea what she's talking about. "Oh my god. I can't . . ."

"I believe in fate, Diana. There's a reason you had that accident. Why your memories were taken away. It was so you'd stop being so stupid and selfish," Harriett says.

"Diana? Did you text me to come over?" I ask.

She shakes her head. "No. Harriett had my phone."

"*I* texted you," Harriett says. "You need to hear it from Jonathan himself, so we can get this all sorted. Tell her, Jonathan. You're finished with her."

"Jonathan?" I say, waiting for him to tell his mother she has no idea what she's talking about.

252

"I'm sorry, Val," he says. "I never thought it would get this far."

"Oh god, Jonathan, you're such an asshole," Diana says. "After all this?"

Jonathan puts a hand on the back of a kitchen chair like if he doesn't hold onto it, he's going to fall down. He hangs his head. I can't see his face, and I guess I really don't want to.

"I'm sorry," he says again.

"You go on home now," Harriett says.

Diana steps toward me. "No. Val. Don't go. You have to hear this. It's about what I was going to tell you in August."

You'd think Diana had punched her in the face, the way Harriett starts to scream. She's flailing and writhing, and if she had the room for it, I'm sure she'd be throwing herself onto the floor to pound her fists against it. I am looking into the face of a woman gone legitimately mad. Harriett puts a hand to her heart, her fingers curling and digging in deep enough to leave dents in her skin above the neckline of her blouse.

"Harriett is—"

But Diana doesn't have time to say more, because Harriett launches herself toward my friend.

CHAPTER FIFTY-NINE

Diana

"Have you lost your goddamned mind?" Val screams.

Harriett catches me with a slap to the face, more by luck than anything else, but I've been in a psych ward for the past three days and detoxing from prescription meds. I'm unsteady as it is, so the second blow to my face knocks me back a step. The kitchen counter hits me in the small of the back, and I let out a curse. I manage to get my hands up in front of me to stop most of the clawing smacks she's aiming at me, but when she goes for my eyes, all I can do is shove her away from me as hard as I can. She's still muttering accusations, unintelligible except for a word here or there.

Baby mother . . . nobody else . . . love . . . mail-order pills . . .

She's seething, huffing and puffing. Her eyes roll. She's fucking unhinged.

Finally, Jonathan steps forward to struggle with his mess of a mother. He has to forcibly push her a few steps out of the way so he can get around the table. He tries to grab her by the upper arms, but she manages to slip his grip.

"Ma, everything's going to be all right. We're going to call for some help."

Val has her phone out, but Harriett is fast. She slaps it out of Val's hands. The phone hits the floor hard enough to shatter the screen and slides far under the table, into the corner. I blink and blink, trying hard to keep on my feet. Harriett is between me and Val, who looks too stunned to move.

"All those pills I got for you in the mail. It's not so easy to buy them, no, but I did! Everything you ate or drank. I knew Jonathan would never eat or drink anything, not with meat in it—oh no. It was all for Diana!"

Jonathan goes pale and we share a look. It makes sense now, the few times he snuck some of his mother's food. How he acted after. How I've been acting for months.

"Were you trying to kill me?" I cry.

Harriett stops struggling in Jonathan's grip and goes very, very still. "If you weren't sick, Diana, how could Mama possibly take care of you?"

Val lets out a breath and mutters what sounds like an exclamation, but I can't hear the words. Jonathan makes a low cry of disgust, puts the heels of his hands over his eyes. Nobody moves.

"I don't understand what's going on," Val whispers.

I don't either. I don't think I want to know. "Harriett, you need serious help."

"It had to be just enough—never too much. I didn't want you to end up like that addict whore who tried to get back on your good side. She was too stupid not to take pills from a stranger, wasn't she? But I suppose she thought we weren't strangers, not after I told her the truth about who I really am. Still, she got what she deserved." Harriett's laugh is cold and cruel.

I want to puke. I can't be hearing this right. "You killed her. You killed my mother."

"I didn't do anything to her she wasn't going to do all on her own. I just helped her out a little. I mean, when life's lemons make lemonade all on their own, what can you do but take a drink?"

"Are you *my* mother?" Jonathan cuts in.

Both of us look at him. Harriett seems to have forgotten he was there, just for a minute or so. Hope rises inside me, but it's dashed when she speaks. "Of course I'm your mother."

"And you're . . . Diana's mother?"

Val grunts. Harriett nods, grinning. She claps her hands together as though this is the best news ever, and not a devastating, disgusting revelation for the two of us.

Thank god we never had kids.

"Yes. I didn't have the pleasure of raising her—I already told you that—but I've made up for it—"

"Shut. Up," Jonathan barks. "Dad is her father? And mine?"

Harriett scowls, her pleasant expression twisting again into the face of a crone. "Yes. Are you stupid? Yes. That's what I'm saying. I took care of his first wife, that sow, and he came around just like he was meant to. We had you. And years later, I was blessed with the chance to get to know Diana. We are a family now, and—"

"But you set us up." He gestures at me. "You set us up to get *married*."

"How else was I going to have both my babies back with me under one roof?" Harriett reaches for him, and Jonathan, maybe too stunned to protest, lets her pull him into an embrace. "It's been so lovely. Our little family. Our perfect family, both of you with me the way it was always meant to be."

This hurts worse than anything else, I think. Because I'd never asked her to try to be my mother. I'd never asked her to love me. I'd just come to believe she did.

"This is sick. It's sick!" Jonathan wrestles out of her grip.

Val pushes past Harriett and gets on her knees in front of the table, trying to grab for her phone. I close my eyes. I hear the clang of metal.

When I open my eyes, Harriett has pulled the biggest knife from the block.

She holds it in front of her, between us, and the fact that her hands are shaking wildly does not bring me any comfort because the blade is waving way too close to me.

I am exhausted, but also I am beyond tired of Harriett's fuckery. The knife scares me, but not enough to stop me from spilling some scalding truth tea all over this bitch. I make sure I look her dead in the eyes.

"We are getting divorced, and we will never, ever, ever be your perfect little family. Not fucking ever, you sick, twisted psycho."

CHAPTER SIXTY

Cole

I'm not completely out of it.

Whatever that bitch put in my coffee is trying hard to push me under, but I'm bigger than she probably accounted for. I've lost some time, though. Not sure how much. Her living room floor is hard and cold under my cheek. The room spins.

I need to get up.

I push myself to my feet and stagger. I have to get this out of me. She's drugged me. That's all I can think, and I don't know why, but it doesn't matter.

In the kitchen, I bend over the garbage can and put my fingers down my throat. I gag and heave, but nothing comes up. I try again, but the iron stomach I've cultivated is my enemy now.

In the trash, yellow padded envelopes addressed to Harriett Richmond. Mailed from Mexico. Canada. Labels in Chinese. Pill bottles inside.

Empty.

I can't make myself throw up whatever used to be in these bottles. I'm going down again, on my knees. I hit the floor with my face. Phone in my pocket. I swipe it but can't get it to open.

I'm passing out.

I try one more time. A voice asks me what's my emergency. I think I answer, but in the end, all I manage is one word.

"Help."

CHAPTER SIXTY-ONE

Diana

"How could you do this?" Jonathan looks defeated, and I have the most infinitesimal shard of pity for him. I mean, nobody deserves to be loved this wrongly. We've both been fucked over. The difference is, I already know what it's like to be betrayed by a mother, and he's only just learning. "You've ruined my life. I can't even look at you."

"*Noooo!*" Her wail seems endless until it's chopped off abruptly by the snap of her teeth.

Harriett is faster than she looks. I am not sure she's stabbed him until the first arterial spray of blood jets from Jonathan's throat. She doesn't stop. Again and again, Harriett's blade raises and lowers, and although the knife skips off him in some places, it catches him in enough others. Blood is everywhere. She is screaming. I am screaming. Val is backed against the wall, covered in blood.

Jonathan clutches his throat, pressing against the tide of crimson spurting out of him, and he can't make a sound.

I grab the blade, but it's the knife end of it, and Harriett slices my palms. Metal clinks on metal; the only thing that saves the fingers on my left hand is my wedding set as it deflects the blade's bite. Still, I let go, because I can't hold onto it. The pain is cold, then hot, the burn of ice on bare flesh. I fall back.

Val lunges forward, but she's not fast enough. Jonathan falls face first, and his head bounces off the kitchen counter so he ends up on his back, sprawled on the floor. Harriett, still screaming, plunges the knife directly into his crotch, and if there was ever a more meaningful action taken by anyone in this life, I don't know what it would be.

The world is graying out in front of me. I fall to my knees. Harriett yanks the knife out of Jonathan's motionless body and turns on me.

"I'm going to tell them you did it!" she screams at Val—just before she stabs herself in the stomach.

EPILOGUE

Diana

ONE YEAR LATER

The police and paramedics showed up, first next door, where they discovered Cole. He was able to direct them to the main house before passing out completely. He was in the hospital for a few days but made a full recovery.

Harriett's self-inflicted wound was not fatal. The one she landed on her son, though, was. Jonathan bled out while I was unconscious. The paramedics found the three of us on the kitchen floor. Harriett had tossed the knife in Val's direction, but of course that wasn't enough to make anyone believe it had been Val who stabbed her.

The frozen leftovers from all the meals she made just for me were analyzed, and it became clear she was dosing my food with medications she purchased online. I didn't need credit card statements or receipts to prove she was the one buying all the wine, but the stupid hag kept them all together in a folder easily discovered on her desk. It turns out she was also regularly messing with the thermostat and changing the settings on my phone. In other words, she'd been deliberately and relentlessly trying to keep me helpless, for months.

My memories still have not come back, and there will always be some mysteries left I will never figure out.

I have Cole, though, and his ability to dig up the past even when it's not conveniently buried beneath a tree in the yard. He was able to find out everything about the adoption and Jonathan's father's first wife. Her death, my mother's, and the similarities between them.

He's got it all in a file, ready for me any time I want to know.

As for the two of us, it's not love. It might have been in the heat of last summer. It might have lasted, too, and grown into something real, if not for the accident. It might still, if we give it a chance, and there are days when I think about it. We'll never know what might have been, but nobody ever can.

Val has moved out of town, and one day she might let me know where she went. She didn't want to take the money I insisted on giving her, but in the end, she did. We owe each other debts that can never be repaid, but as it turns out, death is cheaper than divorce. I could afford to be generous to my oldest friend, the sister of my heart.

We don't talk about those final moments when she knelt beside the man who'd come between us. I would never accuse her of not doing enough to save him, of not even trying. But Val and I both know the unalterable truth.

Letting someone die is not the same as killing him.

For now, it's enough to see my cherry red Camaro sitting in the driveway. You'd never know she was ever broken. Unlike mine, her scars are invisible.

It's also enough that my insane ex–mother-in-law/biological mother is locked up without any hope of release, not in her lifetime. It's enough, too, to know that the woman who raised me did not, in the end, come back into my life and then abandon me on purpose. There's another "what might've been" in that story, but at least this one lets me sleep at night.

Without the bad dreams.